KT-546-492

CLAIRE ADAM

Golden Child

FABER & FABER

First published in 2019
by Faber & Faber Limited
Bloomsbury House
74–77 Great Russell Street
London WC1B 3DA
This paperback edition published in 2019

Typeset by Faber & Faber Limited
Printed and bound in the UK by CPI Group (UK) Ltd, Croydon, CR0 4YY

All rights reserved
© Claire Adam, 2019

The right of Claire Adam to be identified as author of this work
has been asserted in accordance with Section 77 of the Copyright,
Designs and Patents Act 1988

*This book is sold subject to the condition that it shall not, by way of trade or
otherwise, be lent, resold, hired out or otherwise circulated without the publisher's
prior consent in any form of binding or cover other than that in which it is
published and without a similar condition including this condition being
imposed on the subsequent purchaser*

A CIP record for this book
is available from the British Library

ISBN 978–0–571–33982–2

2 4 6 8 10 9 7 5 3 1

For my parents

PART ONE

I

Only Trixie is at the gate when he pulls up. She is sitting on her haunches staring at something across the road, her forelegs planted in front of her, solid as tree-stumps. Probably an iguana, Clyde thinks, or an agouti, judging by the look on her face. He glances in that direction as he yanks the handbrake up but can't see what she might be looking at. There is only bush over there on that side of the road: bush all the way down to the river, and then more bush, until you get to the cocoa plantations. The leaves are shiny with the little rain that just fell, the asphalt road steaming. As he walks down to the gate, he pulls off his t-shirt, wipes the sweat from his face, the back of his neck.

He had a little wash before he left work, but the smell of the industrial estate still clings to him – it is in his hair, his clothes, the creases of his joints. 'Oil-smell,' people call it, or 'petrochemical smell,' if they are better informed. Today, Clyde knows, he smells of grease, ammonia and rotten eggs, because he spent the afternoon going round the plant with the engineer, sealing off valves, hauling open chambers, collecting samples in little plastic bags, and then closing back the chambers and opening valves again. Usually, he would have been wearing a blue coverall instead of his own clothes, and he would have showered at the plant before he left. But since the break-in a few weeks ago, he's switched to day-work – just as a temporary measure – so that he can be at home with Joy and the boys during the night. It doesn't pay as well as shifts, but Joy says she feels safer with him in the house.

Brownie and Jab-Jab come down to the gate, their noses dusty with the red-orange dirt from under the house. 'Aye! All-you been sleeping?' he asks. They stretch and sneeze their hellos, panting in wide, happy smiles. 'Lazy dogs!' he tells them, as he pats them through the bars. 'Lazy!' But they smile and wave their tails: they can tell he is not mad. Anyway, he thinks, what is the point of them being awake during the day? Better they sleep during the day, so they could be awake at night. You can't expect animals to be awake twenty-four hours, even watchdogs.

'Get back, get back,' he calls, as he lifts the top latch. The two pothounds retreat to the scrubby grass at the side of the driveway, but Trixie gets to her feet and stands there squarely, a burly mass of Rottweiler muscle, frowning at the spot where the two halves of the gate join.

'What happen to you?' Clyde says to her. 'You not going out on the road, you know.' He looks again over his shoulder, searching for what might be troubling her. The sun has gone down behind the trees, and the lane is shady and cool and still. The birds have already gone in: there's just that one keskidee left in the guava tree by the gate, the big-talker who's always the last to go in. 'You still here?' Clyde says. 'Everyone else gone home!' The bird blinks, angles its striped head this way and that; then, as if suddenly realising what a fool it is, rushes off.

Clyde opens the gate a tiny bit and grabs Trixie by the collar, trying to push her away. 'I have to bring the car in!' he pleads. She growls: just a low rumble from her throat, eyes fixed on the ground. If he gives her one more inch, he knows, she'll shoot out

[4]

onto the road and they'll spend the rest of the evening trying to catch her and get her back into the yard.

Clyde lets the latch fall and rattles the gate. 'Paul!' he calls. 'Paul! Come and hold this dog for me.'

There's a brief movement at the window – someone waving to say they're coming – and then Peter comes out to the patio. The boys are twins but even from here, twenty or thirty feet away, Clyde can tell that it's Peter, not Paul. Paul tends to slink around – like he playing invisible, Clyde always thinks – but Peter walks with a bold step, his head up, his arms held a little way from his sides, not with the elbows tucked in like he doesn't know what to do with them. Peter is only thirteen, but he is nearly as tall as Clyde already, and as hairy. He has changed out of his school uniform into shortpants, the dents from his socks still marking his ankles.

'Aye,' says Peter, as he comes down the steps. He skips quickly over the hot concrete to the grass on the side, the brown, dried-up grass of dry season.

'Where's Paul?'

'Gone out.'

'Gone out? Gone out where?'

'I dunno. By the river, I think.'

'Hold this dog for me while I bring the car in.'

Peter holds Trixie while Clyde drives into the carport, a shelter at the side of the house built of tall poles and galvanise. When he lets her go, she steps away from him and shakes, as if she'd just climbed out of a wet drain. Then she returns to her position in front of the gate, sitting on her haunches, staring at the bush across the road.

Joy is sitting down when Clyde comes in, the fan set to blow breeze straight on her. The sheets that they laid over the sofa and armchair since the break-in are all smoothed out and organised, but the place still looks terrible. Joy looks hot and tired, her hair greasy, pulled back, her bare feet dusty and black with dirt. He feels too grimy himself to go and kiss her hello.

'Water gone?' he asks.

'Yea.'

'When? In the morning?'

'About lunchtime,' she says. 'I saw the pressure was getting low so I filled up the pots.' She keeps talking as Clyde goes through to the kitchen to put down his keys. He waves away the flies from the dishes stacked up in the sink. 'I couldn't cook,' she calls. 'I took out roti from the freezer and I made up some melongene to go with it. I was going to make curry, but I couldn't cook.'

He comes back to the living room and lifts up the covers of the Pyrex dishes on the table: melongene choka, with plenty onion and garlic, the way he likes it, some cucumber salad, and some warm paratha roti wrapped up in a dishcloth. 'Don't worry, man, this is fine!' he says. He speaks with extra cheerfulness, so that she doesn't feel bad about the simple dinner.

He washes his hands from a bucket in the bathroom and puts on a clean shirt: that will have to do for today, in place of a shower. Back in the living room, he pulls out the chair at the head of the table, but Joy doesn't get up. She is still on her corner of the sofa, her right hand twisting at her wedding ring, squeezing it up as far as the knuckle and then pushing it back down again.

'What happen?' he asks.

Her eyes flick to the clock on the wall, just behind Clyde's head.

'What?' he asks, again.

'I just wondering how come Paul not home yet.'

He sits, takes a roti skin from underneath the cloth and drops it on his plate. 'He'll come back when he's ready, I suppose.'

'But it's going to get dark just now,' Joy says.

Peter comes in, glances at the two of them, and sits down. Clyde takes a bit of melongene, using the back of the spoon to spread it out on his plate a bit, to make it look bigger.

'I's thinking I would phone Romesh,' Joy says, 'and see if he's by them.' Romesh is her younger brother – he lives with his family about a half-mile up the road, in a two-storey house with carpets and air-conditioners. She watches as he tears a strip of roti. 'You don't mind?' she asks.

He pushes the food into his mouth and chews, his forearms on the edge of the table, scowling at the space in front of him. At his side, Peter keeps his eyes down and busies himself with eating.

'Eh?' she asks again, after Clyde has swallowed. 'You don't mind?'

'Me?' Clyde says. 'Why I would mind?'

'I'll just call them and see,' she says.

He is not there. After she hangs up, Joy comes to the table and the three of them eat together in silence.

When he has finished eating, Clyde takes his plate to the kitchen, but there is nowhere to rest it down. The sink is full of unwashed dishes, and the counters are covered by cooking pots, bowls, ice-cream containers, all filled with water. He waves the flies away.

'Clyde, don't worry about this,' Joy says, coming in. 'Go on the patio. You want a cold Carib or something? Look a cold bottle in the fridge there.' She takes his plate from him.

'I'm working early tomorrow,' he says.

'Well, just one not going to kill you. Eh? One wouldn't be OK?'

[7]

'Nah,' he says. 'Just some ice-water. We have ice?'

'Plenty, plenty,' she says. 'Go and relax yourself, Clyde. I'll bring the water.'

On the patio, he settles himself into a chair and lights a cigarette. He can hear the seven o'clock News headlines from next door quite clearly: the usual mix of lies from government ministers, road fatalities, rapes, kidnappings and so on. The same stories day after day.

Brownie and Jab-Jab come up to the little wrought-iron gate at the top step and wag their tails at him, bright-eyed and alert now it's evening. He cranes his neck to look: the street-lamp on their road hasn't worked in years, but he can just make out Trixie's stout shape, still there at the gate.

'The dogs had their food?' Clyde asks Joy, when she comes with the ice-water to sit down with him.

'I don't think so,' she says. 'I think it's Paul's week to feed them. That's why I'm telling you, I'm wondering where he is.'

'He said anything before he went out?'

'No. Not that I remember. But he's hardly opened his mouth since the break-in. You don't find? He's upset about what happened.'

'Well,' Clyde says. 'Upset? Or sulking?'

'Upset,' Joy says.

'You're trying to tell me I was too harsh on him?'

'I'm not saying that. I'm only saying you-all had an argument, not so? And he was upset.'

Clyde clasps his hands over his waist and looks away, out over the front yard. He loosens his feet from his slippers, crosses one foot over the other knee. All these years, Joy has told him he's been too harsh on the boy: now what does she think? Has he been too harsh, or maybe not harsh enough? He takes a sip of water

[8]

and sets the glass back on the coaster. He looks towards the front yard again, waggles his foot. Jab-Jab pricks her ears up at something rustling in the bush, then trots down the steps to investigate.

The break-in happened two weeks ago now to the day. Clyde came home to find the gate ajar, the house dark. He sat in his car, his fingers gripping the steering wheel, knowing what might be waiting for him inside. 'CARNAGE,' the newspapers said, most days, above the photos. On other days: 'MORE CARNAGE', or 'WHEN WILL IT END?' Two neighbours, Mr Chin Lee and Mr Bartholomew, came with him, armed with cutlasses and sticks, and they found Joy and the boys in a heap on the kitchen floor, their mouths stuffed with rags, hands and feet bound with wire. 'Alive, praise God!' Mr Chin Lee said. 'All alive!' Clyde sat by the wall with his head in his hands; neighbours brought wire-cutters, food, Dettol, ice. Mr Bartholomew picked up the phone and called his wife. 'Everybody OK,' he said. 'They were just tied up. Nobody dead.'

The next morning, when he woke, he already had a headache starting. He had planned just to make Joy her tea and go back to bed, but when he came out to the kitchen, he felt the sickening squelch of a maggot under his bare foot. They were all over the floor; Paul, wearing flip-flops, was already working his way around with a scrap of newspaper in hand. 'One blasted day late!' Clyde said. Paul didn't say anything, maybe he bent a little lower to the ground. Clyde felt his anger bubbling up. 'One blasted day late with the rubbish, and this is what happens in this blasted place!' He bit his tongue, but the words continued in his head: *And Joy's jewellery gone, and the house turned upside down, and he's missing a day of work. And Paul and his foolishness! All his damn foolishness!* 'Well, you could forget about going to that fete in Port of Spain,'

[9]

Clyde burst out. The boys had been talking about nothing except this fete for weeks: Clyde was going to drive them up to Port of Spain in the afternoon and collect them at midnight. 'Nobody's going to any fetes!' He waited, fuming, but there was no reply. 'You don't have anything to say for yourself?' But Paul just stood there with that blank look of his; Clyde had to restrain himself from giving the boy one good cuff in his head to wake him up. 'You know what?' Clyde said. He heard the words spilling out. 'Maybe we should have put you in St Ann's one-time in truth.' Paul made no response, but some small change in his posture – a slight droop of the head, maybe, or a sag of the shoulders – told him that the boy had heard and understood.

On the patio, Clyde stubs out his cigarette. The News has moved on to oil prices. His feet wriggle back into his slippers and he walks through the house – through the dark passageway, through the sitting room, then through the kitchen to the little passageway by the bedrooms. He knocks on the boys' bedroom door.

'Yea?' calls Peter. His voice is a deep voice now, a man's voice.

'It's me.'

Peter opens the door, steps back to give Clyde space. Behind him, on his bed, is an open textbook and a copybook, pens, pencils, rulers. The sheets on Paul's bed are smooth, untouched: a pair of khaki school trousers are folded in half on the edge of the bed, the pale blue shirt crumpled on the floor by his schoolbag.

'Did you look in his schoolbag?' Clyde asks.

'You want me to look in it? What for?'

'Just look in it,' Clyde says.

He stands at the door as Peter takes a handful of books out, flips through the pages. 'I don't think there's anything here,' Peter says. 'What do you want me to look for?' He rummages at the bottom of the bag, pulls out what he finds: a dried-up wild-pine; a number of salt-prune seeds; a Caramel wrapper; a chewed straw; a few coins. Peter looks at Clyde for a few moments, the empty schoolbag in his hand, and then he slowly puts the books back.

'Come,' Clyde says, when Peter is finished. Peter glances at the books and papers arranged over his own bed and then he follows Clyde through the house out to the patio.

It's properly dark now – the bats are out. Joy puts on the overhead light, a fluorescent tube that flickers and gives Clyde a headache, but at least it keeps the bats away. Paul, when he was smaller, used to say that this light makes everyone's faces look green. He's right, Clyde thinks, as he sits down on the patio chair and reaches for his Du Mauriers: it makes everybody look kind of sick. Instead of their normal brown, now they all look bleached-out, half-alive. While they talk, insects keep flying into the bulb above, making little shadows scurry over their faces.

'Tell me about this afternoon,' Clyde says. 'What time did he go out?'

'It was straight after we got home from school,' Peter says. 'Around half past four.'

'And what he said?'

'Nothing. He asked me if I wanted to go by the river, and I said no, and then he went.'

From overhead, there is the quiet *bap-bap* of the insects knocking against the light. Joy pinches at her t-shirt to unstick it from the folds of her belly.

'He had anything with him?' Clyde asks.

'No.'

'He had on shoes?'

'Don't think so.'

'I saw the young-fellas when I was coming home,' Clyde says. 'They were playing football in the road by the gas station there. They asked if Peter wanted to come and play, but they didn't mention they had seen Paul or anything like that.'

'Phone the neighbours,' Joy says. 'Phone them and ask if they saw him.'

They listen to the international news, then stock market prices. When the weatherman comes on, Clyde gets up – nobody bothers with the weatherman during dry season: every evening, he takes about ten minutes just to say that tomorrow will be hot with no rain. Peter and Joy follow Clyde to the living room and watch as he dials the number for the Chin Lees next door.

'Hello, goodnight!' Clyde says, when Mr Chin Lee answers. He makes his tone jovial, apologises for calling so late. 'I just calling to see if your water came back. You tried the tap with the tank off?'

He watches first Joy's eyes, and then Peter's, as he listens. Mr Chin Lee has water from his tank; he offers to give Clyde some. 'No, no,' Clyde says. 'Joy put some aside this morning while the pressure was good. But if we run out, we'll send Peter around with the bucket.' As they're saying goodbye, he says, 'Oh, by the way, Paul is not by you, by any chance?'

But Mr Chin Lee hasn't seen him. Clyde tells him not to worry, that Paul is probably just out somewhere around the neighbourhood and didn't notice the time.

He tries the next neighbour on the Trace, then the one further down, at the end. Joy brings him the phone book and he tries people from the new developments, even though he can't think of anyone Paul is friendly with up there. No one has seen him. He hangs up the phone and the three of them look at each other in silence.

'You want me to go and look?' asks Peter.

'You know where he goes?'

'Not really. He used to just go by the river, but I don't know if he still goes there.'

'You don't know?'

'No.'

'Who would know? He's friendly with anyone around here?' Peter shakes his head slowly.

'Tell us,' Joy says. 'They might know something. Who is it?'

'Well, I don't really know,' Peter says.

'Say it anyway.'

'Maybe Sando.'

'Sando?' Clyde says. The man's real name is something else, something very ordinary, but they all take these silly nicknames nowadays.

'I said, I don't know.'

'But you must have some reason for thinking of him. You're talking about the fella with the dreadlocks? And always wearing shades?'

Peter nods.

'And why you think he would know about Paul?'

'I didn't say he would know anything.'

'Well, what is it then? What connection they have?'

'I don't know. Just, like, in the maxi taxi in the mornings? Sando acts like they're friends or something.'

'Is that so?' Clyde says. Is that so, that the man thinks they're friends? This is who Paul is associating with? The man is over thirty years old, and spends all his time at the panyard chatting up women and smoking weed.

'I don't think Paul is doing anything,' Peter says quickly. 'He's not taking drugs or anything, if that's what you're thinking.'

'Well,' Clyde says. He's already imagining dragging Paul in here by the ear. 'When he comes back, I'll find out.' And that fella Sando? He will have a word with that wutless man, and he will say, what business do you have with my son? What business do you have with a thirteen-year-old boy?

'I think the two of you should go across the road and look in the bush,' Joy says. 'Let Peter show you where to go. And he could call out. If Paul hiding, he more likely to come out if he hears Peter.'

Clyde taps his fingertips together, thinking. Why should he drag Peter out into the bush in the middle of the night just to please Paul? It's bad enough that one person has to go and look for him, never mind two! And after the break-in and everything, he doesn't want to leave Joy on her own here. 'No. I'll go by myself,' Clyde says. 'Peter, you stay with Mummy.'

Peter finds him a torch, and Clyde changes into long pants and shoes. Shorts and slippers are no good for that bush across the road. Before, when Clyde was small, he used to go in there barefoot: by daylight you can easily pick your way along, avoiding ant-hills, sharp stones, prickers and whatever else. But it's a long time since he's been in there, and also – who knows what will be out now, at night? Snakes, frogs, agouti, all the night-time creatures, or spirits, or whatever they are. La Diablesse and Papa Bois and all of them. Not that he believes in all of that nonsense, really. But still – the agreement, as far as he is concerned, is that the humans stay in one realm and the spirits stay in another: to think of walking into the dark bush now feels like trespassing. But, as usual, there is nothing else to be done. Clyde, lacing up his shoes in the bedroom, thinks: this is the last time. The last time he's jumping through hoops for this child. Next week, after things settle down, Clyde thinks, he will sit him down and tell him straight out: no more. And just two weeks ago Paul nearly got Joy killed? No more of this nonsense. He will say sorry for what he said, about St Ann's. He never really meant that. He will say: I always said we would care for you at home, rather than put you in that place for god-knows-what to happen to you. But enough is enough. You have to stop this nonsense.

Back on the patio, he flicks the torch on, trains the beam on the stretch of road beyond the gate: the long grass is a weird kind of green in the torchlight, a colour that doesn't exist in the daytime.

'You're going to take Trixie?' Peter asks, on the patio.

'No, no. Better she stays with you-all,' Clyde says. 'Lock up after me. And if there's any problem, phone Romesh.'

Clyde goes down the steps, the little light of his torch bobbing in the darkness, Brownie and Jab-Jab trotting ahead of him. Behind him, he hears Peter close the door and slide the lock shut. Trixie is still sitting by the gate. She turns her head: her eyes catch the torchlight, two ghostly discs in the dark.

2

Clyde crosses the road and steps over the ditch, pushing back the long grass with his arms. Long-time ago, there used to be a path through here: it started by the lime tree and went from tree to tree, so that children used to try to walk along the roots without touching their feet to the ground at all. But as soon as he steps into the bush, he feels lost: nothing is where he remembers it. The long blades of grass are silvery-green in the torchlight, each one as wide as a carving knife, covered with tiny hairs that catch on his t-shirt so that after every step he has to stop to tear himself free. Already, just ten, twenty feet in, he wants to turn and fight his way back to the road, but he forces himself to keep going. He trips over tree-roots and stones, hollow snail shells, bone-coloured, the size of a child's fist. Feathery tips tickle his elbows, sharp prickers in the undergrowth pull his shoelaces loose. He turns the light of his torch to the ground, searching for any sign of Paul, but he sees nothing – only beetles and little lizards scurrying away, and the ti-marie leaves firmly folding themselves shut at his touch, like old women closing their jalousies when they see the madman passing on the street.

This is no place for Paul to be at night. Even long-time ago, before things got how they are now in Trinidad, grown-ups used to tell children to be careful when they came down here. Convicts who escaped from the Golden Grove Prison used this bush as a hiding place: Clyde and his friends had twice found the discarded orange jumpsuits, like shedded snake-skins, under piles of leaves or half-buried in the dirt. Shouter Baptists sometimes passed through here with their long white gowns, ringing bells and lighting candles, or with a fowl in one hand and a cutlass in the other. And there was that other time that Clyde still remembers vividly, from when he was about eight years old, when a crazy naked woman came out of this bush. His father was in the front yard and Clyde was on the patio, and this naked woman just pushed her way out of the bush, looking crazy with her hair all tangled up and scratches all over her. His father said something to her that Clyde couldn't hear – maybe he asked her what the matter was, or offered to call the police. But the woman just stood there, stark naked, shaking her head like she had ants in her hair. 'Hose me down!' she said. That was all she said: *Hose me down! Hose me down!* And then after a while, she turned and went walking down the road fast fast.

He must have already come off the path, if there was a path: every direction he looks, there is just bush reaching way above his head. He tries to pick out landmarks to orient himself – that fallen coconut tree; that low branch that he had to duck under, covered with lichen and wild-pines – but has no idea where he's going. Next thing you know, he thinks, he too will get lost in here, and someone will have to come in and rescue him. He battles with a long vine that has tangled itself around him; he tries to yank it away from his own body but, as he pulls, the upper end of it, somewhere in the trees above, comes loose and brings down a shower of dead twigs and leaves and, a few moments later, a rotten branch with a termites' nest still attached. He runs, drops the torch, madly brushes insects from his face, his arms, his hair. When he has caught his breath, he finds the torch again and shines the light around. The ground is stamped down flat into a circle, with yellow star-shaped flowers scattered around the edge. He makes out a candle-stump, chicken feathers, sticks arranged in the twos and threes of obeah patterns. He steps quickly out of the clearing, hearing the soft snap of big leaves as they break.

'Paul!' he shouts. 'Paul! Where are you?'

Angrily, he flashes his light around, expecting to see Paul's face appear in the strange light, to see him climbing down from a tree, or wherever his hiding place is, for the boy to be full of remorse, regretting pulling this stunt at all. He shines his light at the trees, suddenly suspicious. There are no spirits here, he says to himself, it's all nonsense, superstition. He says it again, out loud. 'There are no spirits here!' He shines his light all around the trees before he walks on.

He makes his way down the slope towards the river. Now that it's dry season, the water is only ankle deep and he could probably leap from one bank to the other if he tried. The sides are overgrown with bamboo; the tall poles leaning over the water from either side make a criss-cross shape like the roof of a tent. He finds his way to the big-stone, the one all the children used to sit on, feeling glad to have found something familiar.

'Hello?' he calls. 'Paul? Where are you?' He stands very still, listening. 'Paul?' he calls again. 'You hiding? Come out, please. Mummy's worrying herself to death about you. You can't go walking around in the bush like this at night-time. It's not safe.'

He looks up at the high branches, imagining the wild-looking face half-hidden behind the long hair, the hair that the boy refuses to cut. Tarzan, they call him, because of the hair; Clyde isn't sure if it's a proper nickname – Paul 'Tarzan' Deyalsingh – or if it's just something that they call him behind his back.

'I not mad,' he calls out, trying to make the words sound convincing. 'You could come out. I not mad. I not going to send you to St Ann's, I was only joking. We could discuss about the fete if you want.'

He thinks of saying, 'I'm sorry,' but then changes his mind. Why should he say he is sorry? It was Paul who was in the wrong in the first place: he shouldn't have provoked the bandits. Even Joy hasn't tried to defend him this time.

It was Joy who told him what happened. It was late that night when she told him, the night of the break-in, maybe two-three o'clock in the morning, after they had said goodbye to all the neighbours who had come over to help, and he and Joy had gone to bed. She lay on her side to face him and whispered everything that had happened: how the bandits had known about the money; that that was what they were searching for. 'And what you told them? You told them anything?' Clyde asked. 'No, of course not. I told them there was no money,' she said. And then she told Clyde what Paul had done: that Paul had refused to get down on the floor when the bandit told him to; that he had cussed the bandit and moved towards the man as if to hit him; that the man had pointed the gun at him. In that moment, Joy said, she only saw black; she couldn't explain it, but it was as if the world went black for her, everything was blotted out by a sort of blackness. She couldn't remember what she'd said, only that she had tried to act normal. She got up from the ground; she stepped in front of Paul and pushed him back. And then the man put the gun to her head, right in the middle of her forehead so that her head tipped back. She fell silent after saying this and, after a moment, reached for Clyde's hand and grasped it tightly.

They lay like this for some time, staring up at the ceiling, side by side in the dark.

The frogs have started up their singing again. It doesn't feel like any other human is here now. Maybe Paul was here before and he crept away without Clyde realising; maybe he was never here. Clyde steupses to himself. The boy playing ole mas: he will walk back in the house tomorrow, pleased with the trouble he caused – and meanwhile, here Clyde is in the pitch darkness looking for him! He sets off in the direction of the bridge, using a stick to swipe left and right in front of him, as if clearing a path. He's wasting his time in here. He'll go by Romesh's house and ask Romesh to bring his car and come with him, and they'll drive around and look. Romesh should have rung him back and offered to come out with him; now Clyde will have to go to Romesh's house and call out at the gate like a beggar to ask for his help.

At the bridge, he climbs up to the road. The street-lamps along here haven't worked for years – some of them are so thickly covered with vines that he can't see which ones are street-lamps and which are just posts for telephone wires – but he knows the road well enough: bush on both sides, and no pavement, but just a ditch at the side of the road that cars are always falling into. He takes out the torch, shines his light into the bushes as he walks along.

A half-mile up the road, a car is on the recreation ground, its doors flung open, headlamps on, the radio thumping out music. Three or four men are sprawled on the grass amidst cricket bats and wickets, bottles of beer and soft drinks. He recognises the song – the one by that woman, the black American woman with the massive head of hair, Tina Turner; one of the men is singing along, screwing up his face the way the woman does in the music video. Clyde raises a hand in greeting as he passes them. He used to play cricket in the evenings with these men, but invariably, once the cricket has finished, the cards come out, then bottles of rum, wads of money. He does not cut through the recreation ground but stays on the road, keeps his eyes fixed straight ahead, his pace steady, until he gets to Bougainvillea Avenue.

The roads in the new developments all have names like this: Ixora Crescent, Hibiscus Drive, Bougainvillea Avenue. When Romesh and his family moved here, Romesh kept trying to persuade Clyde to buy one of these houses, and Romesh's wife, Rachel, kept showing Joy the three bathrooms, the laundry room with space for a washing machine and tumble dryer, the smooth tiled floor, which Joy said would be so easy to sweep and mop. But Clyde didn't see what they had to show off about when everyone knew that Rachel's father had bought the house for them.

On Bougainvillea Avenue, the old pothound in the first house is already at the gate. She lifts her chin towards the sky and makes a high-pitched, repeating call: *ru-ru-ru-ru*. Immediately, the other dogs start barking and rush to their gates; at every house on the road, floodlights suddenly expose front lawns, concrete driveways, tall gates, all with dogs behind them. The pothound keeps her ears pricked as he goes past, her cloudy eyes trying to find him. 'It's only me,' he calls. Her ears flatten, she wags her tail.

The dogs at the next house are purebreeds – some kind of fancy breed with orange-coloured fur and tails that curl over their backs. They bark at Clyde, then at each other, then at the other dogs along the road and then at each other again. On the patio, above the shelter where the cars are parked, the lights are on, people are sitting talking. He can't see clearly past the burglar-proofing over the patio and the flowering vine they have growing over the iron bars, but it looks like the whole family is probably there: the mother and father, the three grown-up children, and the oldest child's husband, a pilot with BWIA. The whole family gets free flights on BWIA because of the pilot: at Christmas they went to Canada; the summer before, to Switzerland. The pilot's car is parked on the driveway. Clyde sees people getting up and looking out towards the road: he lifts a hand and calls out to greet them.

At Romesh and Rachel's house, the Alsatians squeeze their muzzles through the bars, barking and snapping. 'It's me, you fools,' he tells the dogs. 'You think I'm here to rob the place or something?' Their pupils dilate, lock him into focus. He reaches up to grab one of the bars, high up where the dogs cannot bite his hand, and rattles the gate.

He waits, hands on hips, amidst all the noise and the security lights, and people looking out their windows to see what the commotion is. Both Romesh's and Rachel's cars are parked in the carport; above, the patio is dark, the door to the house closed, but Clyde sees a light on in the living room and hears JR Ewing's voice on the TV inside. At the house next door, the one with the two stupid orange dogs, the mother of the family leans over the patio railing.

'Who's that?' she calls.

'Goodnight,' he calls back. 'It's just me. I'm waiting for Romesh.'

She turns and repeats this to the others, and then shouts down, 'Everything OK?'

'Yes, yes, thanks,' he calls.

'Where's your car?' she asks. She has to repeat it several times before he hears the question properly. A few others in the pilot's family come to the balcony railing – the father of the household, a little girl in her nightdress, a teenage son. A woman with shiny

[22]

dangling earrings and a ponytail gets up and carries a stack of plates into the house. Clyde knows what the mother wants to ask: whether everything is OK since the break-in. He gives them a thumbs-up. There is no point asking them about Paul: none of them have anything to do with him. He sees the pilot-man get up – he recognises the man's build, tall, with rounded shoulders. The pilot puts a bottle of Coca-Cola to his lips and tips his head back, drinks; he raises the bottle up to the light to check the bottom.

At last, Romesh comes to his patio door and looks out. Clyde waves. Romesh goes back inside, and then comes out again with a key and unlocks the burglar-proofing door and comes down the steps. He's still in his work-clothes: long pants and the t-shirt with the logo of Rachel's father's business, the sleeves of the t-shirt carefully rolled up all the way so the t-shirt looks more like a vest, and shows off his little muscles. Romesh is not very tall, but he's lithe: one of those smallish Coolie kind of fellas who could hoist up a sack of flour or rice on his shoulder and walk down the highway in the hotsun. He moves with a kind of swagger that women find sexy, and he wears a Playboy bunny pendant on a gold chain around his neck, with a little diamond where the bunny's eye would be. Romesh jangles the keyring on his forefinger as he comes down the driveway. The dogs keep up their pacing along the length of the gate, barking at Clyde from one end and then the other, as if hoping for a gap to appear.

'What took you so long?' Clyde says. He has to shout to make himself heard.

'I was about to go to bed,' Romesh says.

'What?'

'I was about to go to bed!' Romesh says. 'I have to get up in the morning, you know!'

'Put the dogs away,' Clyde says.

'What?'

'Put the dogs away!' Clyde shouts. 'I want to come up and talk to you.' He has to repeat it several times, but eventually Romesh chains the dogs up and comes back to unlock the gate.

Clyde follows Romesh up the steps and through the dark patio into the house. He was expecting to greet other people – Rachel, or some other friend or neighbour or relative – but there is no one here. The chairs are pushed in at the dining table, the plastic table-cloth wiped clean, the condiments gathered into a neat group on a placemat in the middle. On the other side of the room – the room is at least thirty feet long, and most of it is just empty space – the TV is on, the credits of *Dallas* rolling by; next to it, the standing fan slowly turns its head from one side to the other.

'You always have the volume turned up loud so?' Clyde asks.

Romesh turns it down, then sits on one of the sofas – they have three sofas and two armchairs and a pouffe, all in brown corduroy velvet – his eyes still on the TV.

'Rachel and Sayeed home?' he asks.

'Yea, yea,' Romesh says. He motions with one hand towards the bedrooms. 'They're sleeping. Boy, it's late. I'm going to switch this off and go to bed. JR is a real double-crosser, you don't find? You saw?'

'No, I didn't see it.'

'You didn't see it? Oh gosh, I keep forgetting, they took the TV. Sorry. If you had reminded me, I would have taped it for you. You want me to tape it for you next week?'

'Well – OK,' Clyde says. 'Why not? I don't mind missing it, but Joy likes it.'

'I'll tape it for you. You should have told me.' He opens the cabinet that the TV is resting on, pulls out a VHS tape and looks at

[24]

the writing scribbled on the label. 'I could tape over this,' he says.

'Hear nuh,' Clyde says. 'Paul hasn't come back. You could come in the car with me? I want to go and look by the quarry.'

'He hasn't come back? It's getting so late!'

'Exactly. Joy is worrying herself to death.'

Romesh puts the VHS tape on top of the cabinet, next to the TV, and then closes the cabinet doors. The TV is showing an advertisement for Trouble cologne. 'Boy, I going to switch this off,' Romesh says. 'I going to bed.' He pushes in the knob and the image on the screen shrinks to a dot then dies.

'Wait, I want you to come out with me,' Clyde says. 'I didn't want to take my car for it to look like I was out of the house.'

'You want to take my car? You want the keys?' Romesh gets up, stands in front of the fan. 'Lord oh Lord,' he says, 'it's hot for so, eh? I can't wait for rainy season to come.' He presses his chest to the wire grille, lifts his arms. His t-shirt puffs out at the back with the breeze. 'Aah,' he says. 'Coolness.'

'You can't come with me? It'll only be a half-hour or so. I just want to go by the quarry, and drive around on the roads and look for him.'

'He might be in the nightclub, you know. You thought of that?' Romesh says. He turns to face Clyde, pressing his back to the fan.

'What nightclub?'

'The one in Arima. Limin' Soda,' Romesh says. 'Thursday night is the best night, that's when all the young-fellas try to get in. That's what Sayeed tells me.'

'Sayeed? But he's twelve years old! That place is for eighteen and over!'

'Yea, but they all get in, man, how you mean? Nowadays? Anywhere it have a fete? That is where the young-fellas want to be these days. Ent Peter and Paul going to a fete up in Port of Spain just now? At Chinese Association?'

'Yea. Supposedly.'

'How you mean?'

Clyde makes a face. 'Well. Paul won't be going to any fetes after this stunt, I could tell you!'

'Exactly,' says Romesh. 'Right. You is the boss. Show him you mean business.' He nods several times.

'You think that's it?' Clyde says. 'That's where he is?'

Romesh is pressing his chest to the fan again, his shirt puffing out at the back. 'Most likely,' he says.

Clyde settles down on one of the armchairs, reaches forward for the cigarettes and matches on the coffee table. 'You mind?' he asks. 'I didn't bring mine.'

Romesh nods, flops onto a chair, jiggles his knees.

Clyde slides a cigarette out, places it between his lips, lights it with a match. 'Teenagers!' he says, tossing the match in the ashtray. 'This boy is taking years off my life, I swear to God. He'd better be in this nightclub, let me tell you. He'd better not be getting up to any kind of mischief.' He rubs his fingers along the lines of the corduroy fabric, runs his nails along the grooves. 'Hear nuh,' he says. 'I wanted to ask you something. Who has the contract for your security system?' He mentions the name of a man in Arima who has been trying to sell him a security system since the break-in. 'He says he'll give me a good discount. But I don't know who he is! Whoever comes to put in a security system, they have access to every room in your house, not so? They say they're laying wires, but while they do it, they make sure to go round the whole place, looking to see where the drawers are, where the cupboards are, they look under the mattresses, everything.'

Romesh runs his hands through his hair, looks at his palms, wipes them on his shorts.

'Something wrong?' Clyde asks.

'I find it hot. You don't find it hot?'

Clyde shrugs. Romesh gets up and goes to the fan again. He pulls up the knob to stop the fan from rotating, switches the power up to maximum.

'So to be quite honest,' Clyde continues, 'I don't want to let anybody into my house like that, for them to snoop around. And the other thing is, once you start a contract, you're paying them every month. Every single month you have to see these people to pay them their money, and every time they'll be asking all your business. What you think? Who put in your security system for you?'

'I don't remember. I'll find out for you tomorrow.'

'You don't remember?'

'Rachel organises it. It's somebody her family knows who does it for us.'

'Oh, you don't pay?'

'No.'

'Oh.'

'Come, I want to lock up now,' Romesh says. 'I want to have a shower and go to bed.'

Clyde stubs out the cigarette, gets up. 'I'll call you in the morning,' he says.

He goes back through the living room, through the patio, Romesh walking slowly after him. At the gate, it takes him a moment to unhook the padlock from where he left it looped in place; as he is lifting the latch at the top, he glances over his shoulder and sees Romesh already unchaining the dogs. 'Hold on,' he calls, but the first dog is loose, its eyes fixed on him. Clyde manages to get out to the road before the dog reaches him: with one hand he holds the gate firm; with the other, he tries to get the latch in place. He has to lean all his weight against the gate for the dogs not to push it open; their teeth catch at his elbow, his shoulder. At last he gets the catch secure and backs away, his heart racing. 'You couldn't wait for me to get out, man?' Clyde shouts. 'Hey! You hearing me?' But Romesh goes up his stairs without turning his head, and soon after that, Clyde hears the key turning in the lock. Clyde walks back along Bougainvillea Avenue feeling shaky with adrenaline, half-wanting to go back to Romesh and shout at him for his carelessness. The pilot has gone home: his car is gone from the drive, the patio dark, only the security lights on. At the last house, the old pothound takes a few lopsided steps towards her gate and then sits and tries to scratch her ear. In the bright floodlights, Clyde sees strands of her old fur float away like dandelion seeds.

The men are still on the recreation ground, their voices louder than before, their laughter higher-pitched. He makes them out as he gets closer: two men sprawled on the ground, another leaning against the side of the car. There's the Jamaican man who works as an engineer offshore doing six weeks on, six weeks off; another man with bad acne and long fingernails who has a job in the Ministry of Works; another man who Clyde has never seen before, a thinnish, light-skinned kind of man who looks like he belongs in a library.

'Deyalsingh!' one of the men calls, one of the ones sitting on the ground. 'You lost, man? What you doing out here at this time of night?'

'Boy?' Clyde says, with a steups. 'I got sent out on a wild goose chase. One of my boys is playing the jackass and staying out late.'

He kicks the ground, nods at each of the men in turn.

'Pass him the bottle,' the man with acne says, laughing. 'That's what he came here for. He need a drink.'

'You so wound up all the time, man,' the engineer says. 'You can't live like that! All the time just sitting in your house, never coming out to lime? Man need to relax sometimes, you know. Life so stressful!'

'Which child it is?' the man with acne asks. 'Tarzan?'

The librarian chokes on his drink, opens his mouth and lets the liquid fall to the ground. 'Tarzan? You named your child Tarzan?'

Clyde lifts the rum bottle to his lips. He tips his head back while the men laugh, allows a drop to touch his tongue, feels the sweet heat of it spread from there to the back of his throat. He passes the bottle back.

'His name is something else, I don't remember what,' the man with acne says. 'They just call him Tarzan. He has long hair, he's swing around on vines and thing.'

'He's probably in the nightclub,' Clyde says. 'You-all know about this nightclub?'

'Limin' Soda,' the engineer says. 'Everybody knows.'

'Thursday night,' says the librarian. 'Thursday night is ladies' night!'

'How things going, since the break-in?' the engineer asks. 'You got a security system yet?'

'I'm speaking to somebody about it,' Clyde says. 'I'm getting a quote.'

'Put it in,' the engineer says. 'I know somebody who works in security. You want me to organise it for you?'

'No, no,' Clyde says. 'I already picked a company. I already decided.'

[29]

'Oho. OK. Well, as long as you have some kind of protection. You already had one break-in and you got away scot-free, you might not be so lucky the next time.'

'Who broke in?' the librarian asks.

The men fill the librarian in on the details. Clyde takes the torch from his waistband and turns it in his hands, squeezing his fingers around the rubber casing. He looks at the clump of trees just there, behind the swings and the see-saws, scanning the darkness for any sign of movement. To his left, twenty or thirty feet away, is the dark road where he walked earlier. The torch is heavy enough to hit someone with, but if someone runs out of those bushes with a gun, this little torch won't be any use. Clyde looks at the ground, at the path he might take over the men's sprawled-out legs to the far side of the car: he could crouch down to the ground there or even crawl under the car. He holds the torch in one hand, taps it against the other palm.

'You found out who it was? Who was behind it?' the librarian asks. 'That sounds like somebody organised, for them to have a gun, and come with wire in their pockets. They came prepared!'

'I don't know who it was,' Clyde says. 'Why would I want to know? Unless I could go and shoot everybody who does something wrong to me. I'm not into that. I mind my own business.'

But the men talk anyway about who they have heard is behind it: a gang, not just one of the little Boyz on the Block-type gangs, as they call themselves, but one of the more serious gangs, one of the proper criminal rings that have connections in the police, the army, the coast guard. 'But why they're taking an interest in you, that is what I want to know!' the civil servant says. 'You have some drugs hidden under the mattress or something?'

'Me?' Clyde says. 'You mad? I stay far away from all of that.'

'You need that security system,' the engineer says. 'Put it in, I'm telling you. Now for now.'

'Security system wouldn't help him,' the librarian says. He mentions the latest gossip, about the property magnate in Port of Spain whose wife was kidnapped. 'Security systems didn't help him,' he says. 'He had a fence fifteen feet high around his house, and he has private security patrolling the perimeter night and day. And still they found a way to take his wife.'

'Well, nobody will touch his family now,' Clyde says. The property magnate apparently paid the ransom in full to get his wife back, and then two weeks later, so the rumour goes, he sent hit-men to wipe out the kidnappers. Six murders in six locations around Trinidad, all within the space of a few hours.

'The hit-men were Colombian,' the librarian says. 'Professionals.'

'I heard Jamaican,' says Clyde.

'No. They were Venezuelan,' says the engineer. He heard it from someone connected to the businessman's family, someone who knows. 'They came across on a pirogue about midday, they got hooked up with the locals doing the driving, and they went around *bam-bam-bam!*' – he makes a motion as if shooting a gun – 'and then they went back over about six o'clock.'

Silence falls between them. Clyde, suddenly nervous, looks over his shoulder. He says goodnight to the men, sets off back home; he doesn't want to be out here any more, with Peter and Joy in the house alone. What if Paul's disappearing trick is all some kind of ploy to get Clyde out of the house, for who knows what purpose? He reprimands himself as soon as the thought crosses his mind: whatever else Paul might be, surely the boy wouldn't be so evil as to do a thing like that.

But the truth of the matter is, he thinks, as he walks along the roadside in the dark, who knows what Paul gets up to when he's by himself? There was that night, for example, it must have been over a year ago, when Clyde woke with the feeling of a strange breeze passing through the house, of something not being right. He picked up the rock he keeps under his bed and crept out. The kitchen door was wide open, Trixie panting at the top step, wagging her tail at him. And there on the back lawn, lying flat on his back, was Paul. Clyde nearly had a heart attack: he thought, perhaps, that the boy was dead. He went down the steps, feeling he had to get closer, look in the child's eyes; he might see that he was really crazy, really and truly. He drew closer, the rock in his fist. And then Paul sat up and looked around.

'What are you doing out here?' Clyde asked, his voice hoarse.

'Nothing.'

Nothing! Lying down under the sky like a dead man in the middle of the night! 'Come inside,' Clyde said. It was all he could think to say. Paul came inside. Clyde locked the back door and lay down in bed, staring up at the ceiling, his blood pounding. Tomorrow, he thought. Tomorrow he would take Paul aside and ask him. 'What were you doing?' he would ask. 'What the hell were you doing?' But he couldn't find the right moment: one day passed without him saying anything, and then another, and then it seemed too late.

When Paul comes back, Clyde thinks, as he walks along the road – tomorrow, when Paul is back, Clyde will sit him down and get some answers out of him. First question: Where is he, and who is he with, and what possessed him to stay out so late? Second: Does he really go walking around at night like people say? Where does he go? What does he do? Third: Paul had better not be mixed up in anything to do with that rastaman, because if he is, Clyde will set him straight, no doubt about it. Clyde slaps the torch against his thigh as he turns into La Sagesse Trace. He won't put it off, he tells himself: the moment Paul walks in the door, Clyde will sit him down straight away, and he won't let the boy leave the room until he gets his answers.

3

There is no TV any more since the break-in, just a light-coloured rectangle on the sideboard in the space where it used to be; instead, now, Clyde sits in his armchair, watching the curtain gently lift and fall with the breeze. The room feels very quiet with the fan off. From outside, just below the window, there's the quiet snarling of Trixie holding Brownie down at the neck, the click of teeth against teeth. Earlier, the national anthem played on a television somewhere along the Trace: Joy looked at Clyde, as if expecting him to do something. 'Midnight!' she said. 'Eh, Clyde? It's midnight now!' He didn't answer. She can't stop fidgeting: she looks at the window, at the clock, at him, at the window again; she looks at her nails, her palms, the hem of her shorts; she takes a corner of the bedsheet laid over the sofa, wipes her face.

One of the bedroom doors squeaks open: they listen to Peter pause at the threshold and then walk to the bathroom. There's the quiet tap of the toilet seat being raised, the tinkling of him urinating. The pitch changes from high to low to high again as the liquid hits the water in the pan, then the side of the toilet bowl, then the water again. The clank of porcelain as Peter removes the top of the cistern. He must find it full, because he flushes: the pipes shudder as the toilet water flows out, and then there's the harsh coughing sound of the empty cistern trying to refill and failing. Peter fills it back with water from the bucket and returns quietly to his room. Tomorrow, Clyde thinks, he'll tell Peter not to use the water to flush away a – what should he call it? A number one. 'You could flush down the number two, yes,' he'll say. 'But don't use up the water on a number one.'

'I want to decide about this water tank,' Joy says, some minutes after Peter has gone back to bed. 'We have to decide what we're doing. If we're staying here, then buy the water tank and put it in, fix up the house. If we're going to Port of Spain, then let's go, let's just pack up one-time and go, and whatever it costs, we'll pay it.'

Clyde closes his eyes, presses his thumb to his temple. 'You see, that is why I told you to go to bed,' he tells her. 'Because I knew you would start on this. Water tank, washing machine, furniture, curtains, bookshelf . . .'

'They need a bookshelf to put their books in. They can't have them on the floor getting dirty. You think that is how they should treat books?'

'They're not on the floor. They keep them in their schoolbags.'

'They need a bookshelf, Clyde, or at least somewhere to line up the books properly, to organise themselves. Two more years and they'll be doing O-levels! This is serious business, Clyde!'

'I know that. You think I don't know that?'

'Well, that's why I'm saying. You're saving, saving, thinking about the future, but what about today?' She folds her arms, looks towards the window. 'And Romesh keeps telling you he has people lining up ready to buy this house from you? So many people want to buy this house and build on the land! Why we don't sell the house and use the money to rent a place in Port of Spain? That makes the most sense to me. And then the boys wouldn't have to travel so far to get to school. All this waking up at four o'clock in the morning. It's not good for children to operate like that. It exhausts them. Peter looking exhausted. Under his eyes, he has big bags.' She touches her finger to the skin under her own eyes. 'That is exhaustion. I'm telling you. We need to move up.'

'You think now is the time to talk about this?'

'When is the time, then?' she says. 'I'll tell you when. The time was last week. Last month. Last year. All now we could have been living in Port of Spain.'

He reaches for the newspaper folded on the coffee table and opens the paper to the classifieds, where two of the little boxes are circled in blue ballpoint ink. 'Here, look at those and tell me what you think.'

Joy reads out the advertisements: the number of bedrooms; the locations; the level of security in the houses; and the prices, which, he already knows, are more than they can afford. She gets a pen, asks him for numbers – how much will this house sell for? How much will they have to pay for electricity, telephone, water? She does her calculations on the margin of the newspaper and then stares at the answer.

'So if we sell this house,' she says, 'we could live for three years in Port of Spain.'

'More or less.'

'Three years is a long time.'

'And Peter has five more years of school? You think three years is enough?'

'But we could pay from your salary. And in Port of Spain, I could pick up some work.'

He stares straight ahead, breathes out a long plume of smoke as she talks. He does not say that there are other things she hasn't even thought of yet; that he has heard, from other men who have children in Port of Spain, how the children have all kinds of expensive entertainments: they go to the shopping malls, buy things like lamb gyros and frozen yoghurt; they go to the beach, and they can't just go in the water in their clothes like normal children, they must have a bathing costume; that one pair of shoes is not enough, they need different shoes for every place they go. Joy talks and talks, about her father and her grandfather, and about all the things they should spend their money on instead of keeping it in the bank account. His cigarette burns down to the end. He rubs at the scratches on his neck, picks away a prickly burr still stuck to the hair of his forearms. At last, she gives up. Her shoulders slump. With one finger, she slowly traces the lines on her palm.

'What if he's not in the nightclub?' she asks.

'We'll soon see.'

'You should take the car and drive to Arima and see, Clyde.'

'No! I already said no! I'm not leaving you-all alone here in the house.'

'But Peter looked worried,' Joy says.

'Well, he was probably worried because you were worried.'

'I am worried. Of course I'm worried. Aren't you worried?'

'A little bit. But I think he's at the nightclub.'

'Peter said he wouldn't be there.'

'Yea, but how would Peter know? They're more separate now. Maybe Peter doesn't know.'

'But they're brothers,' Joy says. 'They're *twins*. Peter must know.'

'Peter's not responsible for him. I keep telling you this, the same thing, over and over. Why must Peter be responsible for him? Peter has his own life to worry about!'

Joy goes quiet. Clyde knows that Peter, in his bedroom, must be listening. He stubs out his cigarette; the ashtray tips, spilling ash onto his trousers.

'I'll go and lie down for a little while,' she says.

'Sure. You go to bed. There's no point two of us staying up.'

She stares at him as he brushes away the ash, and then she gets up and slowly walks away.

After she has gone, Clyde gets up, pulls back the curtain to look through the window. The dogs must have gone around the back, the yard is quiet. He brushes the dust from the bedsheet laid over his armchair, then pins the sheet in place with one hand while he carefully twists to get into the seat. He clasps his hands at his waist. He doesn't mind sitting here alone. He sometimes sits up for a little while after Joy and the boys have gone to bed; sometimes he pours himself a little glass of rum and spends a while thinking things over until he feels ready to sleep. He crosses his legs, studies the walls around him, the curtains with their blue and green flowers, the Celotex panels of the ceiling, the brown-stained patches where leaks have come through. Romesh has been saying that Clyde can get eighty thousand for this house: people want this land, he says, because of the empty plot on one side and the empty land in the back. People will take a little extra land from both sides, he says, and they'll build a big compound for two-three families to live in together. Several times now, men have approached Clyde – in the grocery store, in the shopping malls, at the T&TEC office while he was waiting in line to pay his electricity bill. 'You're Deyalsingh?' the men said, shaking his hand. 'From up by La Sagesse?' And they asked, 'You want to sell the house yet?' And each time, Clyde laughed like it was a joke and said, 'Not yet, boy, not yet.'

Once he sells this house, he knows how things will be: they will be forever packing up, scrambling to try and find somewhere to live, knocking on people's doors asking to stay a few days, a few weeks, a few months. Clyde spent years like that after he walked out of this house – it was when he was twelve, after a fight with his father – years of carrying his few possessions around in a plastic bag, and sleeping on bare mattresses, or on cardboard and newspaper laid out on the floor, or on two armchairs pushed together. At least this house, here in La Sagesse, belongs to him. Clyde studies the cracks on the walls, the thin ones behind the sofa that look like faint pencil marks, that bigger one in the corner that starts at the ceiling and spreads and branches down the wall. Compared to Romesh's big living room, this place looks like a cardboard box. It only just fits the furniture they have put in: the three-seater sofa against the wall, Clyde's armchair, the standing fan next to him, the cabinet beneath the window. In the middle is the coffee table, a dusty chipped wooden box with carvings of cows along the rim, which he would like to throw away but which Joy wants to keep because it once belonged to somebody in her family. Behind him, in the other half of the room, is the mahogany dining table and velvet-padded chairs he bought from Courts a few years ago. Two months' salary that table cost him – if they move to Port of Spain, what will happen to the table? It will go in someone's pick-up truck, get wet in the rain, or someone will drop it, and a leg will break off. There's no point in buying expensive things, Clyde thinks, not unless you're somewhere stable, somewhere you can say: this is my house, this is where I live, where I'm always going to live.

Somewhere in the neighbourhood, there's the deep throbbing of calypso music playing. Clyde pictures the men on the recreation ground, now with a boombox and a set of women clustered around them, the alcohol flowing. Carnival isn't for a little while yet, but already the feteing has started; every year, earlier and earlier. Clyde said no at first, when Peter and Paul asked to go to the fete in Port of Spain, but then Joy talked him into it, said to let the boys free up a little bit, let them see their school-friends. 'Schoolfriends,' Clyde said, 'and girls!' And Joy said, yes, of course. They're teenaged boys, she said, of course they want to see girls. Clyde agreed to the fete, and he made a little song and dance about them behaving themselves, and said woe betide them if he hears of any irresponsible behaviour; but, secretly, he is glad that Peter wants to go out. Clyde has often wondered if it is really healthy for a boy to be inside all the time, studying studying like Peter does. Sometimes, late at night, Clyde has seen the strip of light under the door of the boys' room – at midnight, one o'clock in the morning – and he's knocked, opened the door, and found Peter sitting on the bed, or on the floor next to the bed, still working. All weekend, when the other boys are out on the road playing football or cricket, Peter stays in his room, or sits at the dining table with his books spread out around him, books full of long words and graphs and diagrams that make no sense to Clyde at all. It is like there are two islands, Clyde thinks, one for people who understand about these things, and another for people who don't understand. Even now, at thirteen, Peter is like a foreigner in Trinidad. Look at what the Principal, Father Malachy, said about him after that prize-giving ceremony a few months ago. Clyde had sat in the chapel pew watching as his son went up to the altar over and over again to collect the wooden plaques: Geography, Spanish, Mathematics, clapping, clapping, clapping. Afterwards, Father Malachy called Clyde into his office for a word. (That was what he said: he tapped Clyde on the arm and said into his ear, 'Can I have a word?') Clyde was nervous as he followed Father Malachy through the school corridors to the office, wondering whether he had done something wrong. Then, in the office, Father Malachy pulled his chair up and clasped his hands over the desk. 'Now,' he said. 'Tell me what you're planning for him. University-wise, I mean.'

'I'm not sure,' Clyde said. He laughed, relieved not to be in trouble. 'I was thinking the States. Or Canada. I have nobody to advise me.' Father Malachy didn't move. He looked very stern. Clyde wished that Peter was here to tell him what to say. He thought of explaining in a jokey voice that the people who used to advise him were all dead, but Father Malachy didn't look in the mood for jokes.

'I will advise you,' Father Malachy said. 'I am advising you now. Go right to the top.' He counted off on his fingers. 'Harvard, Yale, Princeton, MIT, all of them.'

'But Father!' Clyde said, still smiling. 'Those places expensive! How I would pay for that?'

Father Malachy talked for a long time. He said, let me explain. He said, with a boy like Peter, money would not be a problem. He talked about the different scholarships that Peter might win. He called the names of the boys from St Saviour's who had won various levels of island scholarships, what portion of their fees had been paid by the government, where they are working now. 'And then there's the Gold Medal,' Father Malachy said: the Gold Medal had been won by a St Saviour's boy four times in the last ten years.

'Very good,' Clyde said. He said it with a smile, as if playing along at something; he didn't know what else to do.

Father Malachy folded his arms, leaned them on the table; Clyde felt his heart thudding in the silence before the priest

spoke. 'Look here,' he said. 'Look here. I don't think you understand the kind of child you have on your hands.'

The dogs on the Trace are barking: that must be Paul now, Clyde
thinks, getting up. It's after three! He pulls back an edge of the
curtain to look: the footsteps out there don't sound familiar, and
the person is bashing a stick against the ground as he walks. Clyde
waits for the person to come into view: it's just one of the vagrants,
the older one who sleeps in the old bus shelter during the day and
walks around by night. It crosses Clyde's mind to go out to speak
to the man, to ask him whether he has seen any sign of Paul, but
there's no point. The man is completely mad: when he talks, only
gibberish comes out of his mouth. He sits in his chair again; the
sheet slips down and crumples behind his shoulders.

He picks up the newspaper, reads the circled advertisements,
checks the sums that Joy has done in the margin. He knows
that they have to move to Port of Spain; he's not denying that at
all. But buying is out of the question, and the only houses that
they can afford to rent are so small: the back yards are just little
squares of concrete, and in some of the houses there is no front
yard at all – instead, the front porch is pressed right up against
the pavement, so that everyone going by can see what you're
doing and hear what you're saying. Here, in Tiparo, he can sit
on his patio morning and evening, and there is no big set of traffic passing by or people macoing his business, there is just cool
breeze and quietness. It was the same in Mayaro, where Clyde
lived with his auntie years ago: just cool breeze and the sound
of the waves, and the smell of fish cooking on the fire in the evenings. Mayaro was nice. It was a nice place to live, a place where
everybody knew everybody, and the children played all day on

the beach, building rafts out of driftwood and coconuts and bits of fishing net, and the women sat in the shade of the trees for a few hours each afternoon after their work was done. If things were different, Clyde would have thought about moving back to Mayaro and maybe building a house – just a little house, he could build it himself, he didn't need anything fancy – but he knows it is impossible. Nowadays, things are getting harder; a man can't make a living any more on the few fish he manages to pull in from the sea. No, they will go to Port of Spain, that is for sure. It would be nicer to live in a quiet, peaceful place like Mayaro, just like it would be nice to have a new roof and a new car and a new TV. But nice is one thing; essential is another.

He is woken by the sound of choking and spluttering from the kitchen, the water coming back. He hadn't realised he was asleep. The room looks small, dark, empty. He gets up, stretching his back, a cold feeling in the pit of his stomach. The birds are singing. The whole night has passed and Paul is still not back! He fills the kettle, boils water for a cup of coffee. Not that he needs it – he feels wide awake now – but it gives him something to do. The dogs come up the back-steps and scratch at the door, wanting their morning titbit. Clyde stands by the sink watching through the window as morning creeps in. The hills behind the house were just dark shadows a moment ago; now he can make out their silhouettes against the deep blue sky, still speckled with stars.

A door opens: Peter, his hair rumpled, eyes puffy.

'Is Paul home?'

Clyde shakes his head.

'What time is it?'

'I don't know. Probably half-four, quarter to five.'

Clyde can see, under Peter's t-shirt, how much the muscles across his chest and shoulders have thickened, how the lump of his Adam's apple glides up and down under the skin as he yawns. Thirteen years old is already a man, these days – a young man, but still a man.

'You think he would come back from the nightclub so late?' Clyde asks.

'He wouldn't be at the nightclub,' Peter says. 'He's not at the nightclub.'

'Well, where is he then?'

Peter rubs at a bit of dried spit at the side of his mouth. 'I don't know.' He and Clyde stare at each other. 'I don't know,' Peter says again, shaking his head.

Joy is getting up – they hear the bedsprings, and then her footsteps and then she pushes open their bedroom door.

'Paul there?' she asks. 'He's home?'

They both shake their heads. She stands there for a moment in her thin nightie, scratching at a mosquito bite on her arm. 'He's not home?'

Clyde shakes his head. 'Water came back,' he says.

She goes into the bathroom, murmuring to herself.

Clyde sends Peter to get ready for school and then he gets the key from the hook, unlocks the back door and stands in the doorway, watching the sun coming over the top of the hill. Beneath the shining rim of light, the hillside is quiet, still taking shape, grey-green, silver-green, gold-green. The dogs pant and jostle at his knees.

Now Clyde will have to ring Seepersad, his supervisor at the industrial estate, and say that, again, he cannot come in today. Already, Clyde can imagine Seepersad's expression, the steups as he hangs up the phone, how he will sit in his little office, the doors closed against the humming of the machines, the hiss of the gas vents, complaining to whoever is there that people in Trinidad don't know how to work, that every other day people are calling in sick, or coming in late, or leaving early.

All this is because of Paul, he thinks; it is Paul who is causing all this. If he isn't in the nightclub, then where is he? He begins to think now of other places that, he realises, didn't occur to him before. He might have been in an accident. He might have drunk a bottle of Gramoxone. He might have spent the night with a girl – but which girl? And where? And when will he come back? Or what if – Clyde winces at the thought – what if Paul goes with men for money? There is a man like that in Tiparo: his wife left him, and everyone knows why. Men like that offer money to boys to go with them, they pay a lot of money.

The sun is up; the light has hardened into shape. In the high branches of the poui tree on the hillside, the long, hanging nests of the cornbirds sway in the breeze, yellow flowers drift to the ground. Clyde sits on the step, suddenly afraid; the dogs sit with him, push their noses into his hands.

PART TWO

4

Clyde is sitting on the steps in front of the Port of Spain General Hospital, smoking a cigarette and watching the people passing by on Charlotte Street. It's coming up to half past ten in the morning, and he's been here for over twenty-four hours already, waiting for the babies to be born. Yesterday morning, while it was shady, he sat out on the stone steps at the front, watching office workers and schoolchildren go by; at midday, he went down to the vendors on the pavement to buy an arepa and a cold Red Solo; later, he walked across the hot glare of the car park to Reception to use the phone. When dusk fell, the daytime vendors closed up their umbrellas and wheeled their carts away. The waiting rooms cleared out. The night-time vendors arrived, still with umbrellas even though there was no sun, and stationed their carts under the street lights: these ones sold pholourie and bags of pink cotton candy and bottles of Carib. These, too, eventually drifted off. The receptionist and some of the nurses got in their cars and drove away. As Clyde sat out on the steps smoking, sometime around ten-eleven o'clock, the only people he saw were the one security guard, standing in his dark hut, and a vagrant walking down Charlotte Street, singing a hymn and swinging a bottle. Clyde passed the night hours sitting on a chair outside the door to the ward, counting the green tiles on the wall and walking from one end of the corridor to the other.

Now, again, it is morning: the daytime vendors have rolled back into place; women laden with bags get out of maxi taxis and make their way up to the wards to visit sick relatives. Clyde sits on the steps in the shade, watching how the schoolboys, stopping at the vendors on their way to school, eye up the girls; how the girls hitch their skirts above their knees, flick their hair around. A nun passes them and says something, and then they all start tucking their shirts in and holding out their dollars to the vendor to get their soft drinks. Clyde is watching all this, and noticing how St Saviour's boys look different, more intelligent, better behaved than the others, when the door in the corridor opens and someone comes up behind him.

'Deyalsingh?'

He gets up, dusting off his pants. 'Right here.'

'The first baby's born. A boy!'

'A boy!' he says. The people listening on the steps nearby start cheering, clapping Clyde on the back.

'It's your first child?' someone asks.

'First one,' Clyde says.

'He need a drink,' a man says, a fattish man in a red t-shirt. He taps a younger man on the shoulder. 'Go down by the vendors and see if you could get him a cold Carib. Whole night the man waiting here.'

'Hello,' the doctor says. 'Hello. I am talking.'

'Sorry,' Clyde says. 'I listening. You-all, hush. Let the doctor speak.'

'We having some trouble with the second one. But Joy is OK.'

'Good, very good.'

'We'll get it out, don't worry. And then we'll see.'

'OK, doc. You go. I will wait here.'

Clyde comes up the steps. In the corridor, outside the door to the ward, are an older woman with a basket and a pregnant girl in a flimsy pink vest. Clyde puts his hands in his pockets, walks past a few chairs pushed against the wall, past an abandoned mop and bucket, to the far end of the corridor where there is a sick-looking banana tree and a rusted water tank. He turns and comes back: past the bucket, past the chairs, past the woman and girl and the door to the ward. The little crowd of people has drifted away from the steps; a few stray dogs are nosing amongst the rubbish they have left behind. Clyde turns and walks back. Back and forward, forward and back.

'Sit down,' the older woman says to him, after a while. 'You making people anxious.'

She fishes around in her basket, pulls out some food wrapped in tinfoil, hands it to him. It is a sweet-cake, still warm from the oven, grains of brown sugar stuck to the top. The pregnant girl doubles over, gasps. Clyde sits, eats. The girl's face is like a dead person's. Clyde looks away.

'Walk,' the woman commands the girl. '*You*'s the one who need to walk.' The girl walks slowly, resting one hand on the wall. The straps of her vest slip down her shoulders.

'They ent come out to tell you anything yet, boy,' the woman says, after a while.

'No.'

She sucks something out of her teeth, shakes her head.

'What?' says Clyde.

'Something wrong,' she says.

The girl starts crying out. Clyde cannot listen to this. He goes back out to the brightness of the steps outside and sits and watches the people passing in front on Charlotte Street. Office workers in their long-sleeved shirts; ladies in high-heels and make-up, all off to air-conditioned offices; men with produce loaded into the backs of their pick-up trucks, to sell downtown; women laden with shopping bags.

'Mr Deyalsingh,' the doctor calls, behind him.

The stray dogs look up at him as he slowly goes up the steps, draw in their paws and tails to let him pass. The doctor leads him past the ward, through another door at the far end of the corridor, into a small room with no proper window, just one glass louvre high up on the wall near the ceiling. Joy's uncle, Uncle Vishnu, is there: Clyde is used to seeing him in shortpants and t-shirt, but right now Uncle Vishnu is in his doctor's clothes, black pants and a white shirt-jac. He smiles as he shakes Clyde's hand, and says congratulations, but there's no old-talk; Clyde stands to one side, trying not to look at the baby lying in a sort of plastic box in the middle. It's smaller than he expected, with blue veins visible across its chest, its arms, its upturned palms. It's lying on its back, its head turned a little to the side. Joy and the other baby aren't there.

Deprived of oxygen, the first doctor is saying. *Possible mental retardation. Cord wrapped around the neck.* Clyde raises his chin, trying to get some air from the louvre. There should be a proper window in this room. The doctors talk about many things – forceps, heart rates, contractions. *Mental retardation?* His heart is beating very fast. There is nowhere to sit down. While the other doctor talks, Uncle Vishnu's eyes are fixed on the baby. He touches his fingertips all over the small body, pressing, tapping, listening. Clyde starts to sweat. Finally Uncle Vishnu goes to the sink, washes his hands, and then stands back, still looking at the baby, stroking his beard.

'Well?' Clyde says. He speaks louder than he means to. 'What you think?'

For a moment, Uncle Vishnu doesn't reply.

'What?' says Clyde. 'What is it?'

'I don't see any abnormality,' Uncle Vishnu says. But he stands there for a few moments more, stroking his beard, watching the baby. It is as if he knows there must be something wrong with it, Clyde thinks, he just cannot work out what it is.

That week, while Joy stays in hospital recovering, Clyde and Joy's mother, Mousey, get the house ready for her and the babies to come home. He arranges with the foreman to get to work early and leave just after lunch. He goes to the hardware store in Arima, buys cans of paint in 'Apple Green' and 'Baby Blue'; he borrows paintbrushes, rollers, ladders, cloths; drags the furniture away from the walls. While he paints, Mousey stands at the concrete sink outside, just under the kitchen window, doing the washing: curtains, clothes, sheets, towels, diapers, dishcloths, every single thing, she says, must be washed before the babies come home. Mousey has been living with Clyde and Joy in La Sagesse Trace for a while now: it was only meant to be a temporary arrangement while she was getting over pneumonia, but Joy likes having her here so she hasn't left. She's in her sixties, Mousey, small and thin and tireless, with long grey hair that she washes twice a week with sap from a cactus plant and then winds into a bun. She fills the sink with water, taps in the Breeze washing powder and mixes with her hand until there is a sinkful of white suds. Then she gathers the sheets into a bundle between her fists and rubs it against the ridges on the sloping side of the sink. *Frush-frush-frush*, it goes. Clyde finds himself painting in time with her rhythm. *Frush-frush-frush*. She kneads the bundle to let a different part reach the ridges.

Frush-frush-frush.

Knead.

Frush-frush-frush.

The Chin Lees offer their washing line for extra space; so do the Bartholomews next to them, and Mrs des Vignes in the next house down. All along La Sagesse Trace, sheets, blinding white in the midday sun, flap on the washing lines.

Uncle Vishnu brings a cot from Joy's older brother who's finished with it, and a vinyl-covered mattress for the cot, and a brand-new fan still wrapped in plastic. The old women in saris – aunts, sisters, friends; there are so many of them that Clyde loses track of who's who – arrive, with tiny baby-clothes that they hold up to each other and squeal at. They bring big iron pots and jars of spices, and install themselves in the kitchen. When Clyde comes back from the hospital with Joy and the babies, the house is spotless and the big iron pots are full of food: rice, roti, curry chicken, curry shrimp, alloo pies, green salads, macaroni pie.

Joy needs help to get out of the car and up the steps; as soon as she reaches the patio, she grips the back of a chair, all the colour gone out of her face. 'Sit, sit, sit,' the women say, all the women who have taken over Clyde's house. 'Make her sit down.' A plate of food is brought to her. Uncle Vishnu and Clyde eat too, their plates balanced on their knees. When the babies start to cry, the women mix up bottles of milk; others walk, bouncing and shushing. Joy looks for somewhere to put down her plate. Clyde takes it from her.

'Don't let her get up, make her sit,' someone calls. 'Bring her the babies,' someone else says. 'Look, she's fretting. Bring them to her.'

The good baby takes its bottle, settles. The other one twists and lurches, its face turning purple. 'Is that normal?' Clyde asks. 'Is it supposed to look like that?' Milk spills out of the baby's mouth, trickles down its cheek to the folds of its neck. It splutters, turns purple again. 'That doesn't look right,' Clyde says.

Mousey turns to Uncle Vishnu. 'Why you-all don't go out for a drive or something?' she says. 'Take Clyde to get some fresh air.'

Uncle Vishnu, still chewing, puts down his plate, pats his pockets for his keys. 'No problem!' he says. 'Eh, Clyde? Come. You and me will go out. The men.'

'Yes, you men go out,' Mousey says. 'It's better.'

'Anywhere you want to go?' Uncle Vishnu asks, when they get in his car and reverse out the drive.

'Not really,' Clyde says. He wants to stay in his house with his wife, and to show her the rooms that he painted, all the things that he has done.

'Now is the time to give her some space,' Uncle Vishnu says. He waves to the children playing outside the gas station. 'Give her a little room. But don't worry, things will come back like before. It will take a little time.'

'Sure, sure,' Clyde says. He lights a cigarette. He is glad of the fresh air and the breeze through the car window. He is glad to be away from the women and babies, and seeing Joy so silent and weak, and the strange twisting and lurching of the sick baby. This is why men end up in the rum shop, he thinks – in the rum shops and on street corners, playing cards and gambling and going with other women and fathering children all over Trinidad. He doesn't exactly know what he's going to do, what he is supposed to do, but he knows for sure that it isn't that. When he has smoked the cigarette down, he mashes it into the ashtray and brushes the dust from his fingers. He looks at his hands, still covered with speckles of Baby Blue paint.

'Boy, you know, I really have to ask you something,' Clyde says to Uncle Vishnu, after a while. They are out of the valley, coming into town. 'Why you driving this old mash-up car?' The car is an old Nissan Bluebird with the rearview mirror cracked and taped over with Sellotape, the stuffing poking out through cracks in the vinyl seats.

Uncle Vishnu laughs; Clyde realises that he has been staying quiet all this time, waiting for Clyde to feel better. 'Man, I don't need those kind of things,' Uncle Vishnu says. 'What I need a fancy car for? So people will ooh and aah when they see me coming?' He rests his elbow in the open car window, waving frequently to people he knows. 'Man, they already glad to see me! You know how many people trying to get appointment with me and I'm all booked up? Sometimes, at the hospital, I'm still seeing patients at all kind of nine-ten o'clock at night.'

'But that's what I mean,' Clyde says. 'You could have a big house in Haleland Park or Federation Park or one or those places, instead of that little place you live in.'

'Man, I don't need any of that stuff,' Uncle Vishnu says. 'As long as I'm working? I'm happy. People say, Vishnu, why you don't take a holiday? Go Miami, London, all those places? I say – what I want to take holiday for? Holiday from what? I love what I do. I don't need holidays.'

In the parking lot for the grocery, a youngish man comes up to them, in a white t-shirt and flip-flops, and a baseball cap with 'Yankees' written on it in swirly writing. He leans in politely until Uncle Vishnu sees him. 'Hi, doc,' he says. He extends a hand to shake. 'How you keeping?'

'Good, thanks, good,' Uncle Vishnu says. 'How's your mother?'

'She's very well,' the man says, still shaking his hand. 'She's well, thanks, doc.'

Inside the grocery, by a stack of dusty yams, a woman taps Uncle Vishnu on the shoulder. She's lightish-skinned, with grey hair, well dressed. 'Dr Ramcharan? Hi! I thought it looked like you.'

As Uncle Vishnu talks, the woman's eyes examine Clyde; Clyde tries to look respectable. 'And who's this you have with you?' she asks, smiling at Clyde. 'Not your son? I thought you had no children?'

'My nephew,' Uncle Vishnu says, and again Clyde shakes hands.

'You're not a Ramcharan,' the woman says. 'You don't have the Ramcharan face. You must be an in-law?'

Uncle Vishnu explains that yes, Clyde is an in-law. 'But same difference,' he says. 'It's still family. In-law or out-law, no matter!'

The woman laughs. 'I have something to bring for you,' she says. 'I'll drop it next week. OK? I'll put it in the carport for you if you're not in.'

Uncle Vishnu inclines his head graciously. 'OK,' he says. 'I wouldn't say no! Everything you bring always gets eaten, if not by me, then by somebody!'

They say their goodbyes and slowly push the trolley past the buckets of hot peppers and limes. Clyde runs his hand over a big watermelon, cool and smooth, the size of a pregnant woman's belly. In the refrigerated aisle, Uncle Vishnu picks up a chicken, a few damp feathers pressing against the plastic. 'Chicken,' he says. He picks up another one, puts it in the trolley next to the first one. 'Two chickens.'

Clyde follows, his hands in his pockets.

'What about shrimp? You like shrimp?' Uncle Vishnu asks, picking up a packet and inspecting it. 'I'm paying, eh?' he says, as he puts the shrimp in the trolley. 'I will pay for all of this.'

'Well, you get the meat, and I'll get the rest,' Clyde says.

'No, no,' Uncle Vishnu says. He's walking slowly along the refrigerated aisle. He picks up a pack of chicken feet and puts it down. 'You just had two babies, man. Let me give you a little treat, nuh.'

As well as the meat, Uncle Vishnu buys a sack of rice, six tins of Klim powdered milk, a jumbo pack of Crix crackers, Maggi stock cubes, cheese, eggs, macaroni, tomato ketchup, mustard, toilet paper, soap, shampoo, Squeezy, three cases of Carib, tinfoil, ice-cream cones and two tubs of Flavorite ice-cream, one vanilla, one rum 'n' raisin. Vegetables are better at the San Juan market, he says; he's not buying vegetables here. While he's lining up at the tills, another patient comes up to him to say hello, an elderly man with two grown-up daughters and several grandchildren in flip-flops. One of the daughters talks to Uncle Vishnu about someone's liver, while the man and the children look at Clyde and the full shopping trolley. Clyde puts out his hand to the old man. 'Clyde Deyalsingh,' he says. 'Nephew-in-law.'

'Hear nuh,' Uncle Vishnu says, in the car, on the way home. 'I was thinking. Mousey's living with you such a long time now. Let me give you some money to pay for her food.'

'If you want. But she doesn't eat much,' Clyde says.

'I know. And she's good, she works all the time. As long as she could stand up on her two feet, Mousey will work. Cook, clean, she will mind the children when Joy needs to rest.'

'I don't mind Mousey being with us at all. She helps Joy in the house. It doesn't bother me.'

'Let me leave some money for you anyway,' Uncle Vishnu says. 'I don't want to be putting any burden on you, you understand.'

'It's no burden,' Clyde says. 'So far, we managing OK.'

'What's the problem?' Uncle Vishnu says. 'You don't want to take money from me or something?' He looks confused.

'I'm not really in the habit of taking money from people,' Clyde says, tentatively. 'Borrowing, and things like that.'

'It's not borrowing. You don't have to pay me anything back. I just want to give you something to cover Mousey's expenses.' They're out of the town, on a fast stretch of road, but Uncle Vishnu glances towards Clyde every few seconds, waiting for him to reply. 'Eh? What's the problem?'

'Well,' Clyde says. He tries to speak lightly. 'When people give you money, there's usually strings attached!'

'You're right,' Uncle Vishnu says. He nods several times, and Clyde feels relieved that he hasn't taken offence. 'You're right to think twice before taking money from people. Very right. But I am not just *people*!' He says 'people' in a jokey tone, with a kind of mock-disgust. 'I am family with you, man! You are my family. There are no strings attached. I'm not going to come back in a year's time and say, oh, hello, you must pay me back such-and-such amount that I lent you. I am not like that.'

Clyde murmurs, 'Yea,' as Uncle Vishnu talks. There's nothing else he can say.

'Look. I could see you're not sure. You're worried I'm trying to take over. I'm not. But you are my family, man. I don't need all the money I earn! I prefer to give that money to my family, rather than buy things I don't need.'

They're coming back into the valley, where it's green and quiet. Uncle Vishnu goes slowly down the hill, braking often on the curving, narrow road where the bush grows thickly on both sides. When the road straightens out, the bush thins and the valley opens up to a wide green expanse dotted with trees and buffalo and goats, and the bright yellow of the poui trees in bloom. Uncle Vishnu lets the car coast down the slope.

'Let's do like this,' Uncle Vishnu says. 'I'll pay you a little bit to cover Mousey's expenses. You have extra mouths to feed now. All of that is a burden on you. I have seen it time and time again. Trust me, I am right. You might not feel it yet, but it will become a burden.'

In the months that follow, Clyde sees that Uncle Vishnu was right: that the burden on him grows and grows. The babies need milk, toys, clothes; they need bottles, special cups, plastic plates. They need no-more-tears shampoo, they need a pram, they need cream for diaper rash. Joy starts buying Pampers, because the cloth diapers are too slow to wash and dry every time; if there is no water, she can't wash them at all, and they just sit in a bucket stinking up the place. Joy's brothers and their families come over every few weeks, and they stay until late in the evening, and eat and drink and drink and eat. If Clyde does the shopping on a Saturday, by Tuesday the food will be finished again. Uncle Vishnu gives him an envelope full of money which he says is for Mousey's food, and then he gives him another envelope at Divali, at Christmas, at New Year. He starts bringing little extras with him when he comes over: a big sack of Purina dog chow, two dozen eggs. He goes in the back and washes out the dogs' food bowls, hoses down the floor of the dog-house, pours some Clorox, scrubs with the broom. Clyde, sometimes, watches him from the back-step and says, a bit sheepishly, that he was going to do it, and just hasn't got round to it yet, but Uncle Vishnu just waves a hand and says, 'Don't worry, man. I just doing a little bit to help out. You busy with your wife and children. Me, I have time, I could do it.'

As the months tick by, Clyde tries to wait patiently for things to go back to normal as Uncle Vishnu said they would. The healthy baby, Peter, starts sleeping through the night after a few months, but the other one, Paul, still wakes everybody up all through the night, bawling its lungs out. Night after night, the baby wakes up, cries, will not go back to sleep; Clyde sometimes goes out for a drive to get away from the noise. 'It takes time,' Uncle Vishnu keeps saying. 'It's not abnormal.' Clyde waits a year, eighteen months; but when the boys are coming up to two years old, they go to Siparia for the hair-cutting ceremony and things get worse.

Later, he wonders why he bothered going to the hair-cutting ceremony at all, why waste his time and money on this superstition and nonsense. Actually, if there is some superstition behind it, he doesn't know what it is – the truth is that nobody knows what the whole thing is about: why Indian people have this tradition at all, of taking their children to have their hair cut by an old man who, a few times a year, dresses himself in yellow robes and a turban; why it is held next to a Catholic church, when it is supposedly a Hindu tradition; and whether it really is Hindu at all, or maybe it's actually a Muslim thing; or maybe, in some way that the Indians can't understand, the Catholics are trying to entice Indian people to become Christian.

Clyde still remembers when his father took him to Siparia for his first hair-cut, years ago: he remembers his father sitting cross-legged on the ground in the shade of a big tree, all the younger men listening to an older man talking, and although Clyde didn't know what the older man was talking about, he could see that his father was happy, not in a drunken kind of way, but properly happy. Clyde remembers holding a strip of blue plastic ribbon, dancing around a maypole with other children; and he remembers the cotton candy vendor walking around, like a walking tree blooming with pink fluffy flowers, and how he could hardly believe it when his father, who normally refused to spend money on frivolous things, beckoned the vendor over and paid the dollar, and the vendor unclipped the puffy plastic bag from the branch and put it in Clyde's hands. On the day that Clyde and Joy and Mousey pack up the car to drive the two hours south to Siparia, Clyde has a roll of five dollar and one dollar bills in his pocket, ready to give to Peter and Paul when they get there, for them to play lucky dip and piñata, whatever is on offer, and to dance the maypole and for them to have as much cotton candy as they want. He has been telling them for weeks how much fun it will be.

The church is a normal Catholic church with a big cross on the roof and a statue of Jesus with a golden halo set into the wall above the main door. They don't park in the main car park, because the priest keeps that for people who are actually going to Mass; they park in the land next to that, already filling up with cars and people and trucks blasting music. Clyde carries the fold-up chair for Mousey and the basket of food that Joy has packed; Joy carries the flask of tea; Mousey holds the boys' hands. Most of the shady spots are already taken but they find one next to the big tent by the hot-food vendors, and they set themselves up for the day there.

Joy suggests that they go and do the hair-cutting one-time, straight away, so that they can get it out of the way and everybody can relax. They find the hair-cutter and put both boys to line up in front of him. Paul keeps stepping out of the line and trying to cling onto Joy and she keeps taking him by the shoulders and pushing him back. Eventually, Peter holds his hand to keep him in place: the bigger children tease him for being like a girl, and Peter says, 'We're twins. And he's retarded, he needs somebody to hold his hand sometimes.'

Eventually, after Paul keeps running out of the line and keeps having to be pushed back in, another grown-up says, 'Let him go first, you could see he's getting anxious.' Paul is pushed up to the front of the line, and the hair-cutter does his little dance and flashes the scissors around as is his custom, and makes Paul sit on the chair for the hair-cut. Clyde can see it beginning to happen: how Paul's eyes glaze over, how his hands scratch against his own thighs. Joy hasn't noticed yet: she's talking about how the flask of tea has spilt, the bag is all wet. She is rummaging around for a napkin when Paul puts his fingers in his ears and starts to scream. The hair-cutter backs away. The children in the line run to their mothers. Joy puts her hand to her chest. Everyone in the whole grounds, Clyde thinks, all the hundreds of people here, must be staring in this direction. He fights an urge to run back to the car, to get out of here, leave this for someone else to deal with. He forces himself to walk forward.

'I didn't even touch him,' the hair-cutter says, 'he just started, just so . . .'

Clyde puts a hand on Paul's shoulder. 'Stop that,' he says. 'Stop it.' There is no effect. Paul is still screaming; he has fallen into a rhythm: a steady, shrill sound, like an alarm clock, or a police siren.

'Stop that. Stop it, I said.'

'Hit him,' the hair-cutter suggests. 'You have to hit him. He not hearing you.'

Clyde's fingers grip Paul's shoulder. 'Stop it, I said! Stop it!' But still Paul does not stop, only scrunches his shoulders further up to his ears. It is all Clyde can do to keep from smacking him across his face, from grabbing his hair and yanking at his head. Instead, in a fury, he picks him up, scrunched-up as he is, and carries him, this shrieking bundle, away. Somewhere on the way to the car, someone – maybe Mousey, maybe someone else – throws a jug of water in Paul's face, and just like that, the screaming ceases.

Later, when they talk about it, back at La Sagesse Trace, Romesh, Joy's younger brother, says they should put the child in St Ann's, the mental hospital in Port of Spain. 'Put him in there one-time,' he says. 'Something wrong with him. Something definitely wrong with him.'

'Uncle Vishnu said to wait and see,' Clyde says.

'Do it now,' Romesh says. 'That's my advice. The longer you wait, the harder it will get for you.'

'Did I ask for your advice?' Clyde asks, angrily. 'Did anybody hear me ask for advice? No! So keep your ideas to yourself!'

Romesh steupses and says to wait and see; one day, he says, Clyde will wish he had listened to him. Clyde goes inside and switches on the TV, turns the knob for the volume up loud to drown out whatever Romesh is saying on the patio. A children's talent show is on: Clyde lights a cigarette while a little girl in a gold spangly leotard walks on her hands. He tries to remember why he looked forward to this day, why he looked forward to taking the boys to Siparia at all just so someone in a yellow turban could cut their hair. What was the point of it? The girl in the spangly leotard does a sort of dance, with splits and kicks and cartwheels. Clyde can't think straight: whenever he tries to lay one thought down next to the other, he is interrupted by the memory of the screaming, of the shame of walking through the crowd of staring people to collect his child. A little boy in a checked shirt and tie walks on carrying a recorder and starts to play a tune. The day seems to him now not to have been anything to do with tradition or ceremonies but just a set of ignorant Indian people getting together to stuff food in their mouths and drink alcohol and watch the girls dancing in their sexy saris. A white girl does a ballet dance. An older girl with her hair braided with many ribbons sings a song in a whispery voice. 'Uncle Vishnu will tell me what to do,' Clyde thinks. 'Whatever he says to do, I will do.' His eyes stay fixed on the screen, but in his mind he sees himself walking to the gates of the mental hospital with two children, and sending one through the gates, and turning to walk away with only one child left.

5

Uncle Vishnu and Mousey are easy to get along with, but the rest of Joy's family are a different story. They come to Clyde's house most Sundays and public holidays; they arrive anytime in the morning that they feel like, and they're often still on his patio at eleven o'clock or midnight. Joy's older brother, Philip, is a judge who won an island scholarship to study at Oxford; he has a big house in Port of Spain that you would think would be perfect for the family to have lunch in, but they only ever go there once or twice a year because the English wife, Marilyn, doesn't like all the mess they create. When Clyde and Joy first went to their house – this was years ago, before the twins were born – Philip and Marilyn drank wine out of wine glasses; Clyde felt like a fool drinking his Carib from the bottle. When it was time to eat, Marilyn put out a big cut of roast beef on the table. Clyde and Joy stared at it, and then it was Joy who said, 'But Philip, why you cooked beef?' And Philip said, 'What, I thought you-all ate beef now?' And Joy said that no, they didn't. 'What, but long-time now you-all don't go to temple or anything – why you still not eating beef?' And Joy said, 'Well, we just don't.' And the whole thing was an embarrassment. Marilyn said that she was fed up trying to remember who wouldn't eat beef and who wouldn't eat pork and that from now on she would only cook shrimp. Philip ended up going out to get Kentucky Fried Chicken instead, and they all went on the patio and ate it out of the box with their fingers, except for Marilyn who sat by herself at the table with her knife and fork and ate her roast beef.

Romesh and Rachel have a big house too, of course – they have that big house down the road there on Bougainvillea Avenue – but Rachel works at her family's Indian Garments shop in the mall and she says she doesn't have time to cook for Romesh's whole family every weekend. And Joy doesn't like going to their house, because of their dogs. They're only puppies still, two Alsatians, with woolly paws and sharp puppy teeth, but Romesh beats them to make them bad, and Joy says that before you know it, those dogs will eat up a child in two gulps. 'I don't want my children near those dogs,' she says. 'I prefer them to be here, where I could watch them with my own eyes.' And so, the twins never go by Romesh and Rachel's house to play with their son, Sayeed, and instead Sayeed always comes here. Often, Rachel drops him in the morning before she goes to work, and then collects him again in the evening; during the day, Joy and Mousey feed him and look after him, and when it's time to bathe, they put him in the shower with Peter and Paul. If Rachel and Romesh go out for the evening, Sayeed puts on one of Peter and Paul's vests and sleeps in the bed with Mousey.

Clyde doesn't like them coming here all the time, but Mousey and Uncle Vishnu are always saying that the family must get together, that family is the most important thing. Romesh and Rachel drop in all the time, but Philip and Marilyn haven't come down in a few months, because of one thing and another. But it's a public holiday today for Emancipation Day and the whole lot of them are coming over for lunch, which means the morning will be spent in a big frenzy of cooking and cleaning, getting everything ready. While it's still dark, Clyde hears the clanking of iron pots, the *slap-slap* of Mousey's slippers as she moves around the kitchen; when he gets up, a little later, Mousey has already finished getting the roti mixed and kneaded, and the pale balls of dough are lined up on a sheet of wax paper on the counter. Peter is sitting on the white plastic chair that just fits in the gap between the fridge and the rubbish bin, swinging his legs, a Milo-moustache on his top lip.

'Where's Joy?' Clyde asks Mousey.

'She went in the bed with Paul,' Mousey says. 'He started crying when Peter got up.'

Clyde unlocks the back door and sits on the step to give the dogs their morning pat. Trixie gets the step closest to him, proudly breathing her bad-breath into his face, her purplish tongue dripping saliva onto his feet. Through the window just next to him, Clyde hears Joy talking to Paul as she helps him get dressed, one arm through the sleeve, then the other. He tries not to listen: he tries, instead, to look at the greenness all around; everything has come back green again now that it's rainy season. Peter comes to sit next to him on the step, and Trixie, happy, plants a heavy paw on Peter's chest, licks his face. Mousey brings his coffee. Clyde has a long list of jobs to do, but it's still early, and he likes to sit here where it's cool and watch the sun come up.

'That's a golden oriole,' Peter says, pointing at a big bird, bright yellow with black markings, on the roof of the dog-house. 'Right?'

'Is it? How you know that?'

'It's in the book Uncle Vishnu brought. And that's a tanager. A blue-grey tanager.'

'Oho. Very good.'

A grey bird lands on the grass near the coconut tree, the type of grey bird with black markings around its eyes that make it look permanently vex. ('Mockingbird,' says Peter.) The bird gives them a long angry look as if warning them to stay away, then it stabs its beak to the ground, and when it pulls away, a long pink worm dangles from its beak. The bird tilts its head upwards and the worm disappears into its body.

'How do they know where the worms are?' Peter says.

'I don't know.'

'It didn't have to go peck, peck, peck, to find the worm. Did you see? It just went – peck! Did you see?'

'I saw,' Clyde says. He looks at Peter, at the smooth brown skin, the skinny little four-year-old legs, the long thin toes that are just like his own, the Deyalsingh toes.

'Uncle Vishnu might bring some more books for you when he comes today,' Mousey says. She's working the grinder, feeding in green leaves of chadon beni, driving the handle round and round, catching the dark green paste from the bottom. 'Eh? He's coming late, after the races. But he'll come. Vishnu always does what he says.' She holds the grinder steady with one hand, turns the handle with the other. When she's finished the chadon beni, she grinds handfuls of thyme and chive, and red slivers of a scotch bonnet pepper. She spoons the spices into the Pyrex bowl with the cut-up chicken, and then mixes it all up with her hands.

'Come on,' Joy says, walking briskly through the kitchen. 'Work to do.' She comes back a moment later with the broom and mop. 'Peter, you and Paul go outside, please. I have floors to mop here.'

Clyde slides his coffee cup onto the counter and goes down the back-step to get started on tidying up the yard. He starts by the dog-house behind the carport, and works his way round all four sides of the house, scooping up dog-mess with a trowel and pitching it into the long grass in the empty land behind their house. When it starts to rain, he goes inside; he scrubs at the mildewed tiles in the shower, pours bleach down the toilet, hangs the good towel on the rail. When the rain stops, he walks around the yard again, looking at the overgrown hedges, the gap in the fence filled in with a plank of wood, the other gap, the one behind the coconut tree, filled in with the door of an old cupboard. This place always looks messy, he thinks, no matter what he does.

In the front yard, Peter and Paul are crouching by the big hole that the dogs have dug next to the driveway, scooping mud out and slapping it onto the flat concrete.

'Hey,' Clyde says. 'Are those your clean clothes? And you're playing in the mud?'

'It's just mud pies,' Peter says. He straightens up a bit, looks down at his t-shirt. 'It's old-clothes. We'll wash off with the hose before we come in.'

Paul looks up at him too from beside the muddy hole, his hair all over his face. He won't cut his hair, since the thing in Siparia: he looks like some kind of madman. Clyde fights an urge to go and get the scissors right now and cut the hair off.

'Go and make the mud pies in the back,' Clyde says, walking away. 'I'm trying to tidy up the place here.'

After he finishes in the yard, he sweeps the leaves off the patio, brings the stack of plastic chairs from the store room and wipes them down one by one. He takes the cushions from the bamboo chairs and shakes them out over the railing, and then he arranges the chairs the way Joy says, alternating bamboo and then plastic, going round in a circle. It's starting to rain again but he puts on his slippers anyway and walks down the Trace to get ice from the gas station. He passes a few children playing in the ditch: they look like they've come through the bush, barefoot and muddy, scratching at insect bites.

'Playing in the rain?' he says. He recognises most of them from around the neighbourhood.

'Yes, Uncle Clyde,' they say. They tell him about a snake they found in the bush; they describe the colours, the markings, ask him if a snake like that is good to eat. He tells them he doesn't think so, and to make sure to bash a stick in the grass wherever they walk, in case a snake is hiding there.

'Yes, yes, we know,' they say.

'Good,' he says. 'Very nice.'

He puts the ice in the sink at the back, where Joy and Mousey do the washing, and then he gets the beer bottles from the fridge and burrows them down beneath the ice to keep them cold. He puts the dogs in the dog-house and opens the gate, and then it's time to have a little wash and change into his good shirt. When all his work is done, he settles down on the clean patio to read the paper.

Rachel arrives first in her white Subaru, and drives in and parks behind Clyde's car. While she's winding up the windows, Sayeed climbs out and makes his way up to the patio, Rachel calling for him to be quick to get out of the rain.

'Hi, Sayeed, boy!' Clyde says. He opens his arms. Sayeed comes for the kiss, takes a handful of peanuts from the bowl and then races into the house. Rachel comes up, holding her handbag over her head. Rachel is the prettiest of the girls in her family, slim, with D-cup breasts and long curly hair. Today she's wearing tight, light-blue trousers and a sleeveless top with a kind of frill at the neckline that sometimes gives Clyde a glimpse of her cleavage. The women come out and stand on the patio for a while talking about Rachel's outfit, what she did in the shop this morning and the various people she bumped into at the mall; then they talk about Rachel's mother and father and sisters, and the sisters' husbands, and the sisters' husbands' sisters. Clyde returns to his newspaper. Eventually the women drift away to the kitchen.

The rain has stopped again by the time Romesh arrives. He helps himself to a Carib from the back sink, kicks off his slippers and settles down next to Clyde on the patio. Romesh has two streaks of sweat running down his face on his left side: two lines going straight straight down, like tyre tracks. He tilts his head to the side, wipes his cheek against his shirt-sleeve.

'Hot!' Clyde says.

'Boy? Whole day I on the road,' says Romesh. He pinches his shirt just under the neckline and pumps it, to make a breeze on his neck. 'All morning, since seven-eight o'clock.'

He went down to San Fernando this morning, he says, to pick up a crate of ceramic tiles for a hotel, then somewhere else, halfway across Trinidad, to unload, and he had to wait while the client went through every single batch of tiles, counting which ones were wet, which ones were broken. He jiggles his knees as he talks, recounts the falling out with the tiles customer. 'I not able with this kind of work at all,' he says. 'Whole day I on the road, sweating, breaking my back, and people complaining about two-three broken tiles!'

'Well, take the electronics shop, then,' Clyde says. 'Not so Rachel's father wants you to manage the electronics shop? You playing hard to get with him, or something? Take it!'

'Boy, it have money in transport, I'm telling you. All kinds of things need transporting.'

'So I hear,' says Clyde.

'I will transport anything,' Romesh says. 'It doesn't matter to me. All kinds of things need transporting from A to B. Tiles, cement, pig-feed, bottled drinks, fridge, freezer, anything.' He takes a swig of his drink. 'Sugarcane,' he says, with a laugh. 'Coconuts. Anything.'

'Or things in powder form,' says Clyde.

Romesh swings his knees in and out. 'Doesn't matter to me. I driving the same twenty miles in the hotsun either way, regardless of what's in my truck. Not so? But one thing pays me a hundred dollars and another thing pays me a thousand. Eh? I taking the thousand dollars! Not so? If one person offers you a hundred dollars for a job, and someone else offers a thousand dollars for the same job, not so you would take the more money?'

'Watch yourself, Romesh,' Clyde says. 'You're rationalising rationalising there, and you going to land up in hot soup.'

Romesh is on his third Carib by the time Philip arrives in his silver Mercedes. He has to park on the road because the driveway is already full and Clyde can tell he's annoyed by the time he reaches up to the patio. Marilyn is already fanning herself and complaining about the heat.

'You brought a book to read?' Joy asks Anna. Anna's nine, the cleanest-looking child Clyde has ever seen, her hair tied back in a plait, and sandals with buckles on her feet. 'You want to go in our room to get peace and quiet?'

Anna shrugs. Clyde notices how her eyes flick around the room, how they rest on his worn slippers, his dusty toes.

'What you having to drink, Philip?' Mousey asks.

'I'll take a rum-and-coke, thanks,' Philip says. He tucks his thumbs under the waistband of his trousers to keep them in place as he sits down. 'With ice, eh? You have ice?'

Mousey says Clyde bought ice, and she shuffles off to get the drinks.

'If you see traffic out there!' Philip says. The route they initially took was blocked because of an Emancipation Day parade, and they had to go a different way. 'Not really a parade,' he says, 'just random people walking in the road with banners and a bit of tinsel around their necks. If you see how much traffic they caused!'

'I doubt they even know what emancipation means!' Marilyn says.

They talk about traffic for a good while; about landslides and rain, and the latest crimes around the country; and how Philip's work is going, which cases are coming in front of him and what he thinks about them. He can only ever talk in general terms, of course, but he talks about the people who've been in his courtroom ('my courtroom') and who they are and, if they're barristers, where they qualified and who they've worked for, things like that. Mousey gets Philip a second rum-and-coke, and then Philip sips, looks at Clyde over the top of his glass.

'So, how's work going?' Philip asks. 'What is it you're doing at the moment?'

'Same thing, man,' Clyde says, trying to sound casual. 'Construction.'

'Construction! You mean the concrete? You mixing concrete still?'

'Nothing wrong with that,' Mousey says, 'everybody need a house to live in! If you know how to mix concrete you will always find work!'

'Yea, but now you have mouths to feed,' Philip says. 'That kind of work is not reliable!'

'But he's hardworking, and he's determined,' Marilyn says.

She's sitting with one leg crossed over the other so her foot sticks out a bit in front, showing off her perfect white toes and nail-polish. 'He has the right attitude. That's half the battle.'

'Why you don't try to get a job in oil and gas?' Philip says. 'I bet you most people around here are working in petrochemicals now, not so?' He talks about the changes he has noticed around Trinidad recently: how more people now have satellite dishes on their roofs; how everybody nowadays has burglar-proofing bars over their windows and doors; how he has heard, via his contacts on the grapevine, how many expats are coming into Trinidad these days, and how in Point Lisas, by the industrial estate, they're going to build a compound with a swimming pool for all the foreigners to live in.

'Eh?' Philip says, turning to him again. 'I bet if you go and ask, they would have something for you to do. You wouldn't be able to get the really high-paying jobs, because – well. But at least get a foot in the door.'

'You need a university education for those high-up jobs,' Rachel says. 'Physics, Chemistry, Engineering, that kind of thing.'

'Education,' Mousey says, nodding.

'But Philip is right,' Marilyn says. 'It's the foot in the door, that's what you need. And once you're in, you can work your way up.'

'You see, if he had the education,' Mousey says, 'then he could get the high-up jobs!' She starts talking about her brother, Uncle Vishnu, how he got a scholarship to St Saviour's College there in Port of Spain, and then won an island scholarship to England to study Medicine. Clyde takes a handful of peanuts and sits, one foot cocked over the other knee, looking out towards the front yard. He has heard this story many times before, how it all goes back to Mousey's father, Surindranath, and the sacrifices he made. Out on the Trace, children of various sizes are running back and forth, hollering, waving sticks and leaves at each other; Peter and Paul and Sayeed are watching them from the front gate. 'And as you see, my son, Philip,' Mousey says, gesturing to Philip, 'took the same path, and now he's a judge, always in the papers.'

On the patio, while Mousey talks, Romesh drinks his beer, swings his knees in and out. Romesh didn't do well at school at all: he went to a Government Secondary somewhere in Marabella or somewhere, one of those places where the teachers are always on strike and the girls are pregnant by fifteen. Whenever Mousey gets going in this vein, which is often, Romesh refuses to make any response, just acts like it's water off a duck's back. Clyde refuses to make any response either, even though he knows Mousey wants him to be impressed. But what is there to be impressed by? They have two kinds of men in the world, Clyde thinks, two kinds of fathers. One kind works hard and brings all the money home and gives it to his wife to spend on the house and children. The other kind doesn't do that. And nobody can control which kind of father they get. Simple as that.

By five o'clock, the thing is going the same way as usual. When you have men like Romesh and Philip drinking alcohol from morning till evening, this is how it always ends up, with one set of arguing, always about the same old things. A lot of it comes from Romesh, who is the most drunk of all: it starts when he asks Philip for money to help with some debt he's run up, and then things spiral downhill in the usual way with Philip saying self-righteously, 'Never a borrower nor a lender be,' and Romesh telling Philip to stop being high and mighty and acting like he's better than everyone else, and how he should share what he has with them because they are family. Uncle Vishnu, arrived back from the races and sitting with his plate of food balanced on his knees, says how he has already lent Romesh money once and he's not going to do it again without good reason, and he says nothing else on the subject at all. Then Mousey says that she will lend him what money she can, but she argues with Romesh about how he doesn't do enough to help; how he only comes when it suits him; how all he does is eat and leave, and bring the child Sayeed here for her to mind and feed, how Romesh should do something in return; how he should help out. Take, take, take, she says. That is how you are. And Romesh says, you see, I rather get the money from Republic Bank and pay it back with fifteen per cent interest, rather than have to listen to you complaining about all the things I don't do.

Clyde has been trying to stay out of the whole thing, and not say anything at all, but at one point, Romesh turns to him and says, 'But Uncle Vishnu is giving you money. Why he's giving money to you and not to me, that's what I want to know?'

Uncle Vishnu smiles and shakes his head to himself, and he starts picking up empty paper plates to throw away. 'You know why!' he says. 'Why you asking him when I'm right here in front of you?'

'I want to hear from him,' Romesh says, looking at Clyde.

'Hello,' Uncle Vishnu says. 'God helps those who help themselves! You refusing to take a good job that someone is offering you, and instead you want money for free? I already explained this to you. Behave yourself – I'll help you, gladly. Misbehave yourself – no help.' And he takes the stack of paper plates and goes to the kitchen.

'He is not even a blood relative,' Romesh says to Philip. 'I am a blood relative. I don't understand why he is the favourite.'

'I am the favourite?' Clyde says. 'Uncle Vishnu's just helping out with expenses, seeing as everybody always coming here to eat, that's all. You-all are plenty mouths to feed, you know! And I have the boys now too. That's why.'

'But I have a child too,' Romesh says. 'I don't find that fair.'

Clyde picks up a few empty Carib bottles and walks out before Romesh can say anything more. In the kitchen, Joy is scraping leftovers into a pot, the dogs watching from the top step. 'Move,' he tells them, and he pushes his way out and down the steps. He puts the empty bottles into the bottle-crate under the steps, and then takes a deep breath, trying to cool down. It's sunset. The breeze has dropped, the clouds are very still.

'Aye,' Uncle Vishnu says, from the back door. He follows Clyde down the steps. 'Don't let Romesh provoke you, you know.'

Clyde doesn't look at him. He wishes he hadn't had that last Carib. He wishes Joy's family wouldn't take over his house every weekend.

'One day he's provoke you,' Uncle Vishnu continues, 'the next day, he's provoke somebody else. That is how he is. He is not a serious fella. You are a serious fella. You need to focus on your family, don't bother with people like Romesh.' He pauses for a moment, and then maybe he sees the mood Clyde is in, because he says, 'Why you still mixing concrete, man? You see all the people I know? Why you haven't come to me and asked me to help you get a better job?'

'Boy, I don't know,' Clyde says. 'I'm managing.' But he's not managing. Every time Joy's family comes here, they have the same conversations again and again; and every time, the day ends just like this, with him wanting to pour himself a glass of rum, or shouting at Joy, or wanting to throw all these empty Carib bottles against the wall.

'You don't see how many people are offering me favours?' Uncle Vishnu is saying. 'I don't owe them anything, you know. They're trying to thank *me* for something I did for them. You want a job with Neal and Massy? I could get you a job, you know. Just name the place you want to work, and I'll get the job for you.'

'Anywhere?'

'Anywhere! Don't be so shy, man! You're my family, I will do anything for you! I will move mountains! Where you want to work?'

Uncle Vishnu is really distressed. He really wants to help. Clyde feels the decision forming itself in his mind, like something with a will of its own that he has no power to stop.

'Oil and gas, man,' Clyde says.

'Oil and gas,' Uncle Vishnu repeats. He looks relieved. 'No problem. Let me speak to some friends of mine.' As Uncle Vishnu turns to go back up to the kitchen, he says, 'Don't doubt yourself, man. You're doing the right thing. You're providing for your family. Stand up tall.'

Uncle Vishnu is a fast man to act. The following week, he takes Clyde to meet someone down at Point Lisas, and a fortnight after that, Clyde gives his notice at the construction company and fills out the paperwork for Amoco. By the end of the month, Clyde has a sticker on the windscreen of his car that the security guard at the industrial estate nods at each morning; hanging up in the cupboard at home are five shirts with the Amoco logo on the pocket; he doesn't need Joy to pack lunch for him first thing in the morning any more – instead, he goes to the Amoco canteen, where they have all kinds of food: dhalpuri roti and buss-up-shut, chicken wings and drumsticks, pelau, corn-soup, callaloo. At Christmas, his colleagues say, he will get a hamper filled with jams and chutneys, Hershey's chocolates, strawberry Pop-Tarts. At Carnival-time, there will be a family fun-day for the employees and their families, with a DJ, free t-shirts, lime-and-spoon races, tug-o-war.

The next time Philip and Marilyn come for lunch, at Divali, Philip asks Clyde how the petrochemicals business is going, and Clyde gives his insider information about the developments at Point Lisas, and which way oil prices will go. 'It's manual labour, naturally,' Philip says. 'Sweat of the brow!' Clyde isn't sure whether he means it as a compliment or not, but he doesn't really care either way. These days, he has a regular, reliable income: not very much money yet, but enough to put a little aside each month. He's opened a bank account with Republic Bank, and Amoco pays him a salary straight into the bank account on a monthly basis, not cash at the end of the week like the concrete mixing used to. The only drawback now is tax: instead of getting the full amount in the bank account, they're taking some away. But Uncle Vishnu has said he will speak to someone and sort that out.

These days, then, the few minutes that he spends sitting on the back-step with his coffee in the morning are peaceful and contented, and he rehearses in his mind the words he will one day say to Peter when he is big enough. If you are an honest person? he will say. And you work hard? He imagines walking side by side with Peter, the dark, glossy hair of youth, the frame still slender, on the cusp of adulthood. You can achieve what you set out to achieve in life, he will say. People used to say that because I didn't finish my schooling, they said I would come to no good, I would end up washing windscreens on the highway or sitting on the street corner selling nuts. But you see me? I just put my head down and I worked hard, and I didn't get myself all tangled up with doing favours for one person to try getting back a favour from somebody else. No, no. So you see, if you just rely on yourself, and live an honest kind of life, and you work hard? It will pay dividends. Trust me, he will say, it will pay dividends.

6

While they wait for the Hindu school Principal to come, Paul sits
in the hole in the ixora bush by the fence. The dogs made the hole;
they're always sticking their heads in the bush to bark at the Chin
Lees' dogs on the other side. It is a good place to sit because the
bush gives shade, and at this time of day the dogs are all asleep,
so it is quiet. Paul has to be careful not to get dirty because he
and Peter have already bathed and put on their good clothes.
But there is nothing dirty here, the grass is dried-up and prickly
now it's dry season. He picks a little red flower off the tightly
packed bunch just next to him, and sucks the nectar out from the
tiny tube of the stem. Then he holds the stem gently between his
finger and thumb and twirls the flower slowly, then fast, slowly,
then fast, watching how the petals go blurry. While he twirls, he
listens carefully in case Peter is sneaking onto the patio to eat the
Danish Butter Cookies that Mummy put on the coffee table.

When Paul hears the Principal's car turn into the Trace, he
crawls out of the bush and runs through the carport, around
to the back. Peter is already there. Together they crouch down
and look through the gaps between the stilt-legs that the house
stands on, and they watch the Principal waiting at the gate for
Mummy to let him in. He's a dark-skinned Indian man with a
moustache and a normal belly: not one of the very big bellies the
size of a football; a smaller belly, maybe the size of a cushion. A

flattened cushion. 'Where's the bad dog?' they hear the Principal ask. 'They told me you have a bad dog here.'

Mummy says she's tied up. When the Principal comes in, he reaches out a hand to pat Jab-Jab on her head but she shies away. The dogs trot after him up the drive, sniffing the scent he leaves behind. When he comes up the steps, they don't follow him up and stand at the gate panting and wagging their tails like they usually do; instead, they go and lie down in the holes they've dug up in the front lawn.

Daddy stays with the Principal on the patio while Mummy and Mousey come in and out of the kitchen getting drinks. Paul and Peter sit on the back-steps: it is a good place to be, out of the way, not getting dirty, but close enough so that the grown-ups can see you when they want you. As soon as a grown-up wants you, they expect you to be like a genie and *appear!* Paul imagines the grown-up snapping their fingers and Paul materialising out of thin air. Then, next moment, they want you to disappear. *Disappear!* Paul snaps his fingers.

'Peter! Paul! Come!' That's Mummy in the kitchen. They get up, dust off their pants, come up the steps. Mummy holds Paul by the shoulders. 'You feeling OK?'

He nods.

'You'll talk to him?'

He nods again, and follows Peter through to the patio.

The Principal is sitting on one of the bamboo chairs with his knees wide apart. He smells bad: a bad-body smell mixed with Limacol, which helps a little bit but not that much. The tin of cookies is open and Paul sees straight away how two of the little compartments are empty, the little paper cases askew, already being picked up by the breeze.

'The O's are my favourite!' the Principal is saying. 'I always take those before anyone else could get them!' There are crumbs and grains of sugar stuck to his moustache. 'You have some milk? I could stand to take some milk right now.'

Mummy goes to the kitchen.

'So!' the Principal says, sitting forward, his hands clasped together. 'I could already tell who is who!' He points at Peter. 'You look like the bright one. You're Peter. Eh?' Peter nods. He points at Paul. 'You're Paul.' They both nod. 'They told me you-all were twins!' he says. 'Siamese twins! I thought I would come here and wouldn't be able to work out who was who! But look how easy it is. Straight away I could see. You're Peter and you're Paul.'

'We're not Siamese twins,' Peter says. He always has to say this. 'We're just normal twins.'

'They told me Siamese twins!' the Principal said. 'Identical! You-all don't look identical to me.'

'Peter's look more vibrant,' Mousey says. 'He more vivacious. Paul is the quieter one.'

'I see that. Paul is the one who's kind of crazy, eh?' He's studying Paul closely. Paul wants to get out of here, but Peter is warning him not to. 'I hear how he's scream and rock back and forth and thing like that.'

'He used to,' Mummy says, coming back with the milk. 'He doesn't do it any more. Not really.'

'I hear how he's put his fingers in his ears and scream,' the Principal says. 'You heard what the children saying about him, eh? How he's possessed by the devil?'

'Children say all kinds of stupidness,' Daddy says.

'That's nonsense,' Mummy says. 'Children too cruel. What kind of thing is that to say? If my children said that about anybody, I wouldn't allow that. What kind of people are these? Who's saying this?'

'All kind of people,' the Principal says. He waves a hand towards the Trace. 'It's a general thing.'

'It only really happened once,' Mummy says. It's not true, it happened more times than that. 'When they went to do the hair-cutting. You know, the hair-cutting ceremony in Siparia. I don't know what it was, but he must have taken a dislike to somebody or something, and he screamed then, it's true. But he hasn't done it again.'

'Do you remember that?' the Principal asks, suddenly turning to him.

'He wouldn't remember,' Mousey says.

'Sshh! I'm asking him! I want to hear him talk. Hello! You could talk? He can't talk?'

'He could talk, he could talk,' Mummy says.

'I not hearing him say anything.'

They all stare at him. Paul is trying to think what he can say. He can't remember the question. They want him to say something about Siparia, about why he screamed. All he remembers is noise and crowds and being pulled one way and another way, and trying to tell Mummy that he wanted to go home, and she didn't listen to him, and so in the end he put his fingers in his ears and screamed, and then they took him home.

'Gooosh! You could really see something wrong with this child,' the Principal says. 'He not normal. You could see it in his eyes.' He reaches forward and takes another stack of cookies.

At his side, Peter is telling him: *You want them to send you to St Ann's? Quick! Say something!*

'Hello,' Paul says, shyly. 'I'm Paul. I'm five years old, and I live in Tiparo in Trinidad.'

There's a sudden silence. Mummy and Mousey laugh, but nervously. 'See? He could talk. He's a little shy, but he could talk.'

'He's awkward,' Mousey says. 'That doesn't mean he's possessed by the devil.'

When Uncle Vishnu hears about it, he only laughs and says they should go to the Roman Catholic school instead. 'I already went to the Principal,' Uncle Vishnu says. 'I already explained the situation to her.'

'But I will have to pay for that,' Daddy says. 'How much does it cost?'

'I will pay it,' Uncle Vishnu says. 'Don't put Peter in that backward school. He will be wasting his time, trust me.'

'Vishnu knows,' Mousey says. 'Listen to what he says. His education is the most important thing.'

'I know that,' Daddy says. 'I just didn't know it would cost me so much money! And that's times two, if I send both of them.'

'I will pay the fees,' Uncle Vishnu says. 'I'll give you the money for books. Whatever he needs, I will pay it.'

'And Paul? I want them to stay together,' Mummy says.

'I'll pay for him too.'

'You could ask for a discount? Since we're sending two children to the school?'

'I could ask her,' Uncle Vishnu says. 'But you wouldn't be able to get it free. She has teachers to pay, she has to keep up the school buildings, it takes a lot of money to keep the school running. She's only getting a little bit from the government, the school fees pay for the rest. But it's worth it. Trust me. That is education – it must be worth it.'

Now, instead of the Hindu school, they are going to go to

St Anthony's, the Roman Catholic school. Paul is afraid to go, but Peter tells him it is compulsory. Compulsory means you have to do it. 'It's either go to school, or go to St Ann's,' Peter says.

They get the uniform for St Anthony's RC, green pants and a white shirt, and Mummy has to sew a button onto the front pocket to show what house they're in. The Principal, a white nun called Sister Frances, says Peter is in Red house and Paul is in Green, but Mummy calls her up on the phone and says, 'They must stay together. Paul don't really talk much, he's slightly retarded. He needs Peter to help him.'

Peter and Paul sit in front of her, side by side on the arm-rest of Daddy's chair, watching her talk on the telephone, her eyes flicking between the two of them. Mummy just keeps shaking her head. 'Sister, like you not hearing me,' she says. 'The boys are *twins*. They must stay *together*. They together since they in the *womb*.' When she hangs up, she is smiling, and she sews red buttons onto all the shirts.

Mummy takes them to buy the schoolbooks from Khan's at Trincity Mall, and they wait until evening, when Daddy is home, to show him. The grown-ups sit on the chairs on the patio, and the boys kneel by the coffee table. Paul would like to take out his own books, but Peter said it will be better if he takes them all out. Paul's job is to make sure the coffee table is clean: earlier, he wiped it with a J-cloth, scrubbing away the dried bird-mess and the sticky trail of dripped juice that has been attracting ants. Now, he kneels next to Peter at the little table, and performs the final check, brushing away a few leaves and ants. Peter places the bag on the table, and one by one withdraws the books, holding up each one in turn for the grown-ups to see.

'*Junior Mathematics for the Caribbean*,' he says. '*Textbook*. One copy.' He flips the pages so the grown-ups can get a glimpse of what's inside. Paul inhales deeply on the smell of clean, fresh pages.

'Very nice,' says Mousey. 'Look how shiny!'

'*Junior Mathematics for the Caribbean: Workbook*,' Peter says. 'Two copies. One each.' He flips the pages (they are not shiny like the textbook, and smell different, but still good), showing not colour pictures like the textbook, but pages of sums. He passes them to Mummy for her to see. She wipes her hands on her shorts before she takes them.

'*Nelson's West Indian Reader: First Primer*,' says Peter, withdrawing the next one. This one has a bright red cover with a small drawing of a bunch of grapes on the front. He passes it to Daddy, and Daddy opens it and studies it for a moment, and then laughs. 'A is for apple! B is for bat!'

'What's wrong with that?' Mummy says. 'That's how they learn.'

'Yea, but you think Peter really needs to sit in class reading A is for Apple?' Daddy says.

'This is the hymn book,' Peter says. This one is a pale peach colour, with a picture on the front of a golden cross and a white dove.

'Hm!' says Daddy. 'How many of those you got?'

'Just one. We can share.'

'Keep going,' Mummy says.

'Four copybooks,' Peter says. 'Two each.' These are all the same, pale blue covers, their edges sharp and unblemished.

'Very nice, very nice,' Mousey says again. While the grown-ups inspect the copybooks, he and Peter lay out their new things in three piles: Peter's, Paul's, and to share.

'Good!' says Daddy. He sits back, one leg over the other knee, and lights up a cigarette. 'That was everything on the list?'

'Yes,' Mummy says. 'They had everything.'

'Good,' Daddy says. 'Good.'

They go to the kitchen to get some brown Hi-Lo shopping bags to cover the books with: they pick the cleanest ones, with the fewest grease-stains. Then they kneel by the coffee table again, and carefully cut along the creases of the paper bags and flatten out the paper. Paul feels them all watching as he lays the *West Indian Reader: First Primer* down on the brown paper, and cuts away an inch from the edge. He folds and cuts and smooths out the creases, and when it is ready, he lays it on the table again, next to the others. Peter carefully writes their names in his neatest handwriting – 'Peter and Paul Deyalsingh' – then the books are passed around again for another inspection. Daddy studies the hymn book for some time, and then hands it back. 'Right,' he says. 'Everything ready. Go and put them in the schoolbags for next week.'

Paul follows Peter through the kitchen to their bedroom. As they're coming back, Paul hears the grown-ups talking in quiet voices, and they look at each other and creep closer, so they can hear.

'He can read, he can write. He can add and subtract. He'll be wasting his time in Junior Infants. He should go straight into Senior Infants,' Daddy is saying. 'Or even Standard One. Like Sister Frances said.'

'But Paul needs Peter with him, to help him,' Mummy says.

'The boy is not even six years old! Why should he be worrying himself to help Paul, because Paul can't talk, or Paul's too lazy to talk, or whatever it is?'

They can't hear what Mummy replies, but they already know, because they have heard it before. The boys are *twins*. They must stay *together*. In the silence that follows, Paul feels something cold pass through him. He wants to go to the patio and tell them that he doesn't mind not going to school, but Peter frowns at him, the frown that means: *Careful. You want them to send you to St Ann's?* Paul definitely doesn't want to go to St Ann's. He has never been there, or even seen a picture of it, but, still, it makes him afraid. He imagines a big white house on top of a hill, and crazy-people climbing all over the walls, and making *Ooooh! Ooooh! Ooooh!* sounds of monkeys.

That night, when everyone has gone to sleep, Paul lies in bed next to Peter listening to the night-sounds. The dogs are chasing something in the bush around the front; it sounds bigger than a lizard, maybe a rat. Sometimes strange men pass by, walking along the road, or walking fast up the hill, and he can tell by the way the dogs bark whether the men are dangerous or not. Tonight there is no danger. Daddy's snoring fills up the whole house. When Daddy breathes in, he makes a long, jagged, snorting sound, like a pig might make; then there's a pause, sometimes one second, sometimes two or three; then the breath out: a long, loud puff of air, like he's doing breathing exercises. Mummy complains about it sometimes but Paul doesn't mind it. It is nice to lie awake at night and know that, in the next room, Daddy is breathing in and out. Mousey snores too, but just a tiny whistle, and not with every breath like Daddy does, but just every now and again.

On the mattress next to him, Peter has rolled right into the middle of the bed, well past the centre-line. He lies almost on his tummy, but with one knee bent, propping him up a bit. Paul shifts gingerly, careful not to wake him. He only has a narrow space at the edge of the bed because Peter is taking up so much room. He could, in theory, kick him back over to his side: that's what Peter would do, if it was Paul who was taking up too much space. But he doesn't mind. He likes to watch the gentle rise and fall of Peter's back as he breathes.

Carefully, he pulls himself up to his knees so he can look out the window behind the bed. He ducks his head under the curtain and wraps his fingers around the cool metal of the burglar-proofing, his forehead against the bars. The night is bright and cool and still, the moon like a torch lighting everything up. Just beneath the window, in the dogs' water bowl, a big fat frog is resting in the water. It looks like a rock, very still, and the warts and ridges all over its back like the rough surface of a stone. There are a few ants running around nearby, just crazy ants, harmless, the ones that change direction every few steps, like they have no idea where they're going.

The sky is clear. He has noticed this: that on a night with a full moon, the sky is often clear. Uncle Vishnu gave Peter a book about space that showed all the planets and where they stood in relation to the sun and where the moon was in relation to the earth, and diagrams explaining why the moon changed shape. Paul understood from the diagrams about the movements, and the sizes and shapes of things. So things were all much bigger than they looked, he noted. Much bigger. Much much bigger. Much much much bigger. He likes to look at the moon and imagine space. He imagines it to be very silent, very cool. You would definitely need a sweater.

Very quietly, he gets out of bed. Just outside the bedroom door, on the right, is the bathroom. First the toilet, in its own room, and then the shower and sink in the next room. Beyond that, just a few steps ahead of him, is the door to Mummy and

Daddy's room. Paul stands in the dark space listening to the snoring. It is very loud. The door is ajar. Sometimes they close the door, and Paul hears the headboard banging against the wall and the bed springs squeaking. But tonight it is ajar. Very quietly, he creeps forward until he is in the doorway. Through the gap, he can see the window, the curtain moving peacefully in the light breeze. He pushes the door very gently: the hinge squeaks. He freezes into place, his eyes fixed on Mummy's and Daddy's shapes on the bed. If they wake up, Paul thinks, he will run to the bathroom and drink some water from the tap. He pushes the door open a little more, and then a little more again until, by moving sideways and going very flat, he can squeeze through. The snoring gets louder. Daddy is sleeping on the side by the window, the sheet half off, one hand between his legs. Paul comes around to his side, taking care not to trip over the wire cord of the fan. He stands at the bedside silently, looking at Daddy's face: the bristle of stubble on the cheeks, the glistening of oil in the crease of his nose. A curl of hair, matted by sweat, sticks to his cheekbone; its tip makes a sharp point, like the tip of a paintbrush dipped in water.

He holds his breath as he slips out through the door again. He stands in the dark corridor for a few moments and then he goes to the kitchen. Outside, the dogs must smell him, or hear him, because they are up at the top step just outside the back door sniffing and jostling for position. He gets the key from the hook; fits the key in the keyhole; turns. He waits a minute, standing in the darkness, in case the noise has woken anyone up. Then, as quietly as he can, he opens the door. The dogs sniff and sneeze at him in welcome; they know to be quiet when he comes out. He sits on the back-step and watches them race down the steps, tumbling over each other, snapping and snarling quietly as they pin each other down. The sky is completely clear, not black at all, but a dark and beautiful blue, the whole thing, the entire stretch of sky, lit up by the moon. He tips his head back, looking at the bright round moon, the pinpricks of stars.

7

Last year, during Carnival weekend, Daddy took them to Mayaro
to get away from the noise and feteing and immoral behaviour
around the place. It was a very long drive, nearly two hours,
most of it along the east coast heading south, through a thin
road with only coconut trees on both sides. Daddy was in a good
mood, happy to be going to the beach: he drove with one hand
on the steering wheel and the other elbow resting in the frame
of the open window, and he stopped twice on the way, once to
buy watermelon, and another time to buy roast-corn and soursop
juice. The village was small, even smaller than Tiparo: just a few
wooden houses and a parlour that sold drinks and dry goods. To
get to the beach, you left the main road and walked through the
shade of the thickly growing coconut trees, and then you came
out onto sand, soft fine sand that your feet sank straight into. If
you were wearing flip-flops, you would straight away kick them
off and run: it was about fifty steps to get to the water, or twenty-
five if the tide was in. And, if you wanted, you could turn either
left or right and walk in a straight line along the beach, and no
matter how far you walked, there was always sea on one side and
coconut trees on the other, with only the occasional fallen tree or
bit of driftwood here or there to help you pick out that you were
somewhere different to where you had started. Mummy didn't
come with them because she was helping somebody with a new

baby, and Daddy was very happy because he could sit out in the evenings with the men having a little drink. Everywhere Peter and Paul went, people stopped them and said, 'Who are you? I recognise that face!' and Peter said who they were, and the people said, 'You-all are Clyde's sons? Clyde Deyalsingh? But A-A!' And the people asked them how old they were (eight) and where they went to school (St Anthony's RC School, near Arima) and if they were Siamese twins (no, just normal twins). And the people told them stories about the things their father used to do when he lived here, the mischief he used to get up to. At sunset, when the fishermen came in, everyone gathered on the beach to help pull in the seine, and Peter and Paul ran with the other children on the shining wet sand, picking up the little fish that had gotten caught and throwing them quickly back into the water.

Paul had hoped that they could go back to Mayaro again this year over Carnival weekend, but instead they are going to Toco, to Uncle Romesh and Auntie Rachel's holiday house. The whole family needs to be together and to recuperate, Mummy says, after all the misery that happened with Uncle Vishnu and Mousey.

Uncle Vishnu died just before Christmas-time in a car crash. He came about midday that day to collect Mousey to take her to the hospital for her blood tests; when they were coming back that afternoon, a car ran a red light at a junction and crashed into them. All that afternoon, people kept ringing up to ask if Mummy and Daddy had heard the news, and asking who was in the car and if anyone had survived. Uncle Vishnu was killed right away, but Mousey was wearing a seat belt and so she didn't die straight away, but she died after Christmas, in hospital.

Both Mummy and Daddy were out of the house a lot for the few months after that, organising the rites and getting Uncle

Philip to execute the Will. Paul wondered if maybe Uncle Vishnu wasn't fully dead, and if Uncle Philip still had to come and execute him, to be fully dead? But Uncle Vishnu was definitely dead, and had definitely died right away, because the day after the accident, there was a picture in the newspaper of the car crash, with Uncle Vishnu's head splattered open on the ground like an egg. In any case, Mummy and Daddy went by Uncle Philip's house a lot to discuss things, whatever it was they had to discuss. And when Mummy was home, she cooked to keep busy, and while she cooked, she cried and said, 'What is God doing to us? What is God doing to this family?'

It was Uncle Romesh and Auntie Rachel's idea to spend Carnival weekend in Toco, because of how sad Mummy was, and because Mummy was weeping so much about the family breaking apart. They said the whole family should get together, that they don't all get together enough. They have a house in Toco, right on the north-east coast of Trinidad: a fancy house with a pool and security that they rent out to foreigners, but they said the house would be empty for Carnival weekend because all the tourists would be in Port of Spain. When Mummy told Daddy about it, Daddy got angry. 'But every other weekend we have to spend with Romesh and Rachel?' Daddy said.

Mummy said that Philip and Marilyn would be coming too, that Philip and Marilyn would keep things civilised.

'Why we don't go to Mayaro by ourselves? Or Tobago? Go by ourselves without the whole circus troupe coming along.'

'But they're *family*, Clyde,' Mummy said. 'In hard times, *family* must come together.'

Daddy didn't say anything at first, but when he spoke again, he said, 'All right. I suppose we'll go. But I'm telling you now, a day won't pass without Romesh bringing up the money. You'll see. He wants to get us and Philip all in one place so he could ask about it.'

'Well, let him ask,' Mummy said.

They leave early on the Saturday morning, in good time to get away before Carnival traffic builds up: once it starts, Daddy says, roads will be gridlocked and you may as well give up and go home. Mummy has been up cooking since dark, filling Pyrex dishes and tinfoil boxes with food for the weekend. Peter and Paul carry the food to the car, and Daddy packs it all into the trunk, along with clean clothes and towels, bedsheets and pillows, six-packs of Carib, jaliters of Sprite and Red Solo, packets of Chee Zees and Planters Peanuts. This time, Daddy drives with both hands on the steering wheel, and each time a vendor walks past with something – bags of chennets or frozen Orchard Orange juice cartons wrapped in paper napkins – the men just look at his face through the windscreen and walk on to the next car.

It takes a long time, over half an hour, to get to the meeting point, Matura, on the east coast. Everybody fills up at the gas station, because there is no other gas station between here and the north coast, and they set off again, driving in convoy: Uncle Romesh and Auntie Rachel first in the white Subaru with Sayeed; then Uncle Philip and Auntie Marilyn and Anna in the silver Mercedes-Benz; then them in their cream Datsun. The road is similar to the road to Mayaro: straight and thin and flat, with the sea always on one side, and nothing else around but the long, thin necks of coconut trees, their shaggy heads moving in the wind the same slow, dreamy way that hair moves underwater.

The road takes them past the Toco police station, with two navy blue police cars parked in front, and the Trinidad & Tobago flag flying from a tall pole. Two women are sitting on the low brick wall in the front, one fat and one good-looking, both with tight tight jeans and nice tops like they're dressed for going out. Ahead of them, the white Subaru slows down and pulls over, so they pull over too. Uncle Romesh says something to the women through the car window, and one of them slowly gets up and goes in the door of the police station, her big buttocks rolling with each step. A man comes out, wearing the navy blue police pants and a white t-shirt with the sleeves rolled up so it's more like a vest. He has on his shades and his boots and his gun in the holster.

'Hotsauce!' he calls out, to Uncle Romesh. 'Mr Hotsauce Ramcharan!' Romesh and the policeman laugh and shake hands, and the policeman rests his elbows on the open window and leans down to talk to him.

'You see?' Daddy says, quietly, to Mummy. 'This is the kind of thing I mean. It's only gang-members who have these silly nicknames, not so?'

'He has to be friends with them,' Mummy says. 'They keep an eye on his house for him.'

From the back seat of the car, Paul can see round the side of the building. One policeman is shirtless, cooking over a firepit. He takes slabs of meat from a glass bowl and lays them on the wire rack that's propped up over the coal, and wipes his hand on a cloth. A few other men are sitting at a table playing cards, with bottles of alcohol on the ground next to them, or wedged between their thighs. Several turtle shells the size of small rafts are stacked up on the ground.

'Leatherbacks!' Mummy says, after they drive away.

'That is police,' Daddy says. 'One rule for them and a different rule for all the rest of us.'

The house is very fancy, and Sayeed shows them around the whole thing, boasting about how many bedrooms and bathrooms it has, and how many air-conditioners – but the pool is empty. Paul waits for someone else to notice it and tell the grown-ups. They all stop unpacking the cars and come and stare into the empty pool – the little dirty puddle at the deep end, and a few brown leaves and a frog scrabbling at the sides. Uncle Romesh starts swearing about the man who was supposed to have been doing something to the pool and goes out to the gate to ask the security guard whether the pool-man ever came or not. Auntie Rachel looks in her handbag for the man's phone number. Mummy sighs and shakes her head.

'We wouldn't be able to swim?' Peter asks.

'Look in front of you!' Uncle Philip says. 'You have eyes? You see any water in there?'

'I just mean, we're here for four days,' Peter says. 'It might get filled up later today, or maybe tomorrow, and then we could swim.'

'Carnival weekend?' Uncle Philip says. 'You mad?'

'We'll swim in the sea, then. The sea is right there.' Peter gestures towards the little gate where a path leads down to the water. Paul got a glimpse of it earlier through the chain-link fence: it was too steep to see down to the actual beach, but he saw the steep rocky path down the slope, criss-crossed by long slanted necks of coconut trees, and, further out, outcrops of black jagged rock and churning white water.

'You can't swim here,' Auntie Marilyn says. 'It's too rough.'

'Daddy could take us,' Paul says. 'He's a good swimmer.'

But Daddy is shaking his head. Just last week, somebody drowned here, he says. It was a man, a big strong man, a good swimmer, nothing wrong with him except for the fact that he was a damn fool.

Paul is very disappointed about the pool. He is a good swimmer, better than Peter. When Daddy took them to Mayaro last year, he taught them to swim. They walked along the beach, with just the sea on one side and coconut trees on the other, and the three lines of the sea, the sand, and the green of the coconut trees diminishing in the distance to vanishing point ahead of them. When they reached the spot, he sat them on the sand and stood in front of them like a teacher. 'The first rule of the sea,' he said, 'which any child around here could tell you, is, if you see somebody drowning? Don't jump in after them.' He itemised on his fingers the things you could do instead. 'Go and call somebody. Throw them something, a rope, or a lifejacket, or a piece of wood that will float, anything. But don't jump in after them thinking you going to save them. All that will happen is that two will drown instead of one.

'Second rule of the sea, is learn to stay afloat. If you could stay afloat, you can't drown. You have to know the ways to conserve your energy, so you could last in the water for an hour, two hours, a whole day if you need to, until somebody comes to help you, please God.'

Paul waited on the sand while Daddy took Peter into the water to teach him; and then when it was his turn, Daddy stood with the waves breaking around his ankles, hands on his hips, waiting for him to come in for his turn. Paul thought of running in to show that he wasn't afraid; but he might splash Daddy with water or do something else stupid, so instead he tried to walk as he had seen Peter doing, stepping over each frill of wave as it came, but keeping up a steady pace until he was at Daddy's side. Daddy held him by the arm as they went deeper, until the water was up to his shoulders and he felt his toes being lifted off the sandy floor with each slow swell. The feeling was lovely: smooth and gentle and calming; the feeling of it made him think of ice-cream. He let his toes come up and he floated on his back looking up at the sky as Daddy told him. He held his breath and floated on his front; he kicked as Daddy instructed, and it was all so easy, it all made perfect sense. He could see from Daddy's expression that he was doing it right, and that Daddy was pleased and surprised. When they walked back up to the shore, Paul shook Daddy's hand off his arm and walked on his own.

That evening, while the children are watching *Ghostbusters* in the master bedroom, Paul comes out to the kitchen to get away from the horrible clammy air of the air-conditioning. He takes a Styrofoam cup from the stack in the kitchen, cautiously presses the cup to the lever in the freezer door for ice from the ice-machine. Lumps of ice shoot out; he tries to catch them in the cup but several fall on the floor. He puts them in the sink. Then he opens a jaliter bottle of Solo Orange and fills the cup, and stands in the bright lights of the kitchen looking at the shiny fridge, the matching cupboards, all the food and drink and alcohol that the grown-ups brought for the weekend stacked up on the floor or on the kitchen counters. He has another cup of Solo Orange, and a Caramel bar (Auntie Rachel brought a whole box, twenty-four Caramel bars) and thinks longingly of the pool – he can hardly believe that there is an actual swimming pool right there, right outside the door. He imagines walking around the white-painted rim and jumping into the water, if only it had water in it. He tiptoes through the living room and listens to the grown-ups on the porch, trying to gauge whether it is safe to walk that way out into the yard, but they are talking in low voices, which means they are talking about the trial again. Uncle Philip is going to judge the trial of someone famous. Paul goes out the front door to the driveway where the cars are parked. Beyond the front gate, the security guard and another man are smoking cigarettes and old-talking quietly. Paul stoops down and creeps around the cars, and then, instead of just walking along the grass, he keeps close to the little shrubs near to the house which are more in shadow. There is no particular reason to hide but it's fun to pretend to be on a secret mission. The empty pool looks spooky from far away, but by the time he gets up close it just looks like an empty pool. And there are two frogs now, one sitting in the puddle and the other one in the shallow end. He sits on the white-painted rim near the steps and dangles his legs down into the empty space, and imagines the pool being full of water. He goes down the steps (the frog quickly hops away down the sloping floor) and pretends to swim laps of the pool, doing the strokes with his arms.

A little later, when he hears footsteps on the driveway, he quickly gets out of the pool and sits on the edge: it's probably just Sayeed or Peter wondering where he is, or someone getting their toothbrush or slippers out of the car, but he'd feel embarrassed for someone to see him pretending to swim in the empty pool. He retraces his steps, sticking to the shadows, and when he gets near the driveway, he pauses to check all is clear. But all is not clear: there's a man in the driver's seat of the Mercedes. Paul recognises the shape of the man's head, the thick neck, the short-clipped hair, the beret tipped to one side: the security guard who let them in earlier. Paul stoops low to the ground. The overhead light in the car is switched off, but there's a glow from a tiny blue-ish light, maybe from a very small torch or a little bulb on the end of a keyring. The man opens the glovebox, shines his light into it, pulls out a wad of papers. This is not good. He wants to creep away into the house, but he'd have to open the front door and the man would see him going in for sure. He watches the man rest a piece of paper against the steering wheel and hold the light steady while he reads. Not good at all. He has two options: he could either run to the patio and tell the grown-ups that the security guard is in Uncle Philip's car reading his letters, or he could just try to get back into the house as fast as possible without anyone seeing him. His instinct is to get in the house now, fast, but he's transfixed by the dark shape of the man in the car, his thick neck, the tiny glowing light. Then, without any warning, the man quickly stuffs the papers back into the glovebox and steps out of the car. This is terrible; he's in a terrible spot. If the man sees him hiding here in the dark, he'll realise that Paul must have been watching the whole time. Paul stands up, puts his hands in his pockets, and begins to walk calmly towards the pool and the patio, trying very hard to look as if he just this moment walked out the front door and definitely hasn't noticed anything strange. Behind him, the car door clicks shut; his skin prickles knowing that the security guard is watching him walk away. He goes quickly through the porch so nobody has time to ask him why he's not watching the movie, and he goes straight into his room and into his bed and shuts his eyes.

The next morning, when Paul checks, there's a different security guard on duty, fairer-skinned and thin, with sleepy-looking eyes; still, Paul keeps well away from the front gate, just in case. After breakfast, Sayeed starts talking about going down to the private beach – Peter tells him it's not really a private beach, it's just that other people can't access it, which is not the same thing. Sayeed wants to go down to show them, and the children go to the little gate at the back and find that it's padlocked shut. Paul hooks his fingers into the chain-link fence and listens to the crash of waves at the bottom while Sayeed goes to get the key. All the grown-ups come out, saying that they want to see the private beach too. The security guard unlocks the gate for them and then says he will go down first to check everything is OK. He puts on his sunglasses and sets off down the steps, his arms pumping. Sayeed copies him, striding up and down alongside the fence, like Tom Cruise in *Top Gun*, and everyone bursts out laughing.

'All clear,' the security guard says to Uncle Romesh, when he comes back up. 'You could go.'

'We really need all of this security-business?' Mummy says, as they begin to go down. 'You really think somebody hiding down there?'

Sayeed skips down, showing off that he knows the way, Anna follows with the grown-ups, then Peter, and then Paul, trying not to be left behind. It is very windy; his hair keeps blowing in front of his face. The first few steps are easy, the ones made by cutting the ground away in blocks and wedging planks in the horizontals. But soon the ground becomes more rocky, and there's just a ragged length of rope looped around the coconut trees to show the way down. Paul goes carefully, grasping the edges of the rocks with his hands. Through the gaps between the coconut trees, he sees the waves crashing white against the black rocks. He glances once or twice at the security guard behind him and apologises for going so slowly. He wants to tell the security guard to go in front, but the man's face, expressionless with the sunglasses over his eyes, makes him nervous. Then, when he is nearly at the bottom, he feels the man rush up behind him, and he pitches forward, his hands out in front of him grasping at empty space. Then, the strange, burbling sound of underwater and he has no idea which way is up and all he can do is try to hold his breath. He's aware of voices screaming and calling out, but they're very far away and first, before anything, he must get air. He works his arms, trying to get his head above water, but every time he gets close, water goes down his nose, his throat. The waves pitch him forward and back. Rocks are everywhere. He tries to move his arms the right way, to float on his back the way Daddy said, but this water is not like in Mayaro. This water is the wrong kind of water; this water doesn't care about him. There is no shouting any more, just a bubbling, churning sound in his ears.

He's dead?

Move your hand! Your foot! Move something!

That is Daddy kneeling over him; Daddy wet and dripping, his hair sticking to his face. Paul tries to open his eyes, but they are full of saltwater and he shuts them again; he tries to speak instead, to say that he is OK, but he only gurgles warm liquid out of his mouth. Daddy turns him onto his side, holds his head up off the rock.

Later, when he wakes, he is lying on one of the bamboo sofas on the porch, his head on a towel laid over a cushion, Daddy sitting at the far end of the sofa by Paul's feet.

'How you feeling? Open your eyes. Your head hurting?'

His head feels strange: slow and foggy. He puts his fingers to his face, feels the unfamiliar shapes – swellings, cuts, plasters. Red patches of the red-stuff Mummy uses on cuts are painted all over his arms and legs. Gingerly, he stretches his legs, careful to stay on his squares of cushion so that his feet do not touch

Daddy. He closes his eyes again, drifts in and out of sleep. When he wakes up properly, he hears the grown-ups talking around him and senses it must be late. There's an empty rum bottle on the floor and a half-empty one on the table and the ashtray is full of dead cigarettes.

'But I saw the man push him, I'm telling you!' Auntie Marilyn is saying. (Paul quickly closes his eyes.)

'You're imagining things,' says Daddy. 'What reason would he have to kick the boy down the rocks?'

'Ask him when he wakes up,' says Auntie Marilyn.

'You're feeling paranoid because of the trial.' That's Auntie Rachel. 'Everything that happens, you're thinking it's related to the trial, that's the problem.'

'But Marilyn said she saw him!' says Mummy.

'But maybe he tripped,' Uncle Romesh says. 'He's so clumsy. He could have dead, you realise that? See how much trouble the boy is causing you, eh, Clyde? It's one problem after another with him!'

Paul feels the grown-ups looking at him. He pretends to stretch, and turns over so he faces the back of the sofa. He keeps his eyes tightly closed.

'The government is giving me twenty-four-seven security!' Uncle Philip is saying. 'Round the clock!'

'And you trust them?' Auntie Marilyn says.

'But they're all specially vetted,' Uncle Philip says. 'These men are hand-picked!'

'But hand-picked by who?' Mummy says. 'That is the question. Anybody could have hand-picked them, that's what Marilyn means.'

'You're trying to say that I'm being naïve?' Uncle Philip says. 'I'm not naïve. I know exactly what's what. Do you see how many people I'm friends with? The kind of people? Hello, didn't we go to the President's House for dinner just last month? And the month before that, the cocktail party by the British High Commissioner? You think anybody would really touch me or my family?'

'But what Marilyn is saying is that these people don't care about President's House or cocktail parties,' Auntie Rachel says. 'Those are your connections, but they have other connections. I don't think it's safe. I don't think you should do it, to be honest.'

'Well, leave it to me to decide that,' Uncle Philip says.

'I want to go back to England, Philip,' Auntie Marilyn says. 'I've had enough. I just want to go back.'

'But what you want me to do in England?' Uncle Philip says. 'What will I do there? Work in a shop? That's what you want to see me doing?'

The grown-ups all stop talking. Paul feels them all looking at him. He thinks about stretching, pretending he just woke up. He could get up, walk to his bed, get out of here.

'We shouldn't be arguing like this,' Mummy says. 'I wanted us to relax, have a nice time. I didn't come here for people to fight.'

There's a tense silence. He can't get up now. He opens his eyes a fraction, sees Daddy's elbow painted over with red-stuff.

'Hear nuh,' Uncle Romesh says. 'While we're on the subject. I'm still trying to understand where all Uncle Vishnu's money went.'

Paul feels Daddy bristle up. 'I knew that's what you brought us here for!' Daddy says. 'Didn't I say so to you, Joy?'

'Romesh,' Mummy says. 'I just said. I didn't come here to fight with people.'

'I'm not fighting with anyone! I'm only asking a question! I can't ask a question?'

'I not able with this,' Mummy says.

'I'm only asking because I can't believe he had so little

money,' Uncle Romesh says. 'Only a few hundred dollars coming to me, and an old, moth-eaten rug from India? What I will do with a rug?'

'You-all keeping some secret, that is what I feel,' says Auntie Rachel. 'Vishnu had more money than that.'

'Clyde, carry the child and put him in bed, please,' Mummy says. 'I don't know why all-you have to go and spoil everything talking about money, money all the time. You-all have plenty of money, what are you worrying about? You don't have enough?'

'It's not about enough, it's about fairness,' Uncle Romesh says. 'I feel you-all got it all and you don't want to say. Come, get it out in the open! What happened to Uncle Vishnu's money? Why is it such a big secret?'

'It's not a secret,' Daddy says, 'it's just none of your business, that's what it is! What did you ever do for Uncle Vishnu, or for Mousey? Who had Mousey living with them for years, and looking after her, and making sure she got her medicine and did all her blood tests? Not you! So you could stop bringing this up. Just stop it.'

Many voices talk at once: Uncle Romesh, Uncle Philip, Auntie Rachel. Paul feels himself being lifted. In the darkened corridor, on the way to the bedroom, he opens his eyes and sees the underside of his father's chin and the thick black hairs inside his nostrils. He closes his eyes, tries to fix in his mind the feeling of his father's arms around him, his scent, the rhythm of his gait, labouring under his burden. One ear is pressed against his father's chest, and he listens to the slow, steady breathing and the beating of his father's heart.

8

Daddy rang up Uncle Philip and asked him and Auntie Marilyn to come down to Tiparo. Daddy didn't want to call: he said Uncle Philip is too busy for things like this, but Mummy said then in that case she would call him herself to ask. 'He is my brother,' she said, 'and he is the eldest in the family now, of course he must help us.' And Daddy said that Philip has already helped, that he helped a lot, getting the bank account set up in England for them, and buying sterling on the black market and taking the bank draft up to England to deposit in Barclays Bank. 'He might be family,' Daddy says, 'but don't wear him out asking him for help with every little thing.' And Mummy said that he was the eldest in the family, and that he would help.

Now Uncle Philip's Mercedes is in the driveway, the dogs still walking around it and sniffing at the tyres. Peter and Paul are crouched in the space under the house where they can hear, because they know Mummy and Daddy want to talk about them, and about the Eleven Plus exam which is coming up in just a few months' time. They have pulled over their old cot-mattress to sit on and covered it with a splayed-open cardboard box from the grocery. In front, Paul has arranged the roll of wire-mesh, so they're not so visible from the road. Trixie noses around looking for lizards. Every now and again she puts her head down and digs madly, spraying the red dirt into their faces, and they have to reach through the haze and tap her on the rump to get her to stop.

'And if I get my way, we're going to look at schools in Surrey while we're up there,' Auntie Marilyn is saying, up on the patio.

'Oh, schools? For her A-levels?' That's Mummy, trying to sound interested.

'Yes. And I'm going to look at houses.'

'Looking at houses! To live in? So you decided to move up?'

Silence.

'Well, like I've said already,' Uncle Philip says heavily, 'we could go and look. No harm in looking.'

Uncle Philip starts talking about Oxford and Cambridge: this could take a long time. Paul gropes around under the mattress and pulls out an old Milo tin, and then the blade of an old steak-knife that has lost its handle, and prises open the top of the tin, hoping that he's stored something to eat in it, some Crix or a pack of Ovaltine biscuits, but there's just a melted dinner-mint with a few dead ants stuck to the wrapper. He presses the lid back in place with his palm. Uncle Philip is still talking about the great intellectual conversations in the dining hall and the dinner jackets. Paul presses his forefingers against the little flaps over his ear-holes, listening to the workings of his own body: the soft *thud-thud* of his heart, the gurgle of spit as he swallows, the soft dragging sound of air passing through his windpipe as he breathes in and out. Very quietly, he starts to hum, feeling the vibration all around his throat. Peter taps him on the knee to tell him to stop.

'Sister Frances said we should think about which school to put down for Peter.' That is Daddy's voice. 'She said, whichever school we put down for Eleven Plus, he will get his first choice. Guaranteed.'

'What you going to put?' Uncle Philip asks.

'Well, St Saviour's College!' says Daddy.

'What, quite in Port of Spain? For him to travel all that way every day?' Uncle Philip mentions other schools, closer by. 'Those are also very good schools,' he says.

'But why should he go to "very good" when he can get into the best?' Daddy says. 'Why?'

'But – it's a long way, you realise that?'

'I know. That's the only problem. But I'll find a way. First, let him get in. If he gets in? I'll find a way.'

'But the problem is Paul,' Mummy says. 'Paul won't pass for St Saviour's.'

Upstairs, there's a heavy silence. Paul sits on his haunches, his arms wrapped around his knees, staying very still.

'The teachers said he should stay down, repeat Standard Five,' Mummy says. 'They say he harden. Even Sister Frances herself tried to teach him. She kept him in at lunchtimes to do extra work with him, but she said everything does go in one ear and out the other.'

'I keep telling her, let him stay down!' Daddy says. 'The teachers know what is best!'

'But I think they must stay together,' Mummy says. 'Paul – he's getting better. But he needs Peter to be with him.'

'You think that is right?' Daddy asks. 'You think it is right that Peter has to be responsible for him?'

'Well, let Marilyn do an assessment for you,' Uncle Philip says.

'Exactly,' Mummy says. 'An assessment. Do an assessment on him.'

Under the house, Paul looks at Peter to see if he knows what this means. He was listening out for 'St Ann's' or 'expelled': those are the words that normally make him feel sick – now, here is a new one. His stomach begins to lurch. He will need to get out from under here soon, back to the sunshine and the breeze. Peter puts a finger to his lips.

'That is what I wanted to ask you,' says Mummy. 'If you could spend some time with him, work out where he's having difficulties, try to help him.'

'I don't know how much I'll be able to help him,' Auntie Marilyn says.

'Yes, but it's better to know one way or the other,' Mummy says. 'If something truly wrong with him, if something wrong with his brain and he will never be able to learn – then OK, maybe he's wasting his time being in school.'

A car drives past – an unfamiliar car, not one that belongs to anyone around here. It slows down as it passes their driveway, and then it must turn at the end of the Trace, because it comes back again in the other direction, still moving slowly. The grown-ups stop talking upstairs. Uncle Philip says he's getting bitten by mosquitoes, and they all get up and go inside. Peter and Paul dust off their pants and quickly crawl out from under the house, and go and sit instead on the back-steps, trying to look as if they have been there the whole time.

The following week, Mummy carries them in a maxi taxi to Port of Spain, and then a private 'H' car to Uncle Philip and Auntie Marilyn's house. The 'H' car drops them right at the gate, and the watchman comes out from his little hut and puts on his cap. He's fattish, almost bald, with a gentle face. Paul hasn't seen this one before; the government sends different people all the time.

'Hello,' Mummy says to him. 'We're family. I'm just dropping these two boys.'

'Which family?' he says. 'The one working in oil and gas? Or the ones with the shop in Trincity?'

'Oil and gas,' Mummy says. 'And living in Tiparo.'

'Twins!' he says, looking from one face to the other.

'Just normal twins,' Peter says.

The watchman goes to the pillar on one side of the gate and presses the button for the intercom. 'Miss, it's your family,' he says. 'A lady and two children.' Auntie Marilyn says OK, and the watchman unclips a key from his belt and unlocks the gate, and stands back to let them go in. The driveway is proper black tarmac, with white-painted concrete at the edges of the lawns, like a pavement. The grass on the front lawn is green and perfect, the type of grass that people actually plant, with thick blades, the edges ruffled, very springy underfoot. There are supposed to be rose bushes in the flowerbeds bordering the driveway, but the plants are dry and brown, with just a few drooping yellow roses. The silver Mercedes isn't in the carport.

'Hello, hello, come in, come in,' says Auntie Marilyn, when she comes to the door. She's wearing face powder and lipstick and her hair is pulled back on one side with a tortoiseshell clip. She stands back to make space for them to come in.

'No, no, I won't come in,' says Mummy. 'I'll just leave them.'

'Joy, come in and have something to drink. You look so hot.'

'No, no, I'm fine.'

'Come on, Joy. Come in. Sit down for a few minutes.'

'No, no,' Mummy says again. She says she is going to do some shopping, even though Paul knows this isn't true, and that instead she is going to find a shady spot to sit while she waits.

Auntie Marilyn leads them down the corridor towards the patio. Peter and Paul peek into the other rooms they pass on their way: the laundry room, with the ironing board standing in the middle, and a short black lady doing the ironing. They're about to smile and say, 'Hello, Auntie,' to be polite, but Auntie Marilyn just walks past. Then the kitchen, with all matching white cupboards and black countertops, and cactuses on the windowsill above the sink. Past the dining room, with its enormous shiny dining table, and the cabinet with crystal ornaments. They follow her through to the patio at the back, with bamboo chairs and a glass-topped bamboo table, and a ceiling fan and an aquarium with goldfish swimming around. The grass in the back garden is perfect, green and smooth, with none of the usual fruit trees that grow in everyone's gardens, just perfect, smooth green grass.

'Right!' says Auntie Marilyn. 'Paul, don't look so scared!'

'I feel sick, Auntie,' he says. 'I think I have a fever.'

'You shouldn't be scared of tests,' she says. 'Tests help you learn. And anyway, you're not doing a test today. It's just an assessment.'

'You might not call it a test,' says Peter. 'But it's still a test. Right?'

She doesn't say anything, just pulls out the chairs for them to sit in. 'Do you want to sit together or separately?'

'Together,' says Peter.

'OK.' She has photocopies – pages stapled together. It *is* a test, Paul thinks. Why did she try to tell them it wasn't a test? She slides one test to Peter and the other to Paul. Peter starts to read his.

'Wait, don't start. I have to time you,' Auntie Marilyn says. She takes off her watch and puts it on the table. 'Forty minutes,' she says.

'Auntie,' says Paul, his voice weak, 'I told you, I feel sick.'

Auntie Marilyn looks like the Muppets on *Sesame Street* do when they're angry – their mouths go all crumpled up. 'Paul. It's going to take less than an hour. It's not a test. Could you just read the questions and answer whatever you can? You don't have to answer them all. I don't expect you to finish the whole thing.' After she stops talking, she just stares at him. Paul stares back. He picks up the pencil and grips it hard like he's going to snap it with one hand.

'OK, I'm starting the clock now,' she says. She leans over to look at the watch, and then she walks out of the room.

Peter opens the booklet. 'You want to copy mine?' he whispers.

Paul shakes his head. He slips his feet into his flip-flops and they go *slap-slap-slap* as he walks past the kitchen, past the ironing room and out the door into the open. The warmth of the sun feels good after the clamminess of Auntie Marilyn's cool house. He doesn't bother to try opening the gate, he just kicks the flip-flops off, grabs hold of the bars and starts climbing: one, two, three movements and he is at the top, negotiating the spikes, and then one, two, three down the other side. There's a creaking from the guard's little hut: he comes out, fanning himself with his beret. 'What happen?' the man asks.

'Nothing.' The tarmac is scalding his bare feet. He reaches through the bars for his flip-flops and puts them back on quickly.

'You looking all het-up,' the man says. 'You fight with somebody?'

Paul shrugs.

'Who? Your brother?'

'No.'

'The lady?'

Paul doesn't answer. He wanted to walk out of Auntie Marilyn's house and just walk away, straight down the road. But he will get into big trouble for that. He sits down on the edge of the pavement in the full glare of the hot sun, his feet in the shallow gutter.

'Come, come, come,' the man says. 'You'll end up with headache there.' He points at the patch of shade cast behind his hut. 'Be reasonable.'

Paul hesitates, but he's already feeling his skin begin to sizzle in the heat. He won't be able to sit here for an hour, or two hours, until Mummy comes back. He gets up and sits in the shade of the hut, where the man indicates. The man goes back into his hut and after a while he turns up the volume on his little radio, and they listen to the broadcaster commentating on the Test match playing at the Oval, Australia vs the West Indies.

At home, that evening, Peter and Paul come into the living room as casually as they can, and take up their seats on the sofa, to watch *The Cosby Show*.

Daddy turns the volume down on the TV. 'Peter, I hear you did well in the test,' he says. 'Well done.'

Everyone holds their breath while he turns to Paul. His voice is matter of fact. 'You should have done what Auntie Marilyn asked you to do, Paul,' he says. 'You're not keeping up at school. The teachers are trying to help you, but they said to Mummy they're not making any headway. I can't help you. Mummy can't help you. Marilyn was trying to help you.'

Paul stares at Daddy, trying hard not to blink or to show anything.

'You might not be as bright as Peter,' Daddy continues. He's said this before: *you might not be as bright as Peter, but that's OK!* 'I've given you the same opportunities as him. I'm paying school fees at St Anthony's for *both* of you. I didn't send him to the good school, and you to the other one. No. I trying to treat you both the same. Your education is the most important thing.'

Paul knows that Peter, next to him, wants to say, 'I'll help him, Daddy,' and he, in his turn, would like to say, 'Yes, Peter will help me,' but they both know not to.

'How you will get a job when you're older, if you don't go to school? How you will support yourself when you're older after Mummy and I are gone? There's only so much I can do for you.'

Daddy stares at him. Paul's heart beats very fast.

'You should have let Marilyn help you, that's all I'm saying,' Daddy says. And then he shrugs, like he's done with that, and he gets up and turns the volume back up on the TV. Paul turns his eyes to the screen. He sits very still until the advertisements come on, and then he gets up as casually as he can and he slips away.

A few days before the Eleven Plus results are due out, Mummy gets a phone call from Sister Frances. She sits on Daddy's armchair in the living room, the phone at her ear, her eyes wide, flicking from Peter to Paul and back again. The twins perch shoulder to shoulder on the sofa, watching her.

'Ah hah. Ah hah. Yes.' Her eyes are on Peter and a smile slowly spreads across her face. 'You sure? OK. Yes, I'll tell him.

'Yes. Yes.' Now she is looking at Paul and the smile is fading. 'Ah hah. Ah hah. You think they will do it? Ah hah. Ah hah. OK. Well, I'll speak to Clyde about it when he comes home.'

Finally, she hangs up. She rubs her face with her hands and says, 'Sister told me that Peter got into St Saviour's. Paul, darling, you didn't get it, I'm sorry. But Sister said they going to do a recheck for you.'

'So what did I get?' Paul asks.

'I don't know, darling.'

'Did I get the second choice?'

'I don't know, Paul. Sister only said they're going to do a recheck.'

Later, when Daddy comes home from work, Mummy tells them to go outside to play. They crawl past the brick pillars to the space under the house where they can hear, and stoop on their haunches, Peter poking at the loose dirt with a stick. Paul can picture the scene: Daddy on the green armchair, sitting forward with his knees wide apart, smoking; Mummy on her corner of the sofa, winding the hem of her skirt around her forefinger.

'So what did the teacher say?' they hear Daddy say, upstairs.

'She said the Ministry called her and said that how that Peter came first.'

'How you mean first?'

'First. First in the two islands.'

There is a long silence.

'First in the two islands!' Daddy says again.

There is another long silence.

'They sure?'

'Yea. But what we going to do about Paul?' Mummy says. 'I don't want him to get separated from Peter. They have to be in the same school so Peter could look after him.'

'Don't you worry about that. I will go into St Saviour's. I will sort all that out.'

'But how you going to do that?'

'You have to understand people, Joy. You see me? I understand people. I am telling you, I will sort it out.'

9

When Paul was younger, he went through a phase of being afraid of cutting his hair: after the whole thing in Siparia, he thought hair-cutting meant crowds and noise and the hair-cutter flashing his scissors and saying he might cut your ears off. Later, when he realised hair-cutting wasn't like that generally, he still refused: he liked having his hair shaggy and overgrown – he felt it made him distinctive. And when the Boyz on the Block started calling him Tarzan, he didn't mind. They all had nicknames – he could be Paul 'Tarzan' Deyalsingh. Yesterday afternoon, though, while Mummy was ironing their new school uniforms, Daddy gave Paul a look and said, 'Listen here. You're not going into St Saviour's looking like *that*.' Paul knew better than to argue: he took Daddy's little round shaving mirror and the kitchen scissors and went out to the back yard and cut his hair. It wasn't perfect, a bit zogged up and jagged, but at least it was short, and Daddy said, 'I suppose that'll have to do.'

This morning, they were up at half past four, and ready to leave the house well before six. In truth, there wasn't that much to do: their clothes were already hanging on the hooks; underwear, belts, shoes and socks laid out. Now, in the cool golden light of morning, with the birds still singing in the tamarind trees, the boys stand at the side of the road opposite the gas station, waiting for the maxi taxi to come. Every few minutes, Paul feels in his pocket for the ten dollar bill Daddy gave him, to pay for the journey to Port of Spain and back, and to buy lunch from the tuck-shop at St Saviour's.

When the maxi taxi comes, the rastaman, Sando, is sitting in the front seat next to the driver. He leans through the window and calls out, 'Aaaaay! Today is the big day, eh?' Sando lives in Arima, as far as they know, but he has friends in Tiparo so he often limes around here. He has long dreadlocks and is always wearing shades, and he spends all his time growing ganja on the mountainside. Sando gets out of the front seat, slides back the main door of the maxi, and stands there like a chauffeur, gesturing for them to go in. Peter and Paul get a seat behind a lady who looks like an office worker, and Sando takes the seat across the aisle, and smiles at them with his big white teeth. Paul can see his own reflection in Sando's shades.

'Whiteboys!' Sando says. 'Come and talk to me a little bit. I could take some education. What is two plus two?'

Peter rolls his eyes.

'Eh? You don't know? How come you don't know? I hear you is a real brainbox.'

'Don't call us whiteboys,' Peter says. 'One, you're being sarcastic, and two, it's not accurate.'

'Sarcastic?' the rastaman says. 'No, I'm speaking the truth! Not so? Not so you're upgrading yourself?' But Peter doesn't answer, only shakes his head and looks out the window, ignoring him.

'Tarzan!' Sando says. 'You cut the hair!'

'Yea,' Paul says. He's not feeling very well. He doesn't like the smell in here: a mixture of sweat, incense, cigarette smoke, coconut oil and talcum powder. He feels like he might vomit. He slides the window open and sticks his head out as far as he can, to get some breeze.

'Hello, don't vomit on me, you know,' says a lady behind him, one of the ones covered in talcum powder. She quickly pushes her window closed. 'You should take ginger root if you get travel sickness,' she says. She starts to explain what the leaves and fruit look like, how and where to find the plant.

A schoolgirl next to her says, 'Actually, they have tablets nowadays for travel sickness.'

'You see?' the woman calls to him. 'You could take tablets for it. Why you don't take the tablets?' She tells the schoolgirl to write down the name of the tablets for him, so that he could take them before he gets in the maxi taxi. 'Otherwise,' she says, 'better you sit in the row behind me, so at least if you feel sick, you don't get the vomit on *me*.'

'It's nerves,' Sando says. 'That's all. Nerves! First day of new school, man! And with all the whiteboys? And you coming from out here, where it's only bush-and-bandits?'

'They're not all whiteboys,' Peter says. 'All kinds of boys go to St Saviour's.'

'You're right,' Sando says. 'It's not whiteboys. It's brightboys!' He slaps his knees and laughs, and then he hums a tune and rocks his head back and forth in time with the beat.

The maxi drops them at the top of Charlotte Street, outside the hospital. They know approximately which way to walk, but people give them directions anyway: across so, down so, five-ten minutes maximum. They smooth out the creases in their clothes, adjust their bags on their backs and head down the road. There are a lot of other schoolchildren walking the same way – past Memorial Square, or the National Museum, heading in the direction of downtown – boys, in the same khaki pants and light blue shirts as themselves, and girls with dark blue skirts and white blouses. A bigger boy, fattish, with glasses and a smiley face, taps them on the shoulder as they pass Deluxe Cinema. 'Form Ones?' he asks, and when they nod, he points down the road and says, 'This way. We going this way.' He looks from one face to the other and says, 'Oh gosh! Twins!' And as he walks along, he tells them about other boys at school who are twins, and that twins are very popular because of the opportunities for pranks.

'Not today, though,' Peter says, to clarify.

'No! You're mad? Definitely not today!' the boy says, laughing.

They walk next to a little square, green and shady, with gates at each corner and paths criss-crossing through it. Wandering around inside is a vagrant: old, ashen-coloured, with overgrown dreadlocks and dirty, smelly clothes. He's singing a hymn, mumbling the words he doesn't remember, and bawling out the ones he does: 'Crea-tor! Ten-der! Praise Him!'

As they walk alongside the fence – iron bars standing up straight, gold-tipped like spears – Paul feels the vagrant's eyes fix on them. 'Schoolchildren!' the man shouts. The smiley boy waves to the vagrant, snickering, and under his breath, he says to Peter and Paul, 'This guy is OK, as long as he's on the *other* side of the fence to you.' The vagrant laughs loudly, and then starts chanting a few words from the calypso 'Hurry, hurry, come for curry'. He chants the chorus over and over, his feet chipping in time with the rhythm. When the boys reach the end of the square and go to cross the road, Paul sees a lady in high-heels go through one of the gates to walk across the square. The vagrant turns to follow her; he takes out his thing and waves it at the woman, still chanting the words of the song. The woman ignores him, clip-clops away out the other gate.

In the classroom – he's on his own, the smiley boy led Peter somewhere else – Paul chooses a desk not right at the back, but almost, and near the doors to the corridor. At the front of the room is the teacher's desk on a raised wooden platform. Behind the desk is a blackboard, not grey as blackboards usually are, but very black, freshly painted, with an unopened box of chalk in the groove at the bottom. On another wall is a green-felted notice-board, where someone has used the coloured thumbtacks to spell out a big HELLO. The teacher is at the desk, leafing through the register book in which, Paul can see, all their names are typed. The bell hasn't rung yet, there are still people passing in the corridor talking loudly, but in here it is quiet, just a few boys whispering to each other. Paul already feels exhausted, and it's not even eight o'clock in the morning.

One boy lifts the lid of his desk, takes out a new exercise book, closes the lid, and places the book on his desk. Someone else copies him, and then everybody starts opening their desks and taking things out: exercise books, pencils, pens, rulers, and laying them out. Paul does the same, furiously studying the teacher's face, trying to work out whether he's nice or strict, and at the same time trying to look casual. He wishes he had some chewing gum; he'd like to sit back in his desk with his elbows over the back of his chair and chew his chewing gum and act like this is all no big deal, like he couldn't care less. But he's afraid the teacher will give them a test or, worse, call people up to the blackboard to answer questions. He wishes he wasn't here; he wishes Mummy and Daddy hadn't organised for him to come here. This is terrible. If the priest asks Paul a question and he can't answer it, or he asks him to come up to the blackboard, he thinks, he could pretend to try to answer it, and when he can't, he'll say he feels sick, and he'll ask to go home. He reaches for his schoolbag at his feet and takes one of the canvas straps in his hand. He's right by one of the doors. He could pick up his schoolbag and just walk out right now, before it happens. The school gates might still be open: he could walk out quickly, before they're closed, and once he's out on the road he won't have to come back. He'll find somewhere to sit in the shade until school has finished, and then they'll work out what to say to Mummy and Daddy on the way home. But all his new books are here – in his bag, in his desk. Daddy spent so much money on all these new books. He can't just walk out. Beads of sweat have been breaking out all over his body while the priest has been slowly turning pages at the front of the room.

The priest is white, the very white colour of a foreigner. He has light brown hair cut short, an oval-shaped kind of face, the cheeks very smooth and young-looking. He might be nice, it's hard to tell for sure. When he looks up, he doesn't smile, but he doesn't look extremely stern and angry like some priests do. In the front row, one boy squeezes his shoulder blades together, angles his head to the left and then to the right, like someone about to run a hundred metres race.

The bell rings; the whole school falls quiet. The priest closes the register book, clasps his hands over it, slowly looks around the room. Paul's heart speeds up. The priest gets down from the platform and stands in front of the blackboard, facing the class. 'Good morning,' he says.

A few boys open their mouths to repeat, but the priest raises one hand to stop them. 'I am Father Kavanagh,' he says. He looks at them, then raises both hands, like a choir conductor.

'Good morning, Father Kavanagh,' the boys chant. Paul chants with them.

The priest takes a stick of chalk from the box on the desk and writes: 'Father Kavanagh.' Paul watches as a few boys open their exercise books and copy it down. The priest steps up onto the platform again, sits at the teacher's desk and opens the register book. 'When I call your name, I want you to stand, and say, "Here".' He looks around. 'When I call your name, what will you do?'

'Stand and say, "Here",' the boys reply.

'Good.' The priest takes a ruler and positions it under the first name in the register book, his pen poised. 'Aboud.'

The boy sitting right in front of Paul stands up, a lightish-skinned boy with dark curly hair, tall for an eleven year old. 'Here, Father.'

'Just "Here".'

'Here.'

He nods, and the boy sits down. The priest makes a little mark in his register. He goes through the list slowly, taking a good look at each boy before he nods for him to sit down. Paul feels his heart speeding up as the priest reaches the Ds. D'Abadie. Dalla Costa. Dennis. Devenish. Deyal.

'Deyalsingh,' the priest reads. His eyes look around the room. 'Paul Deyalsingh.'

Paul stands, trying to summon the feeling as if he couldn't care less about all this. If he were chewing gum, he'd blow a bubble right now, a big bubble and then let it go *pop!* while the priest is looking at him, as if to say: *There, take that!* He puts his weight on one leg, crosses his arms, stares straight at the priest's face. The priest looks straight back. Paul feels hot and cold at once, in different places. He unfolds his arms, slowly lets them drop to his sides. The priest nods. Paul sits down. He waits until the priest has reached the Fs before he picks up his exercise book and fans himself with it, to cool the sweat away.

Problems come, of course, as he knew they would. It happens just before recess, as the whole class is working quietly, each boy's head bowed over his book, and Father Kavanagh is pacing slowly up and down the aisles between the desks. Paul feels himself get hot as Father Kavanagh draws close, then comes to a halt at his side. He smells of Imperial Leather soap. Paul sprawls over his book, trying to look deep in concentration, but the priest taps a forefinger silently on his desk. Slowly, Paul sits back. He doesn't look up – he knows that most of his answers must be wrong. After what seems like a long time, the priest takes the pencil from Paul's hand and writes, in the margin of his copybook, 'See me at recess.' He puts the pencil down and walks on at the same slow pace, and soon after that, the bell rings.

At lunchtime, Paul picks up his bag and makes his way down to the staff room. He wants to have his bag with him in case he's being expelled; he might have to go to the Principal's office, and then they might tell him to leave, and in that case he'd rather have his bag with him so he doesn't have to go back up to his class. He doesn't sling it over his shoulder, just holds it in his hand like it's a thing he has to carry somewhere, like a wet cloth or a bucket. He finds Father Kavanagh's desk and stands there, steeling himself for whatever it is. A female teacher, young, pretty, with red-brown hair, is at the desk opposite Father Kavanagh's. Nearby, another teacher is sucking the meat off a chicken drumstick.

'Hi, Paul,' says Father Kavanagh. He lays down his pen, pushes some books aside, finds a diary, one of those leather-look diaries with a page per day. He opens it to today's page, finds his glasses, picks up his pen again. The pretty teacher smiles at Paul kindly from her side of the desk. 'Are you going home?' she asks.

Father Kavanagh looks up. 'What?'

'Are you not feeling well? Why do you have your bag?' she asks.

They're both looking at him, and so is the man with the chicken bone.

'Are you feeling sick?' Father Kavanagh asks.

'No,' says Paul.

'What is it?' asks the pretty teacher.

'I thought – I thought you're probably sending me home?'

'Sending you home? Why would I send you home?'

Paul doesn't answer. He wishes he hadn't said anything; he wishes he hadn't brought his bag. He hates his bag. This bag is causing him all these terrible problems.

'Why would I do that?' the priest asks.

Paul feels his face go bright red; no words come to him at all. It is the worst. He wants to go home, he wants to just disappear.

Father Kavanagh points to a spot by the wall and tells Paul to leave his bag there, then he gets up from his desk and walks quickly down the corridor towards the courtyard. Doubtfully, Paul follows. Father Kavanagh pokes his head into a classroom, where a few Form Six boys are sitting on the desks, one of them strumming a guitar – the boys slip off the desks, call after Father does he need the room, but he's already moved on. Paul wonders if Father Kavanagh always walks like this, or if he's in a particular hurry.

'I'm looking for somewhere quiet,' Father Kavanagh says to Paul. 'There's nowhere quiet in this school!' They pass classrooms, stairwells, the basketball court, the science labs. Eventually, they are by the entrance to the chapel, and Father

[127]

Kavanagh says, 'Let's try in here.' Inside, it's dim and cool, quiet except for some boys up in the loft at the back playing on the steelpan, not really playing seriously, just tapping notes at random, practising rolling the sticks.

'Now,' Father Kavanagh says. They sit in the front pew. 'Tell me what's the problem.'

'There's no problem.'

'There is a problem,' Father Kavanagh says. 'Why would you think you were being sent home?'

He thinks of saying, 'I don't know, Father. Nothing, Father,' in a deadpan voice, and repeating it until the priest gives up and leaves him alone. But only one morning has gone by: there's still the afternoon to go, and then tomorrow, morning and afternoon, and the same again the next day, and the day after that. Perhaps it would be better to own up, get it out in the open, and then let him go back to Tiparo and explain to Mummy and Daddy that they didn't want him at St Saviour's after all.

'I didn't pass for St Saviour's,' Paul says. 'My brother passed, but I didn't. My father had a meeting with Father Malachy and organised for me to come, so that me and my brother could stay together. My brother is a genius.' He glances at Father Kavanagh. He swallows, makes sure his voice is steady. 'Also, I'm slightly retarded. Because I had some problems at birth.' He glances at Father Kavanagh again. He looks very serious, but not angry. Paul shrugs, as if to say: that's it.

'Who told you this?' Father Kavanagh asks.

'I don't know. It's just – it's just how it is. Nobody said so, it's just so.'

'But somebody must have said it to you, for you to think this? Your mother? Your father?'

'Yes. And also my mother's uncle, Uncle Vishnu. He was there when I was born. He said so.'

'Well,' Father Kavanagh says. 'Well. I don't think you look retarded.'

'Not a lot,' Paul says. 'Just a little.'

'No,' Father Kavanagh says. 'You're not. Not at all. It's very plain to see that you're not.'

Paul nods, thinking that he'd better agree with him so Father doesn't get angry.

Father Kavanagh takes a hold of his arm, just above the elbow. He grips it hard. 'Listen to me. You're not.'

Out in the courtyard, the bell is ringing. The music from the steelpan is replaced by the sound of footsteps thumping down the wooden steps. Paul doesn't look back to see who the boys are, but he hears them whisper to each other, feels their eyes on his back.

'You're going to need extra-lessons,' Father Kavanagh says. 'You need to catch up.'

'I've had a lot of extra-lessons,' Paul says. He feels he may as well be honest, so that Father Kavanagh doesn't feel, later, that Paul has misled him. 'A lot of people have tried.'

'Well, they haven't tried the right way, then,' Father Kavanagh says. 'Maybe I'll find the right way.'

He looks at Paul as if expecting an answer, but Paul can't think of anything to say. The priest is looking at him in that way that priests always seem to look at people, as if they see something that you can't see. The second bell rings. 'Time to go back to class,' Father Kavanagh says. 'Find me later, and we'll organise a day for your extra-lessons. I'll help you. You'll see.'

'OK,' Paul says. He nods. Father Kavanagh nods back. Paul

gets up. 'OK, bye,' he says. Father Kavanagh only nods again, and Paul feels the priest watching him as he weaves through the pews to the door. When he reaches the brightness of the outside, quiet now that the boys have gone back to class, he sprints across the empty courtyard and climbs the steps, two at a time.

10

Father Kavanagh had expected to be lonely at first. When he arrived in Trinidad in August, he knew only the name of his supervisor who would meet him at the airport, and not another soul. Now, it is December; only a few short months have passed and, already, when he walks around the Savannah in the cool of the late afternoons to stretch his legs, he is constantly waving to people, saying hello. Joggers tap him gently on the shoulder as they pass: *Hi Father!* Arms stick out the windows of passing cars, and wave madly: *Father Kavanagh! Hi!* Men playing football on the grass, boys ambling along with their shirts untucked, ladies with children in prams, sitting under the big trees for shade: *Hi Father! You out for your walk? How you going, Father?* When he comes up past the old colonial buildings on the western side of the Savannah, the coconut seller, Johnnie, picks out a coconut from his cart, hacks it open with his cutlass, and hands it to him solemnly. 'You looking hot, Fadder. Drink *dat*.' The first time, he used the straw that Johnnie gave him but he realised, as the weeks passed, that this is just for foreigners. Now, he does it the way everyone else does, with the rough husk pressed to his lips, the sweet milky water dribbling down his chin.

Today, when he comes back from his walk, only the retired priest, Father de Souza, is at home, sitting out on the patio with the newspaper folded up on the little table next to him. He's eighty, although he looks much younger, with toffee-coloured skin and a ring of tufty white hair like a halo. Father Kavanagh pats their little dog, Zelly, on his way up the steps, and he tells the older priest about his day: how many students got detention for ogling the girls at the school across the road; that he tried to pay a bill at lunchtime, at the post office on Abercromby Street, but that the queue was so long and so slow that he gave up; that the teachers brought him a snack from one of the street-vendors at lunchtime, a spicy thing called 'doubles', which was very tasty but had too much pepper for him. Father de Souza listens with great delight to all his stories and questions and troubles. It is Father de Souza that Father Kavanagh has gotten to know best in these few months that he has lived in Trinidad: the other priests are often out at this time of day – at committee meetings or functions, visiting the elderly, the bereaved, the sick.

A brick wall separates the garden from the pavement just in front: it's not high, perhaps four feet, and the taller passers-by can easily see over the top – indeed, some of them crane their necks as they walk past, to get a proper look. A slender, muscular man, wearing only a pair of shortpants held up at the waist by a length of rope, stops at the wrought-iron gate and looks up the path towards them.

'I hope you-all praying for me!' the man calls.

'Yes, sir,' Father Kavanagh calls back. This man passes by most evenings, and calls out the same thing every time.

'Pray for our country!' the man says. 'Only God can save us!'

'I hope you're praying too!' Father de Souza says, cheerfully.

'Yes, Father. Father*ssss*. Of course. Every night! I's get down on my knees and pray to the Lord for salvation.' They wave again to each other and the man walks on; he's completely crazy, of course, but harmless, as far as Father Kavanagh can tell.

Later, as the afternoon rainclouds gather, the priests go to the kitchen and lift the lids of the pots on the stove, ladle out the chicken stew and rice that the housekeeper cooked earlier in the day. In the fridge is a bowl of the thing they call 'pumpkin', although Father Kavanagh hasn't seen anything resembling a pumpkin in the markets here. It is very nice: a similar consistency to pea purée, but orange, spicy and quite delicious.

'That little bit you're taking?' Father de Souza says, as Father Kavanagh fills his plate. 'You're not hungry or something? You're feeling sick?'

'No, I'm fine. But we should leave enough for the others,' Father Kavanagh says.

'There's plenty food there!' Father de Souza says. 'Take more, man! Look how much she made! Take, take!'

Father Kavanagh, obligingly, takes a little more. The food here really is very tasty. Father de Souza nods approvingly, then takes the peppersauce from the cupboard and sprinkles it liberally over his own plate.

They settle down on the patio to eat, where they can watch the rain come. It's nice out here, breezy and cool, with the same polished teak floorboards as the rest of the house, and with a little low railing all around the edge which people sit on when there are not enough chairs. A flower-laden bush hangs over the railing, offering a little privacy from the passers-by on the street. The grass on the lawn is very green, a different green to grass in Ireland, darker, more tinged with blue, and darker-looking again, with the sun now blotted out by thick cloud. The dog, Zelly, pricks up her ears as frogs hop out from under the hibiscus bushes and birds gather in readiness on the lawn. The first raindrops splatter down – then, in a warm rush, it is here. Father Kavanagh has tried many times to find the words to describe this rain which visits them every afternoon, but it is Father de Souza, as usual, who teaches him the words he needs. The older priest sits in silence for many minutes, observing the spectacle, then he nods his head slowly and says, with a tone of great respect, 'Rain!' And Father Kavanagh says, in answer, 'Rain.'

When seven o'clock comes, the priests go to the living room to watch the News. It is a pleasant room, with tall bookcases at the far end of the room, and a big wooden table where they may read, write or work, and windows whose thin curtains seem to inhale and exhale as the air moves through the house. On this side, near a window to the patio where they sat earlier, sofas and chairs in faded blue velvet are arranged around a coffee table and a TV. They watch an advertisement for Harricrete concrete, with the catchy jingle that Father Kavanagh has already learned, and then the thudding music of the News programme starts, accompanied by a montage of moving images: the Red House, cool and stately, with the Trinidadian flag in front, waving in the breeze; a street in downtown Port of Spain, filled with vendors and taxis and shoppers; smiling children dressed as butterflies, in paint and glitter and feathers; men in blue overalls and goggles and hard hats, standing in front of a chemical processing plant. The newsreader appears, a serious-looking young man with glasses and a little moustache, holding a sheaf of papers in his hand, and announces that it is seven o'clock.

He starts, as always, with the worst news. Every evening it is the same: road fatalities, domestic murders, missing people being dragged out of the bush in bodybags, or their charred remains found in burnt-out cars. Father Kavanagh finds he has to brace himself through this part, and he tries to block his ears against the

[134]

language the newsreader uses, about people being 'chopped up' and found 'in pools of blood'.

A photograph of a silver-haired man in a suit and tie appears on the screen behind the newsreader. Father de Souza sits up, his clasped hands at his mouth. 'This is your student's relative,' he says. 'The one you're tutoring? His uncle.' Father Kavanagh sits up too, pays closer attention. The man was Justice Philip Ramcharan, the newsreader says, a prominent judge who was preparing to hear a trial of a 'well-known drug-lord' down in southern Trinidad, a man who is reputed to oversee the transport of drugs and arms from mainland South America through Trinidad. 'Justice Ramcharan was found dead at his home early this morning, apparently strangled to death by bandits,' the newsreader announces.

The programme cuts away to a segment that must have been recorded earlier, of a reporter with a microphone, sweating in the midday sun, in front of a white-painted house with the galvanise roof and burglar-proofing painted in grass-green, two shiny cars in the carport, and drooping rose bushes bordering the driveway. Yellow tape is pulled across the open gate, and there is a little wooden hut to one side. The reporter says that the watchman had gone home with an upset stomach, and that the house was unguarded for a few hours during the night. The murder most likely occurred at about half past six, when, according to the man's wife, Justice Ramcharan went downstairs to make his breakfast. The wife heard an altercation break out; she locked herself and her daughter into an upstairs room and called the police, and remained unharmed. By the time the police arrived, shortly after seven o'clock, the bandits had fled. Behind the reporter, one policeman stands by the yellow tape across the gate; another one, perhaps not realising he is on camera, pats a neighbour's dog through the fence.

'What judge will take this trial on now?' Father de Souza says. 'Ramcharan was one of the honest ones. The only person who will take it on now is someone who will take a little bribe from the drug-lord, and lo and behold, everybody will be not guilty.' He shakes his head, still looking at the TV, where the weathergirl has appeared on screen, tapping with her pointer at a map Sellotaped to the wall, saying that tomorrow it will be hot with a high chance of rain.

At Assembly the next morning, both boys are there – Paul, and his twin, Peter – squashed into the pews with their classmates. Paul looks as he usually does, Father Kavanagh thinks, or almost as usual – maybe a little stunned. Father Malachy, at the lectern, mentions the murder; the whole school prays for God to watch over the judge's wife and daughter, and the other members of his family, including two of our own students here amongst us. Father Malachy prays for the murderers, that they turn their backs on evil; that they turn, instead, to God and find God's love. And he prays for the country, that its leaders find the strength and courage to lead this country out of these dark days of crime and immorality. At recess, when Father Kavanagh walks by Paul's classroom, he sees both Peter and Paul at the centre of a ring of students, all the boys' faces serious, open-mouthed, aghast. It is not until the end of the school day, when Paul comes for his lesson, that Father Kavanagh has a chance to talk to him.

'I thought you might not have come in today,' Father Kavanagh says. They are in their usual place, a Sixth Form classroom across the corridor from the staff room, with windows to the basketball court on one side. He puts his books down, pushes two desks in the front row together. 'I'm very sorry about your uncle.'

Paul nods quickly, a kind of nod that, Father Kavanagh thinks, means he doesn't want to talk about it. He slaps his books on the desk with a sigh, then sits, slouching, his hands in his pockets. His hair has grown shaggy in the months since Father Kavanagh met him. Sometimes he ties the hair back with an elastic band: Father Kavanagh is amazed that the other boys don't tease him for looking like a girl, but then again, Paul has a little bit of a swagger about him when he needs it, a little bit of a macho-man act, which maybe fends off the teasing.

Father Kavanagh sits next to him. Slowly, he opens his book, presses the pages down. 'Did you speak to your aunt last night?' he asks.

'No,' Paul says. 'But Mummy and Daddy went by Uncle Philip's house to help out.'

'I see.'

'They went to bring Auntie Marilyn and Anna back by us, for them to stay by us last night, or in Auntie Rachel and Uncle Romesh's house, because they have more room than us,' Paul says. He shakes his head back to get the hair out of his eyes. 'But they didn't want to come. They stayed with neighbours in Port of Spain. And Auntie Marilyn already bought plane tickets for her and Anna. She said as soon as the funeral is done, she's going back to England one-time.'

'I'm sorry.' Father Kavanagh recalls hearing this on the News last night, that the judge was married to an English lady. 'It's terrible news. The other priests told me that Mr Ramcharan was your uncle.'

'Mummy's brother,' Paul says. 'Her older brother.' His eyes glaze over for a moment, and then he seems to pull himself together, his eyes refocus and he looks at Father Kavanagh properly. 'Well. What's done is done.'

Father Kavanagh slowly brings out the flashcards he has made for the lesson today. He bought the coloured paper last week from the art-materials store nearby, and sat at the table in Rose House cutting it into little squares, and then writing on each square in black marker. Now, he stacks the cards up, and shows them to Paul, one by one: big, jig, dig, wig. Paul hesitates a moment for the first word – he's probably still distracted – and then reads the others fluently. Small, fall, call, mall, tall: no problems. The next batch – fight, might, sight, light – are more difficult. Father Kavanagh has written them like, 'f-igh-t', and drawn an eye over the letters in the middle. 'When you see these letters together,' he explains, 'say "eye". M-eye-t. Might.'

'M-eye-t,' Paul repeats, obediently.

'That's right. It's always like that, every time you see those letters together. Sigh. High.'

'Cry, fly, pie,' offers Paul.

Father Kavanagh hesitates. 'Sort of. They're a bit different. We'll get to them.'

Paul nods briefly, then turns back to the flashcards and reads under his breath: 'F-ight. Fight. Fight. M-ight. Might. Might.' He squeezes his eyes shut. 'Fight. Might.'

That afternoon, after the lesson has finished and Father Kavanagh has had his walk around the Savannah, waving and greeting everyone, he comes back to Rose House and sits again on the patio with Father de Souza and the little dog. Dinner tonight is a special dish, a thing called pelau, with rice, pieces of chicken and the peas they call 'pigeon peas'. Again, they eat their dinner, talk a little bit about the news of the day, watch the sky change colour. Again, the clouds appear, seemingly out of nowhere, then birds, then frogs, then rain. And while the rain is falling, the shirtless man comes to the gate and calls out, the raindrops dripping off his eyelashes, rolling down his chest, that he hopes the priests are praying for him, that every night he gets down on his knees and prays to the Lord for salvation, and that only God can save us now.

They've been on hurricane warning for the past few days. It's only Father Kavanagh's second rainy season in Trinidad, but even he, still unused to the rhythms of the tropics, feels a sudden unease when the wind picks up during the night. He sleeps badly, awoken often by the sound of things clattering down the road, by the constant barking of the neighbourhood dogs. In the morning, his bedroom floor is littered with detritus blown in through the louvres and the open windows: leaves, flowers, scraps of rubbish, twigs; a whole host of crawling wildlife has blown in, like something washed in on a tide. At school, all morning, the boys are distracted, ogling the girls at the school across the road, whistling and clapping when skirts are lifted by the wind. Papers fly around the courtyards and down the corridors, chased by laughing boys. Father Kavanagh is glad when, at lunchtime, the Ministry finally gives the order to close the schools and send all the children home.

The boys who live in Port of Spain are the first to leave: their mothers come in shiny, air-conditioned cars and whisk them away. Fathers appear at the school gates in their office clothes, ties flapping in the wind, rubbish swirling in eddies around their feet, and collect their sons. The boys who live a little further – Diego Martin, Maraval, Westmoorings – gather in the Big Hall downstairs, and sit cross-legged on the floor, calmly eating their lunch, or beating a quiet rhythm on their knees while they wait for someone to come for them. Parents straggle in, or aunties, uncles, grandparents, neighbours; drops are arranged for those who live nearby to one another.

Peter and Paul come to the office and join the queue of boys waiting to use the phone.

'Who's coming for you?' Father Malachy asks.

'We can travel, Father,' Peter says. Paul is next to him, his shirt untucked, his hair loose, falling to his shoulders.

'You,' Father Malachy says, to Paul. 'Tie that hair back. You think just because you're going home early you can start to get on wild?'

Paul reaches a hand into his pocket for his hair elastic, and ties his hair back, his expression vacant.

Father Malachy glares at Paul and then turns back to Peter. 'I can't just let you walk out of here without knowing how you're getting home,' he says.

'We'll go straight and get the maxi,' Peter insists. 'We won't go anywhere else. I promise.'

'I know, but what if the maxi isn't there? Maybe the driver went home already.'

They agree to phone, and ask the boys' mother what to do. Father Malachy speaks to her, explaining. She has heard the news on the radio, she knows the schools are closed. But she cannot drive, she says, and her husband is down at Point Lisas. Even if he leaves now, he won't be able to get to Port of Spain for several hours, and anyway, she has no way to contact him.

'We can walk,' Paul murmurs. 'Tell her we'll walk.'

Father Malachy puts a hand over the receiver and hisses, 'Paul! Be sensible! You're not walking all that way in the middle of a hurricane.'

'It's not a hurricane,' Paul murmurs again. 'It's a tropical depression.'

'I'll take them,' Father Kavanagh says. 'You can spare the car, can't you? We'll leave now.'

He knows the way out of Port of Spain: downtown, past the big ships swaying in the docks, and under the flyover. The gas stations are backed up with cars queuing for petrol, but most other places are quiet. The street-vendors along the highway have abandoned their little huts. The stray dogs that normally patrol the area have mostly disappeared: the few that are left are gathered in pairs or little groups, as if holding worried conferences on what to do. Once they get onto the highway, heading east, he gets a good view of the clouds straight ahead of them, massive and dark as if the water had been lifted from the bottom of the sea.

'Goooooood!' exclaims Paul, sitting forward to see through the windscreen. 'Check rain coming, boy!'

'Hm!' says Peter.

Paul gives directions, pointing out landmarks as they drive past: there's the Kentucky Fried Chicken; there's the new 'drive-thru' cinema that's just opened up; there's the big furniture shop where they bought their dining table and chairs. They stop at a red light at a junction, where barebacked men walk along the lanes of cars, selling fruit in little plastic bags.

'Wind up the window,' Paul advises.

'Why?'

'Just wind it up,' Paul says. 'These fellas look like they want to give you trouble.'

They are just turning off the highway towards the hills when the rain meets them. The windscreen wipers going full tilt reveal only a blurred, watery picture of green on either side, and the dark, winding strip of road in the middle. He slows to a crawl; the boys have to shout their directions to make themselves heard. It is good that they know the way, because he wouldn't have much hope on his own. Straight, they tell him; follow the road. Careful on this turn; watch out here where there tend to be landslides; this deep water won't last long, the road will begin to go uphill again in a moment. Once or twice, they pass cars going the opposite way; Father Kavanagh would like to stop the other drivers, ask what the road is like up ahead, but he decides against it. The engine has been making strange, lurching noises, and if he were to bring the car to a complete stop, he might not get it going again. And who can tell who might be in the other car? Father Malachy instructed him, before he left Port of Spain, to carry the boys directly home. 'Don't stop to help anyone,' he said. 'No matter how innocent anybody looks – just keep going!'

The boys seem untroubled, calmly looking through the fogged-up windows in the back seat, but Father Kavanagh, in front, is sweating, gripping the steering wheel hard. He had expected this to be easier, to drop them home and then quickly drive back to Port of Spain, maybe after a cup of tea; he hadn't expected to feel his stomach clench every time he thinks of the precious cargo he is delivering, of the two human lives entrusted briefly to his care. In the past, he has sometimes wondered what it might have been like to be a different sort of father – a father with a wife, children – but the idea, now, is terrifying. He thinks of the boys' father, Clyde, who he met last year at the parents' evening; he thinks of what it is like for him to carry this burden all the time.

'How much further now?' Father Kavanagh asks, as casually as he can manage.

'Not long,' Peter assures him.

'We could walk from here if anything,' Paul says.

They do have to abandon the car and walk, towards the end, because the boys' road, La Sagesse Trace, is well under water. He leaves the car by the gas station at the intersection where the ground is higher, and they complete the last hundred yards or so on foot, their shoes in their hands, their trousers rolled up to their knees, covering their eyes against the wind and the rain.

The boys exclaim cheerfully at the strength of the wind and point at things in the bush, but Father Kavanagh looks down at the brown rushing water and feels panic grip him. It only just covers his feet right here, but in some places it is darker, with deep swirling eddies. Sticks and leaves float by, bits of rubber tubing, election posters, feathers. Slippery things catch on his ankles; he is sure he feels some wriggling thing brush against his toes. He plants his feet to the ground, trying to brace himself against the sucking, rushing flow of the water.

Paul, who has gone on ahead, looks back at him and then wades back with big purposeful steps, his hair pushed away from his face, his shoes tucked under his arm. 'You scared, Father?' he says. 'You want me to pull you?'

Father Kavanagh cannot think of anything to say; he tries to force his legs to move, but the water keeps pushing him back.

'Walk in the middle of the road,' advises Paul. 'Follow me.' He holds a hand out encouragingly; Father Kavanagh takes it. He tries to step boldly, as Paul is doing, but sometimes he hesitates, and then Paul turns and says, 'You OK, Father? Nearly there!' Paul looks different with his long hair swept away from his face rather than hanging over his eyes – perfectly at ease. With his rolled-up trousers, the shirt sticking to his back, his face turned down against the rain, he reminds Father Kavanagh of pictures of men in old storybooks ploughing fields with their horses or pulling nets in from the sea.

In the boys' yard, with the dogs sniffing him, he sees a woman crawl out from under the house and wipe her hands on her skirt, leaving smears of red-brown mud. 'You reach!' she calls.

'That's Mummy,' says Paul.

She's not much older than him – mid-thirties, maybe, and he now twenty-seven. She has jet-black curly hair tied back with a butterfly clip, a ragged t-shirt that's beginning to cling to her in the rain and a denim skirt that reaches above the knee. Below the skirt, her legs are brown and mottled with scars that he recognises now as being from mosquito bites. Her feet are bare, flat, coated in mud. She watches him come up the driveway, and when he reaches her and holds out his hand, she smiles, showing slightly crooked front teeth.

'I'm Father Kavanagh,' he says.

'I know,' she says. 'Only somebody from Ireland could be as white as you!'

He gets changed in the bathroom, into clothes belonging to Clyde: a pair of checked shortpants and a t-shirt. When he comes out to the kitchen, Joy puts him to work, filling buckets and pots and pans with water, and finding places to store them and things to cover them with. The dogs keep coming in and out, leaving muddy footprints and wet smears on the wall as they push past each other. And the boys come in and out too, carrying things and taking them to another room somewhere in the house: lengths of rope, a mop, a dog's bowl smelling strongly of dog food, planks of wood, a broken chair.

[145]

As he fills the pots at the kitchen sink, Joy stands at the counter next to him, calmly buttering bread. 'You like tuna, Father?' He says that he does. 'With a bit of onion in it?' She means for the sandwich filling: their housekeeper at Rose House does it the same way. He assures her that he does. 'And peppersauce? You take peppersauce?'

'Only a little bit,' he says, doubtfully.

She laughs. 'I'd better do yours without,' she says. 'Foreigners can't take pepper.'

When he has filled all the pots and pans, she says, 'Keep going, keep going. Fill up everything.' She points with her knife at another cupboard where, she says, there are mixing bowls, ice-cream containers. The big Rottweiler sprawls against the kitchen wall, mouth wide open, panting, showing her many sharp teeth; the other two – littler ones, with slender, dainty, ladylike paws – are on the top step. As he works, he notes how very humble their circumstances are: in the bathroom, he twists open a tap, and as he waits for the bucket to fill, takes in the hard scrap of soap in the soap dish, the threadbare towel hanging on the rail, the tiles framed by black mildew. Still, there is something lovely about being here with them; lovely to see the boys helping; lovely to be in the kitchen with the boys and their mother, here in the darkened house with the rain drumming on the roof.

'Paul's enjoying the lessons,' Joy says. She's standing at the counter buttering bread for sandwiches. 'He always looks forward to a Thursday when you-all have the lesson.'

'I'm glad to hear it,' Father Kavanagh says. He smiles at Paul, who blushes and pats the Rottweiler vigorously.

'Mmm-hmm. You see me, Father, I never had much book-learning, Clyde neither. I only went to school on and off until I was ten. Clyde left school at twelve-thirteen. My mother never went to school, my father didn't think girls needed education.' She's always smiling, her eyes crinkling, showing off the crooked teeth. 'Now is better, people know better. Now both girls and boys go to school. But still, it's more important for boys. They are the ones who have to support the whole family. I work too, I cook for functions, I do whatever work I could pick up. But really, it's Clyde who supporting us, you understand.'

She opens cans of tuna, adds mayonnaise in dollops, chops onions. Occasionally she lifts one foot and brushes it against the other ankle, to dust the grit off. The boys sit on the floor – Paul by the wall with the dog, Peter in the doorway, looking out to the back – with the air of people who have heard this all many times before, but don't mind hearing it again. Joy talks about her mother, her father, uncles, aunts and grandparents, all now dead. Her mother lived here with them, she says; she helped a lot with the children when they were small, especially when they were first born and Paul wasn't very well. She says the words again, the same ones that Paul said in the chapel, that he is slightly retarded, that he was deprived of oxygen at birth. The phrase has the ring of often-repeated words that have lost their meaning, like the prayers he used to recite himself as a child, that, at the time, were just collections of syllables with only the vaguest of meanings attached to them. He wants to halt her, to raise a hand and say, 'No, stop, you are wrong,' but he misses the moment and decides, instead, just to listen, to not interrupt the flow of her story, and to come back and correct her later. She goes on talking: about family members who are now dead, how she fears the family is breaking apart, and how it is a sad, sad thing, because family is the most important thing. 'My mother? Dead. Uncle

Vishnu? Dead,' she says, itemising on her fingers. 'Car accident.' She explains the situation, the relative directions of the cars, the time of day, the injuries they had; that the man named Vishnu died instantly, and that her mother died in hospital some weeks later. The boys' faces have turned sober. 'My brother, Philip? You probably heard of him, Father, if you were living here last year. He was a judge, a famous judge, always in the newspapers. Philip Ramcharan. Dead.'

'Yes, I heard. I'm sorry.'

She relates details that he has heard from the other priests since the murder took place last year: that the men broke into his house, that they were probably in the house for a few hours by the time her brother came downstairs to his kitchen, and that they strangled him. 'And the whole thing was silent,' Joy says. 'No gunshots, no screaming. All Marilyn heard from upstairs was the scuffle, and she went straight into the bathroom with Anna and locked the door.'

She presses the sandwiches down, covers them with a cloth. She fills the kettle, puts it on the stove and then stands, her eyes turned to the window, watching the rain.

'I'm sorry. And have you any family still? Is there anyone left, aside from you?'

'Just my other brother,' Joy says. 'That's something. At least we have *some*body.'

An hour or so later, Clyde comes in, soaked, and a towel is brought to him on the patio. 'I'm afraid I may have to trespass on your hospitality tonight,' Father Kavanagh says. 'I thought I'd be able to get back, but it doesn't look like it now.' He feels slightly stupid saying these words, under the meagre defence of their little house; the rain is obscuring the trees not fifty feet away, just across the road, the road flooding. 'I hope I'm not being a burden to you.'

'No, no,' Clyde says. 'Of course not. Excuse me a moment, Father,' he says, and Father Kavanagh looks away as Clyde strips off his t-shirt, then his trousers – 'Sorry, Father! I'm embarrassing you?' – and dries his body with the towel. He wraps it around his waist and says he'll go in to change. As he passes Joy, he murmurs, 'You've given him anything? Coffee or something?' and Joy says that he has had tea, and the sandwiches are made, ready to eat. 'Good, good,' he says. 'Just a minute, Father, I'll be right back.'

He comes back in fresh, dry clothes, smelling of Limacol, his hair combed, and they all gather at the table to eat the sandwiches. Father Kavanagh closes his eyes before he eats, and says grace; his eyes flick to the clock on the wall with the picture of Jesus; the boys have told him their family is Hindu – 'kind of Hindu,' Peter said, whatever that means – but he decides not to ask.

By six o'clock, the power has cut off, and so has the water. They sit in the living room, gathered around a candle on the coffee table: Clyde on his armchair – it is obviously his armchair – calmly smoking a cigarette; Joy and the boys on the sofa; and Father Kavanagh on a chair that he has pulled over from the dining table. The only other furniture in here is the wooden sideboard that the TV is on, which Joy has pulled away from the window to stop it getting wet. The windows here have wrought-iron burglar-proofing, and flimsy glass shutters that are dripping a good quantity of rainwater onto the floor. But in the candlelight, all these things recede into shadow, like spectators at the theatre when the lights are dimmed.

'My father built this house,' Clyde is saying. 'He built it with his own two hands. Did all the electricity, plumbing, everything.

And you notice how it's kind of on stilts, Father?' He has to raise his voice above the sound of the rain outside, but it doesn't hold him back.

'I saw, yes.'

'Because, before? The house that used to be here, it used to be flat on the ground.' Clyde holds out one palm and slaps the other one on top like he's making a sandwich. '*Bam!* And every rainy season? It used to flood. So then my father said, he said he didn't want to live in a house that was always flooding, mashing up all the furniture. And the previous house was made of wood. He said he wanted a house made of bricks so it wouldn't blow over in the wind, and he put it on stilts like this so it wouldn't flood. And in fact? We never had the house flooded yet. Not so?' He beams at Peter.

'That's right,' says Peter, as if on cue.

Joy tells a story about her grandmother, about the bangles she used to wear on her arms, that used to go from her wrists right up to her elbows, and how she had to have someone help her, every time, to take them on and off. Her great-grandmother, or maybe it was her great-great-grandmother, she can't quite remember, brought her jewellery when she came on the ship from India: bangles, rings, earrings, anklets, all gold and precious stones, opal, turquoise, amber, ruby, each stone reputed to mean something – health, wealth, love, purity – but she doesn't remember which is which. 'But they each had a meaning,' Joy says, proudly. Most of the jewellery has been lost now, divided up between relatives over the years, but Joy still has some which she keeps hidden in a shoebox in her bedroom. 'I have eleven of the bangles,' she says, 'and a necklace and some rings.'

Clyde tells them about somewhere he used to live, a place on the south coast of Trinidad, where men, in the afternoons, used to gather in a ring to practise stick-fighting. Everyone used to sit in a circle to watch them, he says, all the children from the village, to watch as two men at a time took their turn in the ring. 'It was nice,' he says. 'They were very skilled, those men. Very elegant fighters.' They ask Father Kavanagh about his childhood, and he finds himself telling them about growing up on a farm with his six brothers and sisters; about getting up on cold dark mornings and going out to get the hay from the barn. During quieter moments, when no one speaks, the children make shadows on the walls with their hands: dogs, ducks, cats. Joy and Paul, putting their hands together, make a swan. In this way, the hours slide by, unnoticed.

Eventually, Joy and the boys disappear to bed. Clyde gets himself the bottle of rum, and says that he will stay up in case looters come; Father Kavanagh accepts a half-glass of rum to be sociable. They talk about this and that for a while: the state of the roads, the upcoming elections, the latest crimes that have been reported in the newspapers – all standard fodder that Father Kavanagh hears picked over so frequently in conversation. Clyde, with the rum warming him up, seems more than willing, now, to talk at great length on any subject at all.

'Philip was good to us,' Clyde is saying now. He's halfway through his second glass of rum, and Father Kavanagh can see how, when he looks at the candle flame, his eyes lose focus. 'Marilyn didn't like us at all. She was jealous because Peter was so bright. She thought her child should have been the bright one! After Philip was killed, Marilyn and the child went back to England, and we're not really in touch any more. They send us a Christmas card, that's about all. But there it is. What's done is done. But Philip, when he was alive, he was good to us. Philip and Uncle Vishnu, they were both good to us.'

Clyde pauses, and seems to be thinking about those things, whatever they are, or some plan that he's mulling over in his head. He only comes to when a gust of wind through the louvres makes the candle flame tip horizontal and threaten to go out.

'Rain!' Clyde says, his attention drawn to the outside.

Father Kavanagh waits a few moments to allow Clyde to resume, and when he doesn't, he asks, 'Joy mentioned Vishnu as well, earlier. Somebody's uncle, was he?'

'Joy's uncle,' Clyde explains. 'Also very well known in Trinidad. A very prominent person. A doctor.'

'And he was good to you, you say,' Father Kavanagh says.

'He was good, yes. He helped when the boys were born. You're aware Paul had some problems, right? And that's why he's slightly retarded?'

'I have heard this,' he says slowly, gathering his thoughts. He's not going to let this pass again: something must be said to these people. 'But I have to say, Paul strikes me as quite normal. I'm not sure I'd be so quick to label him as retarded, to be honest.'

Clyde eyes him over the top of his glass. 'You think I've been quick to label him?'

'Sorry. Quick is probably the wrong word. I apologise. I just mean that he strikes me as quite normal.'

'Is that how he strikes you?' He says it again, his tone disbelieving. 'Is that how he strikes you?' Clyde pauses only long enough for Father Kavanagh to nod, abjectly, knowing he has said the wrong thing. 'Hello. Look here. How long have you known him?'

'A year, I suppose. A little more.'

'A year. One year. And you're sitting here telling me what he is and what he isn't? I have been quick to judge him?'

'I only meant that he strikes me as a normal child.'

'He strikes you as normal?'

'He does.'

'And what about his schoolwork?'

'He's making progress. Slowly. But it's progress, I think.'

'Slow progress. So, what you mean is, he's harden. Eh? He seems normal to you aside from being a bit harden?'

'Harden?' Father Kavanagh asks.

'Harden. A dunce. Nothing stays in his head. He's like that?'

Father Kavanagh thinks carefully. He wants to answer the man honestly, and yet he feels an inclination to say that Paul is doing better than he is. There are times during the extra-lessons when he feels he's made a breakthrough with him, where Paul gets through his work with very few mistakes; and other times where he feels they've made no progress at all. 'I think he can learn,' Father Kavanagh says. 'I think he wants to learn.' They sit in the dim light of the candle flame for some minutes.

'I am not an educated man,' Clyde says. 'Maybe there's something I don't understand. But how it seems to me is, the boy can't learn. That is how it seems to me. All his teachers have tried, all through primary school, they all tried, one after the other. You're trying. My sister-in-law, Marilyn, she tried. Everybody has tried, and he's still not learning. And to me, that says that something is wrong with his brain. Not so? Is that the wrong conclusion? Tell me if it's the wrong conclusion. You tell me.'

'He might not be as bright as another boy,' Father Kavanagh says. 'But does that mean there's something wrong with his brain?'

'Well . . .' Clyde sighs, aggravated, throws his hand up. 'You're telling me that you don't know either, but you're trying to tell me

I'm wrong? How can you say I'm wrong when you don't know either? Eh? Answer me that.'

'I don't know,' Father Kavanagh says. 'I don't know how to answer you.'

'What more can I do for him?' Clyde says. 'I already had to pull some strings to get him into St Saviour's, I don't know if Father Malachy told you, Father, I had to go in and pull some strings, because he didn't get through with the Eleven Plus. He got a junior secondary school out in Marabella. And Joy and I discussed it – we couldn't send him there. He would only get in with a bunch of timewasters and saga boys there. All of them in gangs, and the teachers don't even bother to come in, and they do things like start fires and all kinds of stupidness. We didn't want to send him there. So I went in and spoke to Father Malachy, and he agreed to give Paul a space.'

Clyde taps his fingers together, musing, before he continues. 'Father Malachy spoke to me about Peter not long ago. He probably mentioned to you. He said I need to be putting money aside for Peter to go away.' He joins his palms together thoughtfully, touches his fingertips to his nose.

'How much money?' Father Kavanagh asks. He feels bold asking such a question, but people here are very bold, and Clyde seems to want to talk.

'I need thirty thousand US,' he says. 'About two hundred thousand TT.'

'I see.'

'Plenty money, eh?'

'Plenty.'

'You would think I had that kind of money, to look at me?' Clyde straightens a little in his chair, as if to present himself for inspection.

'Perhaps not.'

'That's right. You see this country? Any bit of money you have? You have to hide it away. I don't have a fancy house, or a fancy car, none of that. To look at me, you would think I have nothing. I see people looking at me, people in Port of Spain, or wherever, I could see them looking at me and thinking I'm poor. And I only laugh to myself. I probably have more money than them! But it's not in Trinidad. You can't keep anything private around here. If people hear how I have that kind of money? I will have people knocking down my door asking me to give them some. All kind of people claiming to be relatives would come out of the woodwork, saying, oh I am Vishnu's niece, or I was his godson, or whatever, and everybody would be holding out their hands, wanting money. Uncle Vishnu left it to us, you see – when he died, he left it to us, for Peter's education.'

'Just for Peter?'

'Well, for everything – Uncle Vishnu and I understood each other, you see. He could see I was an honest fella, a serious fella, and that he could trust me. So what he did, he asked me to look after Joy's mother, which I did, and he said to encourage Peter. He took an interest in Peter from small, you see. Even from two, three, four, he was seeing how Peter was developing. So we put it in a bank account in England. Philip helped us do it. Philip and Marilyn.' The tip of his cigarette glows orange as he sucks on it, then he gives a little shrug.

'Do you have the money you need, then? This three hundred thousand, or however much it is?'

'Yes. I'm telling you this in confidence, by the way, Father, eh?'

'Of course.'

'Not many people know about it.'

'I understand. I won't repeat it.'

'Right. I didn't think you would, I was just saying it, to be sure we understood each other.'

'It's a huge amount of money,' Father Kavanagh says, tentatively. 'You could do a lot of things with that amount of money.'

'What kinds of things?'

'Well. There might be things that Joy would like. And things you'd like.'

'And Paul? Is that what you're getting at?'

'Any of you. You, Joy, Paul. All of you. Paul has mentioned that you're planning to move to Port of Spain. Maybe the money could go towards a new house there. That's all I mean.'

Father Kavanagh stares at the candle flame, the way the milky-white ribbon of flame thins to vaporous, smoky nothingness. It makes a vague, swirling shadow on the wall.

'Father. Let me ask you something. What it is you getting at?'

'I'm not getting at anything. I'm only trying to understand.'

'It's easy to sit down there and judge somebody else, you know! It's easy to judge from the sidelines!'

'No, no . . .'

'Because let me tell you. I'm very grateful for the help you're giving both of them. And if Paul is talking to you about his business, well, I'm glad to hear he's talking to somebody. But, you see me?' He points at his own chest. 'I am their *father*. Twelve years now, I have been sitting down in this chair watching them. Every day of their lives, since the day they were born, I am *watching* them, and *observing* them. I may not look very clever, but I watch, and I observe. Paul may be improving – fine. But don't you, who has known him for just over a year, don't you try and tell me he's normal. He's not. He's not.' Clyde's voice has steadied; his eyes are focused, despite the rum. 'You could think whatever you like,' he says. 'I know you say you're not judging me, but you are. I could see it on your face. You go ahead, it doesn't bother *me*.'

They sit in silence for a long time after that, listening to the scrabbling and barking of the dogs, and the wind and rain drumming on the roof. Clyde gets up to turn over the towel that Joy laid down under the window. Eventually, the conversation turns back to other things: to Father Kavanagh's thoughts on the various scandals ongoing at the Forestry Division, the Ministry of Infrastructure and the Ministry of Health. Sometime after two o'clock, Clyde says, 'I think things quietened down outside,' and gets up to let the dogs out. 'They're not doing any good locked up in there if anybody comes to break in,' he says.

Father Kavanagh gets up, stretching his back. 'Ah well, bedtime then,' he says.

'Yes, yes, yes, go ahead. Don't let me keep you up,' says Clyde. He is feeling his way along the wall towards the store room where the dogs are locked up.

'Aren't you going to bed?' Father Kavanagh asks.

'No, no. I'm staying up. I'll stay up until it's light.'

The dogs rush out to the yard, and Clyde locks the door after them and comes back to the living room.

'Goodnight, then,' Father Kavanagh says.

'Goodnight,' Clyde says, over his shoulder as he settles back down in his armchair. He reaches towards the rum bottle and then stops and says, turning, 'I hope you didn't take offence at any of that, Father?'

'Who? Me? No, no.'

'I was only giving you my honest opinion. That is me! I don't tell lies, Father!' He laughs a little at his own joke. 'No, but seriously, I appreciate how you don't mind just sitting down for a little old-talk, Father. And you not trying to *convert* me, or any of this kind of nonsense.' He waggles a hand in the air as if to repel the very idea.

'My pleasure,' replies Father Kavanagh. He can't help smiling. 'I enjoyed our chat.'

He finds his way to the spare room that Joy has prepared for him. As he gets into bed, he thinks of Clyde, sitting alone in the dark, keeping watch over his family through the night.

12

It is February, dry season again, and the whole country is gearing up for Carnival. The maxi-taxi driver plays his music at full blast all the way from Port of Spain back to Tiparo, and when the boys get out by the gas station, the deep throbbing of the bass is still vibrating all through their bowels. They walk down the Trace together, keeping to the shady side by the bush. Paul undoes the top buttons of his shirt; he strips a banana leaf from a tree and uses it to fan his neck.

'Where're the dogs?' Paul says, when they come up to the gate.

'Gas man,' Peter reminds him. Daddy put the dogs in the dog-house before he went to work this morning, Mummy must have forgotten to let them out again. Paul throws his schoolbag on the ground.

'What're you doing?' Peter asks.

'I feeling hot,' Paul says. He slips the shirt off, twirls it over his head like a lasso.

'Oh gyad,' Peter says, holding his nose. 'Deodorant, man. Those armpits.'

Paul laughs and runs after Peter, holding up his arm, as if to put the smelly armpit in his face. Peter bats him away.

'Seriously, man,' Peter says. 'If you smell like that at the fete, I go stay far away from you. I don't want anyone thinking I'm related to you.'

'Girls like it, man!' Paul says. 'They find it sexy. You think they like fellas who's smell like flowers?'

Upstairs, Mummy says that the gas man still hasn't come, and she's been waiting in for him all day. The boys change out of their school uniforms. Paul pats the dogs through the bars of the dog-house, fills up their water bowl. He wants to sit on the back-step and relax for a while, but Mummy tells him to get started on his work while it's still light, in case power goes.

They're both quietly working at the table, Mummy humming and peeling potatoes in the kitchen, when Paul hears the sound of the latch of the gate being very quietly lifted. He looks up, locks eyes with Peter across the table. They listen to the whine of the hinge as the gate is opened. Paul pushes back his chair and looks out the front window: the front gate is ajar, the driveway empty. He presses his cheek against the burglar-proofing, catches a glimpse of someone in a green t-shirt and torn canvas sneakers slipping around the corner.

'Lock the door, quick, lock the door,' Paul says in a hoarse whisper. The dogs are already barking. They race to the kitchen and Paul slams the door shut just as the men – there are two of them – reach the bottom of the steps.

'What happen? What happen?' says Mummy. Potatoes drop to the floor.

Paul is bracing himself against the door, his feet skidding for-ward. He sinks down, trying to find something to anchor himself against. Peter finds the key, but it is too late. The men push their way in. Mummy drops the knife, puts her hand over her mouth. She picks up the knife again, holds it out in front of her.

'Relax yuhself, woman,' the man in the green t-shirt says. 'Take it easy.'

He looks serious, like he's the boss. He's a lightish-skinned black guy with short, tidy hair and a gold tooth that you can see when he smiles. The handle of a gun sticks up above the waistband of his pants. The other one is taller, wearing sunglasses and a baseball cap, and with a t-shirt tied under his nose. He spins round and points his cutlass at Peter. 'Haaa,' he says. Then he swivels, points it at Paul. 'Haaa.'

The man with the green t-shirt takes the key from Peter's hand and locks the door. 'Only you-all here?' He has to raise his voice above the barking of the dogs.

Mummy hesitates. 'Yea,' she says. Paul can tell she's fighting to keep her voice steady. 'But my husband coming back just now. Who you looking for?' She looks straight at the bandit, but Paul feels she's sending them a silent message to follow her lead, to act calm.

'Check the other rooms,' the one with the green t-shirt says to the other one.

'Don't try no tricks, eh!' the taller one says, and he goes down the corridor to the bedrooms, holding his cutlass in front of him like a sword.

'Come on,' Mummy says. 'What it is you-all are up to? Breaking into my house like this. Who you looking for? It's my husband you want to speak to? He'll be home just now.'

'Just now, eh?' the one with the green t-shirt says. 'I don't think so, doux-doux. Not so he's working down south now? He wouldn't be home until late, that is what I hear.'

She turns back to the sink and picks up a potato. 'Look, I have things to do, you hear? So you better tell me what you after, and then we could fix up. What you looking for? Money? Money to buy your drugs?'

She makes as if to start peeling while the man comes up to her. He takes the knife and puts it in his back pocket, the blade pointing up. 'Hello. This is serious business you know.'

'OK. Well, tell me what you looking for!' she says. 'You talking talking, and I ent hear you say it yet.'

The one with the cutlass comes back in. 'Nobody in there,' he says.

The boss points to the archway to the living room. 'Check in there.'

They all wait, standing where they are, while the cutlass one checks in the living room, down the corridor, the store room, and then on the patio. They hear him close the door to the patio and turn the key in the lock. The house feels dark, with both doors closed. Paul's heart sinks.

'Right,' says the man with the gun. 'All of allyuh, down on the ground.'

Peter, standing by the door, crouches down. Mummy sighs and gathers up her skirt to sit. The man looks at Paul, and Paul looks back at him. The man flicks the gun towards the floor. Paul hesitates. He's not sure if it's better to just meekly get down, or to stand up to the man. But Mummy grabs his hand and tugs it, so he gives the man a cut-eye and gets down on the ground.

'Right. Stay there,' the man says. 'And don't try no tricks.'

The cutlass-man takes his time, working through the bedrooms, the store room, the living room – everywhere. The boss stays with them. From where they are huddled on the kitchen floor, they hear the sounds of furniture being dragged around, drawers being opened and closed, thumps and crashes as things are thrown on the floor. Eventually, the man with the cutlass comes in. 'I can't find anything, boy,' he says.

The gunman nudges Mummy's foot with the toe of his sneaker. 'Where allyuh keep your money?'

'What you talking about?' says Mummy. 'We don't have any money.'

The man steupses. 'Don't tell me lies,' he says. 'Tell me where you keeping the money.'

'What? Where you hear that?' says Mummy. 'My husband, he's working as an operative at Point Lisas, before that he was mixing concrete, driving forklifts, things like that. We don't have money! If we had money, you think we would be living in a house like this?' She gestures around the room.

'Shut up. You think you could fool me?' he asks. 'You think you could fool me?'

'What you going to do?' Mummy asks. 'Shoot me?' She steupses and looks away, smoothing down the hem of her dress. 'You still wouldn't find any money because we don't have none.'

'Shut up,' the man says.

The one with the cutlass goes into the living room and starts tearing it up. It's horrible to watch. Paul puts his arm around Mummy; he feels her heart racing and it makes him feel scared so he takes his arm away again. The man pulls the cushions from the sofa and armchairs, and makes a hole in the fabric of one of the cushions with the tip of the cutlass and then he lays down the cutlass and puts his two hands inside the hole and pulls hard until the whole thing comes apart. All the stuffing comes out, little cubes of yellow and white foam. After he has done all the cushions, he starts tearing up the frames of the armchair in the same way. The stuffing inside there is like a thick grey cotton wool. Little bits of fluff fall out, and little crawling bugs. He takes off his sunglasses to look at them properly.

'Weevils!' he says. 'Or maybe termites.' Then, kicking aside the foam cubes and torn bits of fabric and tufts of grey cotton wool, he turns the furniture upside down and uses his cutlass to tear open the thin fabric lining the base of the armchairs and sofa. A few cents fall out. And some used matches, and a chewed-up lollipop stick and some faded scraps of sweet wrappers.

He unplugs the TV carefully, then pulls out the cabinet it's standing on and looks behind it. He opens the doors of the cabinet and starts pulling everything out: the telephone book, an open box of candles, a bag of red and white after-dinner mints still in their bag, all melted. He picks up the phone book, holds it upside down and shakes it. Then he wipes his face with the t-shirt and takes a swipe at the upturned armchair with his cutlass.

'Nothing here, boy,' he calls.

The one with the gun hesitates. 'You sure? They said this fella has money in his house for sure.'

The one in the living room shakes his head. He lifts the t-shirt that's over his mouth and wipes the sweat from his forehead. The stubble on his cheeks is scraggly, uneven.

'Only the kitchen left,' says the man with the cutlass.

The one with the gun shouts at them again. 'Move,' he says, and he beckons with the gun. Mummy lifts herself stiffly, her knees cracking, and they huddle together on the floor in front of the sink.

'Right, now stay there,' says the man with the gun. 'If anybody moves, I'm shooting you. Understand?'

'I understand,' Mummy says. 'I'm not deaf.'

'Don't give me no backchat.'

'All-you going to mash up my kitchen now?'

'Well, if you tell us where the money is, we wouldn't mash it up,' says the man.

'I really think all-you get some misinformation,' says Mummy. She sighs and leans her head against the edge of the sink. Peter gives Paul a look and Paul makes his face go blank, to not give anything away.

The men begin opening cupboards in the kitchen, glancing inside and jabbing at things with their fingers.

'What you think?' the one with the cutlass asks.

The boss one shrugs. He seems to be changing his mind. He tells the other one to go and get the TV, and to get the jewellery from the bedroom, and he goes into Mummy's handbag and roots around for her money. He finds three blue bills, and holds them up to her. 'Eh heh! You don't have any money, eh? You always walk around with three hundred dollar bills in your handbag?'

'It was to pay the gas man,' Mummy says.

The man pockets the bills. The other one comes in, carrying the TV.

'All right,' says the boss man. He looks irritated, like he's annoyed at wasting his time. 'We're leaving for now, but we're going to find out about that money, you hear? And then we're going to come back.'

He reaches into his pocket and unlocks the back door. The dogs, who have been quiet for a while, start back up.

'Those blasted dogs!' says the man with the gun. 'Listen to that blasted noise!' He turns suddenly and pulls the gun from where it's wedged into his belt.

'Leave them!' Paul shouts. Peter grabs his arm to keep him down, but Paul shakes him off. 'Why you have to kill them? They're locked up, they won't harm you.'

The man whips round and just like that, the gun is pointing at Paul. Paul shakes his hair out of his face. He looks straight into the man's eyes above the barrel of the gun. 'Shoot me, nuh,' he says, taunting. 'Shoot me!'

'Gooood! Check out this big-man, boy!' the boss man says. 'How old are you?'

Paul rolls his eyes, like he can't be bothered to answer such a stupid question. 'Thirteen.'

The man smiles and he begins to walk forward, still pointing the gun. Paul holds the man's gaze steadily. Then Mummy gets up, slowly, like she's in no rush, and steps between them.

'Go,' she says, to the man. 'You're finished here. Take the TV and go.'

The man comes closer and presses the tip of the gun to her head, right in the middle of her forehead. The force of it pushes her head back slightly.

'You-all making me vex,' he says. He pulls out a roll of fence-wire from his pocket, and pushes them down to the ground. Then, with the other man holding the gun and the cutlass, the boss man makes them lie down on the ground and ties their hands and feet tightly with wire.

The dogs bark furiously again, and they all wait for the sound of the gun, but it never comes. There's just a quiet rattle as the men push through the front gate, and then nothing.

Late that evening, after Daddy has untied them, and the Chin Lees and the Bartholomews have gone home, Peter and Paul are in their beds when Mummy knocks and comes in. She sits on the edge of Paul's bed, pats his knee. Her hands are swollen, the marks of the wire still on her wrists. She moves her hands to her lap.

'I want to talk to Paul,' she says. 'But Peter, you need to hear it too. It's for both of you.'

Paul sits up straight. He tries not to look at Peter.

'I'm not mad,' Mummy says. 'But what you did, it was dangerous. You realise that now?'

Paul nods.

'You're getting so big now. Both of you. You're big. Almost full-grown. And what I want to tell you is: you-all are big enough now, you must start looking after yourselves. Eh? You won't always have a Mummy-and-Daddy running after you looking after things. We wouldn't always be here to spoon-feed you. Time will come when I can't fix things for you any more.'

'I'm sorry,' Paul says. He clears his throat, shakes his hair back. 'I'm sorry.'

'I know, darling. But it's not about sorry or not sorry. What I'm saying is I can't keep protecting you all the time. You have to learn to protect yourself now. You understand?'

Paul can't bring himself to speak, but he nods, to say that he understands.

PART THREE

13

Paul is sitting by the riverbank. He shouldn't be here. He should be inside doing his homework: his schoolbag is full-up with homework for him to do. But he can't make. *I overs*, he says to himself. *I'm done.* He would like to lie down on the ground and fling his arms out at his sides and say it out loud: *You see me? I overs. I cyah make at all at all at all.* But you can't lie down on the ground around here because of the ants. Right now, he's sitting on the big-stone with his knees drawn up to his chin, but even so, he has to brush away ants that come and crawl on his feet, and slap at mosquitoes, and pick out wriggling congorees that land in his hair from the almond tree above. Something else lands on his knee – red and black, mandolin-shaped. It closes its wing-case smartly and waggles its antennae. He can't be bothered to flick it away. *I overs*, he says to himself, again.

They finished the lesson with Father Kavanagh early today. Already, Father was in a bad mood when they started: he and Peter could both tell, and they were trying to be extra good and not aggravate him. Peter just opened his textbook and started working through maths problems – he only comes because Daddy told him to, because Daddy thinks it's good for him to be around educated people. Father asked Paul what homework he had to do, and Paul said Geography, and Father said OK, let's read through the questions together. Paul tried to read, but he was nervous because of Father being in a bad mood. The chapter was about natural resources in Trinidad. 'Fidel?' he tried. 'Flint . . . leaf . . .' He could feel Father Kavanagh beginning to bubble up next to him, like a kettle on the stove. 'Foiled. Foiling.' And then Father started rubbing his face with his hands. Peter stopped what he was doing, and looked up with that warning look, and so Paul stopped speaking and rested his hands in his lap and tried not to aggravate anybody. 'It doesn't even begin with F,' Father said. 'It begins with O. Oilfields. Oil – fields.' Then Father Kavanagh just sat there with his hand over his eyes. Peter and Paul didn't dare look at each other. And then Father said he had a headache, and they could go home early.

Maybe he can leave school after Form Five, he thinks. Plenty of boys in other schools leave after O-levels. But even that – that would be three more years! If only he could start to work now, and start to earn his own money. If he was making his own money, he could buy some Ray-Ban sunglasses, and a pair of those fluorescent shortpants like Marc Aboud has and some of the other boys in his class have, the ones that are loose and reach down to the knee, and come in all kinds of fluorescent colours. Baggies. He would even buy some for Peter, if he wants – all the rest of the money he would give to Mummy for groceries. He imagines coming home in his brightly coloured baggies, the Ray-Bans on his head, and handing Mummy a big wad of cash. Maybe he will look for a job in the summer holidays, he thinks. The thought of three more years of this seems unbearable: the other boys feeling sorry for him, and trying to copy from Peter in secret, and struggling and failing at tests, and Daddy always being mad.

Father Kavanagh said he's not retarded – Paul still remembers how Father Kavanagh squeezed his arm, how he looked him straight in the eye: *Listen to me. You're not.* For a while afterwards, Paul had felt different: a little less sick in his stomach, getting dressed for school; a little less afraid when teachers spoke to him; a little more willing to elbow people out of the way in the tuck-shop at lunchtime. But the weeks went on and Father Kavanagh never mentioned it again, and eventually that good feeling wore off. Every now and again, he repeats those words to himself, trying to remind himself of what it felt like when Father Kavanagh spoke them.

The thing is, if he can understand what a question is asking, he usually knows the answer. His Maths has been getting better: in his last test, he got nineteen out of twenty, and Father Kavanagh said, 'You see? You see how practice makes perfect?' But practice isn't making perfect for anything else. He still can't read like other people do. Sometimes the letters all arrange themselves and make sense, and other times they just look like ants crawling around on the page and he has to try to guess, from the pictures, or from the other words he can understand, what all the other ones mean. Paul feels ashamed to imagine what Father Kavanagh was thinking today. *All this time, and still the boy can't even read a simple word!*

His hair feels strange, short: his head feels lighter. Definitely cooler. Before he came out here by the river, he took the scissors from the drawer in the kitchen, and went out to the back yard and cut his hair: he does this every so often, when his hair starts driving him crazy, or being too much effort to tie back, or wash. He stood near the coconut tree, grabbing handfuls of hair and chopping close to the head, then he slid the scissors back onto the kitchen counter, and went round the side of the house and out the front gate.

Sando commented on his long hair this afternoon, in the maxi taxi home. 'Tarzan,' he said. 'It's time to cut that hair, you know. People going to start questioning if you're male or female. You understand what I'm saying?' Sando has been friendly with him for a while now, since that night a few months ago when Paul was out walking and Sando drove past him in his car. Sando slowed down and looked through the window at him and said, 'Who's that? Tarzan? What you doing out here at this time of night, boy? Like you want to dead or something?' And Paul said, 'I just taking a walk, man. Getting some fresh air.' Sando offered to give him a lift home, but Paul said no, and Sando said, 'Very wise. Don't get into any stranger's car.' And before he drove off, he said, 'You're the one who's a bit . . .' and he put a forefinger to his temple and gave a little twirl. 'A bit crazy, eh?' He wasn't being cruel, he was just asking to clarify. Paul said, 'Yes, it's me. But I'm not crazy.' And Sando said, 'Nothing to be ashamed of! Boy, if you look at history, all the brightest people were a little crazy!'

While Paul has been sitting here, one hand has found its way to his groin, slid up through the inside of his shortpants. The bush is the only place where he can get a little privacy these days: right now, his forefinger is gently stroking the soft hairs, feeling the way they curl at the end, assessing their thickness, their length. He can't remember when those hairs appeared – one day he looked at himself in the shower and he saw some hairs, and then there were more, and then the whole thing was covered in hair. It's not a huge shock or anything, Mummy and Auntie Rachel are always talking about 'puberty': puberty is a hard time for boys! Sayeed hitting puberty fast! These days it does happen younger! And at school, all the Form Twos were called into the Audio Visual room to watch a film called *Puberty – a time of growth for young men and women*. There were diagrams of 'Male Reproductive Organs' and 'Female Reproductive Organs', which for some reason made Paul think of aliens, like if an alien were to come to Earth, it might look like the picture in 'Female Reproductive Organs'. Everyone sniggered at the word 'organs', and at all the other words that came thick and fast – vagina, breasts, penis, scrotum – and there was uproar at 'wet dreams', everyone trying to laugh louder than the next one to hide his embarrassment. All the boys were glad when it was finally time to push open the doors and get back out into the open air of the passageway.

Sometimes when he is sitting with Father having his lesson, for no reason at all he feels the blood rushing to his groin, and his penis beginning to swell. He swings his knees in and out or jiggles his legs, to try to distract his body from what it is doing, to get the blood to flow away. Sometimes it works; other times he has to ask if he can go to the bathroom. Father raises his eyes to heaven and makes a little nod, to say yes. As soon as he gets up and walks a few steps down the corridor, he feels it subside; but still, he walks all the way to the bathroom, down past the laboratories, past the tuck-shop, washes his hands, and then walks back.

Paul holds still while a green-bodied dragonfly, hovering a few inches in front of his face, inspects him; he feels a tiny breeze on his cheeks from the buzzing wings. *Food? Not food.* It zooms away. He smiles after it. Batty-mamzels they are called: that is the other name for them, the local name. He says them both in his mind, first one and then the other, slowly, listening to the sound each one makes. Dragonfly, batty-mamzel, dragonfly, batty-mamzel. Dragonfly doesn't seem like a good name, because they don't look anything like dragons. Batty-mamzel seems more right – something about the *batty* matches the way their wings flit, and the *mamzel* is something feminine, as if the creature is really a woman pretending to be an insect, and she might tell you to go and wash your face, or respect your elders, or come in before it gets dark.

Sometimes local words are better, but you have to know the proper word as well, otherwise people in Port of Spain laugh at you for being from the bush. Like when he and Marc Aboud were talking to the girls on the street corner last week after school. 'Living out in the bush there,' Renée said – she was the one that Marc liked – 'Out there where it's only bush-and-bandits, you does hunt iguana and mongoose and thing? And go out the back to the *latrine*?' She cackled but she wasn't being nasty or anything. He made fun of how she talked too. 'Yuh does go by obeah-man when yuh sick?'

'Yea, how you mean,' Paul replied mischievously. 'Everybody does go by him. They have particular plants in the forest by us, he could make real good potions. Anything you want, he could find the right plant, and make a potion.' He spoke in a low voice, the voice you use to tell stories about that kind of thing, and they all drew a little closer.

'Boy, that is nancy story,' said Candace. She made like to push him away, and her hand brushed against his stomach, just above the belt.

'Is true, is true!' said Marc. 'Bush-men does have real big things, you know. Because obeah make potion for them!' He jerked his head towards Paul's pants. '*Real* big.' He raised his eyebrows several times at the girls and the girls burst out laughing.

'How do you know?' Candace asked. 'Why you looking at yuh friend's thing?'

'I didn't look!' Marc exclaimed. 'I just know! Well, I hear so! Why you think these fellas from all kinda Penal and Fyzabad and

Basse Terre so popular when they come up to town for Carnival? You ever see how many women does want to wine-up with them fellas?' Everybody burst out laughing again. Paul's tummy was still tingling where Candace's fingers had touched him.

If he was making his own money, he could go up to the fete in Port of Spain. He and Peter already got their tickets – they cost fifty dollars each for entrance and chicken and chow-mein dinner. Before, Daddy gave them the money without any fuss, but then after the break-in, Daddy was mad and he said, 'All-you could forget about that fete!' But fifty dollars is a lot of money: a week's worth of maxi-taxi fare and lunch money put together, and it would be stupid to waste the tickets when they're already paid for. Paul hasn't told Candace yet that he can't go; he's still hoping maybe he can work something out – ask somebody to give him a lift up to Port of Spain, maybe. Or he could just walk. He could say to Daddy, 'Fine, you don't want to drive me? Fine! I'll walk!' It would take a long time: four, maybe five hours, but he could pack his clothes and go to Marc's house to shower first. He can imagine Daddy in a fury, his fists clenched, looking like he can hardly restrain himself from giving him one cuff. 'If you walk out that door, I don't want to see your tail back in here again!' And Paul would shout back, 'Fine! That's fine with me!' but he wouldn't really mean it. But what's the point of always trying to please Daddy? Only Peter can please Daddy. Everything Peter does is perfect, and everything he does is wrong. Paul steupses quietly, thinking about it. *You see me? I done with that.*

For weeks now, he has been looking forward to asking Candace to slow-dance. If it's going well, he's been thinking, and if he definitely has fresh breath, he might try to kiss her. He could borrow some of Marc's father's cologne: just a little dab, so he wouldn't notice any missing. Daddy doesn't have any cologne. He says all of that is nonsense – deodorant and cologne and after-shave and all of that. In their bathroom, all they have is Jergens shampoo and a bar of Lux soap.

If he was earning money, he could buy whatever soap he wants (Imperial Leather, maybe – Father Kavanagh uses Imperial Leather, he can tell by how he smells), and any cologne, as well as the baggies and the Ray-Bans. Maybe he will do it in truth. First he will find a job, and when everything is secure, he will tell Mummy and Daddy he's not going back to school. Didn't Mummy tell him, after the break-in, she said, 'I can't keep on looking after you. You growing up: you'll be a big-man just now. You have to look after yourself.' So he will do it! He will get a job, and he will look after his own self. 'I can't keep looking after you,' she said.

It probably was a bad idea to shout at the men, Paul thinks. He didn't think the guy would actually come and point the gun at him like that. While the man was holding up the gun, Paul stared straight back at him, giving him one cut-eye, and saying, 'Shoot me, nuh! Shoot me!' the same way that when you saunter across a road, you say to the driver honking at you, 'Bounce me down!' You have to show people you not just going to take that, just so. But then Mummy came up and pushed him behind her, and then the gun was pointing at her instead of him, and then Paul was scared. And then, after the bandits left and Daddy came home and untied them, Mummy said, 'I can't keep on looking after you. You have to look after yourself.'

A couple of cornbirds are moving from tree to tree, making the branches above him sway and crackle as they brush against each other. Dead bits of branch fall, get caught further down the trees; little bits splinter off and shower to the ground. There's the dull thud of some heavy fruit falling to the ground: not the sharp, knocking sound that a coconut would make; a duller, softer sound, bigger than a mango or a shaddock. A breadfruit, maybe, although he can't remember any breadfruit tree anywhere nearby here.

He hears the shushing of raindrops landing on the canopy above; just a little drizzle, bouncing off things and splattering at odd angles, willy nilly. He breathes in deeply, filling his nose with the smell that's rising up from the ground. That is a real nice smell, the rain on dry ground. Already, he feels much better than he did earlier – it's so nice and relaxing to sit here. He doesn't say this kind of thing to anybody, not even to Peter, or Father Kavanagh, or Marc Aboud. If he said he liked to walk in the bush, or sit down by the river and daydream like he's doing now, they would say, 'God, you turning into Tarzan for true!' He knows well enough by now what he can say to people and what not to say. Look how just the other day Daddy mentioned St Ann's again. Daddy said, 'We should have put you in St Ann's one-time.' Paul didn't say anything, he just switched off his face so he wouldn't aggravate Daddy, but in his head he was thinking, 'Go ahead! Try and put me in St Ann's! I will mash up everybody who tries to lay their hand on me!' And that night, after Daddy said that, Paul lay awake in bed thinking about how he could run away, if he had to. He could walk to Arima and from there he could get a taxi to take him anywhere in Trinidad. And he could go down south to Icacos or Cedros, and get a pirogue to Venezuela, and then he would really be gone, and Daddy would never find him. Let him put that in his pipe and smoke it.

The parrots are beginning to go in. Sunset already? Just five more minutes, he thinks. Look, the rest of the birds are still out

and about, still chattering before it's time to go in. Five more minutes, Paul says to himself: five more minutes, just to daydream
about Candace a little bit more. Maybe he could ask her to the
movies. He could call her on the telephone and ask if she wants to
go to Deluxe Cinema in Port of Spain. His eyes glaze over, thinking about what it will be like to sit in the velvety seats in the dark,
with Candace's arm on the arm-rest between them.

14

He senses trouble the moment before it starts: maybe he feels the dogs' hackles rise, or hears the scrape of their claws against the concrete as they dash down the drive. Jab-Jab's voice: high-pitched, fast, urgent; Trixie making that deep, snarling sound that she hardly ever makes; and Brownie, with a thin high-pitched bark that lengthens at the end to a howl, not directed at the men – because it must be men, for them to be barking like that – but directed somewhere else, towards other people, as if calling for help. Paul is already on his feet. This means Trouble. Big Trouble. Big Big Trouble. His eyes and ears scan the bush; his heart is pumping hard, ready to pelt out of here. But which way to go? Back to the road or onward down the riverbank? There are so many dogs barking that he cannot pinpoint where the danger is; he cannot tell which is the right way to run.

Feet are tramping through the bush, big feet, feet with boots. Handle it, he says to himself. It might just be a vagrant, or a hunter. He sits down again. The men's clothes are red, green, brown. He stands up. He should have run, but it is too late now. Handle it. Look them in the eye. Act casual. They might just be normal people.

When they appear in the clearing, still twenty, thirty yards away, he is standing on the stone, ready to look towards them as casually as he can, even to lift his chin as if to say hello. But there is no point: they are the same ones as before, he knew it from the way Trixie barked. Even without the sunglasses and t-shirt, he recognises the one who had the cutlass last time: taller, with patchy bits of beard on his cheeks. His hair is the same, scraggly and overgrown. The other one, lighter-skinned, who had the gold tooth – if he put on a shirt and tie, he could look like a Ministry official. Act calm, act calm. Oh, he should have gone in before! If only he had gone in five minutes ago, like he meant to! He glances behind him, at the riverbed with its trickle of water: just a few hundred yards along is a rope where he could climb up to the bridge. But he sees how the dark one's eyes light up, how the man's eyes measure the distance between them, how the man scans the ground nearby, looking at which way Paul might jump off the stone: the man wants him to run, so that he can run after him, pin Paul down as if he were a manicou or a lappe. 'Aye,' he says. His voice is a little quiet. He tries again. 'Aye, fellas,' he says. 'You're looking for something?' The dark man almost laughs: it is almost working. But the serious one lifts one arm and snaps his fingers, as if to tell the dark one to behave himself. The men widen out, break into a run. Paul forces himself to stand his ground. 'Hey,' he says. He puts his hands up, as if in surrender, still calm, still smiling. 'Hey, fellas.' But it does not work. As the serious man comes closer, Paul tries to look in his eyes: that is the only thing now that might help. But the man doesn't look back, only grabs Paul's wrists and pins them behind his back.

It is happening. Someone wraps an arm around his neck from behind, getting him in a choke-hold; there's the screeching of duct-tape being pulled from a roll. He is struggling without really meaning to. He wants to put his hands up and say, 'I surrender,' and to say, 'I'm not going to fight,' but he can't help but try to get out of the grip. He pulls at the man's arm, manages to get his chin down far enough to bite him. He digs his teeth in and tries to hold on, but the man lands a big cuff on the side of his head and then everything is swimming, and he puts his hands out to stop the ground, but it gets him anyway – *whack!* And then they're pinning him to the ground, one by his knees, the other on his back. There's no need, his body has gone slack.

Everything is dark; stars are dancing in front of his eyes. The duct-tape is sticking to his cheek, screeching over his mouth, winding around to the back of his head, over his ear, and his cheek and his mouth again. His hands are being tied behind his back. The man leans in to bite the edge of the tape: between his teeth are pink flecks of coconut cake.

He is on the ground, trussed up. Way above him, they are discussing something. He wants to pay attention, to catch their names, to find out who they are, where they are taking him, but they seem too far away, impossibly far away. It is like being small again: like being small, and looking up at grown-ups talking, and not following anything they say, and them seeming so very far away. When the grown-ups used to do that – Mummy used to stop to talk to someone she ran into in some crowded place, the mall, or the bank, or in town – he used to hold onto Mummy's skirt in those moments so that he didn't get left behind. People used to say it was babyish of him, but Mummy didn't mind. His head feels foggy. He cannot tell what is real. Is he really five years old, standing behind his mother's legs? Or is he really on the ground, tied up, his face pressed into the mud?

A foot nudges him in the ribs. 'Get up,' the gold-tooth man says. He catches hold of Paul's arm under the armpit and pulls roughly. 'Get up!' Paul tries, but he is still dizzy. And his hands are tied behind his back. It is real. This is real. His heels are really digging into the soft mud; he is really struggling to get his balance. He needs to pull himself together, wake up, try to get out of this. He imagines Mummy walking away – in his hand is a scrap of her skirt, he can just see her disappearing into the crowd. If he runs after her now, he will catch up. The man is yanking Paul up by the arm; his legs won't hold him up, his feet slip in the mud. He squeezes his hands shut, first one, and then the other: there is no scrap of cloth. This is definitely real. *Come on, come on. Handle it!* The man is trying to yank him forward by his shoulder; he stumbles, without his arms to steady him.

'What I said? I said, don't try no tricks!' gold-tooth says again. He shoves Paul in the direction the men came from, and gives him a dig in the back to get him walking. Paul walks a few steps, then stops. He turns to face in the direction of home: just there, not far away, Peter is doing his homework at the table, Mummy is getting dinner ready. That is where he must go. That is the right direction. To walk in any other direction is to leave a part of himself behind, to walk out of his old life, maybe to walk out of his life altogether.

'Where you think you going?' gold-tooth asks. 'Go, I said! Boy, I losing my patience with you, you know!' He grabs Paul by the arm again and spins him round, and gives him one lash with the back of his fist, across the side of his face, by his right eye. Everything goes dim and then he is on the ground again, prickly with dry leaves and sticks. He can tell, somehow, as though it is happening far, far away, that he is being hoisted up over the man's shoulders, like a dead deer. He catches a whiff, before he passes out, of the tick-shampoo that the cattle-men use, and Drakkar cologne.

He is aware, vaguely, of being put into the back seat of a car: of one man at one end, sitting him down on the seat and pushing a shoulder to lay him down; of the other man, at the other end, getting a hand under each armpit to drag him further along. They go to the back, open the trunk, discuss. Their manner is calm, unhurried. They might be discussing whether they have everything they need for a day at the beach. Something is laid over him, a blanket, maybe, or a towel. He closes his eyes. They wind the back windows up, slam the doors shut. The car sinks as the first man gets in; sinks a little more with the other. Doors slam, one, two. The key slides into the ignition, the engine wakes, revs. Pop music plays on the radio.

So this is what it feels like, Paul thinks. This is the part you never hear about. The part after the person disappears. The pictures in the paper, on the News, can only ever show the before and after: the smiling person, a picture taken on a happy day, a birthday party, first day of school, a wedding; and the after – the bodybag being carried out on a stretcher between clumps of bamboo, or the body on the ground, the limbs all askew, something dark on the ground that looks like oil leaked from a car, but which you know must be blood. In between those two moments, the before and the after, is here.

At first, he tries to follow where they go. Straight, left, straight, around. The car goes over a pothole that feels familiar – something about the shape and depth of it, the loose gravel that sprays behind the tyre. But he cannot quite remember where that pothole is: it might be on the road out to Arima, or the back-road out of Tiparo that goes part of the way through the mountains. Straight, left, curving this way, curving that way; he lies on his side, brings his knees further up to his chest to anchor himself down, to stop sliding around. The towel has already slipped off him. The man in the passenger seat glances back; Paul keeps his eyes closed. The radio goes scratchy. There's the BBC World News on the AM radio; then the fast jabbering sound of a Spanish station. 'Ya-ya-ya-ya-ya-ya,' the passenger-man says, mimicking the voice. He's the joker, the one who had the cutlass when they broke in. A Trinidad station comes back with the sea report: a woman's voice reads out the times of low tide and high tide in the north, west, east and south, the speed and directions of the winds, the heights of the waves in open areas.

Paul opens his eyes a fraction, looks, blurrily, through his eyelashes. Beige vinyl upholstery. In the seat pocket behind the driver's side: newspaper, empty juice boxes, a Barbie doll stuck head-first into the pocket, the legs sticking up. On the floor: squashed Orchard Orange cartons, chewed straws, Sunshine Snacks wrappers – the blue ones, for Cheeze Balls, and the red ones, for Chee Zees. In the passenger seat in the front, the joker rests his elbow in the window, his scraggly hair blowing in the breeze. Through the windows, Paul can see the sky, the still-glowing colour of early-evening blue. The parrots have long gone in.

The car-smell is making him feel sick: a horrible mix of oiled vinyl and air freshener. But his mouth is taped up and he must not be sick; if he is sick, he will choke. He braces his back against the seat, reaches his legs forward and kicks the back of the seat in front. The man turns and looks at him.

'What?'

Paul tries to speak. He mimics being sick.

'He's trying to say something,' the passenger-man says.

'What you think he's trying to say?' the driver says, irritated. The driver is the one with the gold tooth. 'What would you be saying if it was you? He's trying to say, let me go!' The driver ste-upses. 'Treats, sometimes I wonder about you, boy. You ignorant in truth.'

The DJ on the radio announces the next song, 'Smooth Opera-tor' by Sade. The driver turns up the volume, hums along.

Paul slides his body towards the door, wedges his toes under the lever to open it. He yanks on the lever, then presses hard against the door with both feet. The men look around: the passenger-man, the one named Treats, reaches an arm over the seat-rest and swipes at him.

'Stop that,' he says. 'Behave yourself.'

The door needs two hands: one to pull the lever, and the other to press against the door while the lever is still pulled. He slides the toes of one foot under the lever, and pulls, and he tries to instruct the other foot to do the opposite, to push. He feels the catch loosen, the door budge a few inches. Treats is swiping at him, but it doesn't matter: all he needs to do is get this door open and get out of this car. He thinks only of his feet: the left toes must do *this*; the right toes must do *that*. The door swings open: the out-side, dark greens and browns, rush by in a blur. He tries to wriggle towards the open door. The door swings half-closed, wide-open, half-closed, wide-open. Then the car comes to a sudden halt, and Paul thuds forward into the footwell. The driver-man slides his seat back to jam him in: Paul's head is caught underneath, the metal struts pinning his head to the ground. It is like that time when he pushed his head through the bars of the front gate at home and then, stupidly, got stuck there. Then, it was a terror of what Daddy might have said that made him squeeze past the pain of the iron bars, feeling the blood trapped in his ears, back through to freedom. He pulls his head free, his skull tingling.

Treats gets out, slams the door closed, presses down the lock. The car sinks again as he gets back in. Through the gap under the seat, Paul watches the driver's feet stepping on the pedals: clutch, gas, first gear; clutch, gas, second; clutch, gas, third. Breeze comes in the windows. One of the men turns up the volume on the radio. The man's sneakers are muddy. On the left foot, resting on the ground, the shoelace is loose. Slowly, Paul turns over onto his back. Above, he can make out dark spots of mildew on the ceiling. He can see through the driver's window that it is still light, but only just, the sky a purplish blue, the light draining away like water down a plughole. Already, the street-lamps are on. All over the mountains, the birds will be settled into warm nests. Soon, they will fluff their feathers for sleep, tuck their beaks into their chests; whatever wants to come out at night will be readying itself to come out.

He must try again; he must keep trying until he is out of this car. He must get away. Sometimes – not sometimes: often, it happens often – there is no news headline. Sometimes it's easy. There have been plenty of stories of people being kidnapped, and the stupid kidnappers doing things like stopping at the rum shop or the roti shop, and the kidnapped person getting out of the car and walking away, shaking his head in disbelief. At school, when these stories are told, the whole thing is like a big joke. Even the criminals in this country are incompetent! And people gather, in the tuck-shop, in classrooms or in corridors, acting out scenes from *Die Hard*, Bruce Willis sweaty and sexy in his white vest, kicking down doors and entering rooms, pointing his gun in that fast way, left-right-left! Dat is how to kidnap people, boys laugh. Dem need to watch more movies to learn the right way to do it.

They are on a main road: there are other cars driving by now, the rattle and clank of trucks, the barking of dogs, voices out on the street talking, laughing. Music: 'What's Love Got to Do with It?' This is where he must get out; this is where he must open the door, get his body out of this car and out onto the road. People will point, exclaim; people will pick him up, untie his hands and feet. The men will drive quickly away, and he will be safe – scratched and bruised and aching, but safe. He needs to get the door open again. He tucks his knees up to his chest, uses all his strength to roll forward, to bring himself to a sitting-up position. His feet support his body; he moves to the seat. There's a commotion in the front seat: swearing, arms reaching over to grab him, the driver mashing first the gas, then the brake, then the gas again. He tries with his chin to push the knob up to unlock the door, but it is hopeless. He needs his teeth. If he had his teeth, he could do it. Treats reaches behind, grabs his arm, yanks him forward.

'I told you! Behave yourself!' Treats says. The man's hand is at his throat. Paul feels his eyes bulge, his whole face begins to swell with blood. 'You want to go in the trunk? We'll put you in the trunk, you know.'

From somewhere outside, a woman's voice cries out, 'Look! Look! He's tied up!'

'Oh my God!' another voice says. 'Look!'

Treats throws him back onto the seat; the other man puts the car into gear and takes off, *voom*. The insides of his head are all out of place; the sensation is like water sloshing. He closes his eyes, listens to the bubbling and gurgling of his body, of things trying to get back to their right places. He doesn't know if they will get back there or not. He doesn't know his own name, or what day it is, or if he's even here at all. Maybe he is dead. Or maybe he is back in the water at Toco, the water tumbling him

[189]

over and over like a washing machine. If he gets to do it again, if he is back in the water at Toco, this time he will get himself out. He doesn't know how, just that this time he will make his body find the strength to do it, and he will do it.

Gradually, the sloshing subsides. There is a throbbing at his neck where the man's fingers held him, and the smell of the waxy oil on the vinyl, and the sliding forward and back as the car moves. He is not in Toco, walking proudly up the rocks; he is not at home eating dinner with his family. He is still in the back seat of the car. The radio is playing late-night music, easy-listening.

If only he had waited until they were on a busy road before he tried to get out, he would have made it, surely. With the door open, the people on the pavement or in other cars would have seen him. People would have stopped the car, they would have pulled him out, untied him. Instead, he was hasty and used up his good chance in a place where no one was there to help him and then the second chance was wasted. He must wait for the next opening, the next opportunity, he thinks; all he has to do is wait for it, and when it comes, take it, take it fast, and then there will be no picture in the paper, and he will walk again down the road and he will tell the story of how he got away from the men. Doesn't he know how to handle himself? He knows how to handle himself, much more than Peter. For so long now, he's been walking around at night, learning his way around, learning how to handle situations – he never really knew for what purpose, but now, here is a purpose.

Since he was small, he's been giving himself challenges: to walk around the yard; to walk to the end of the Trace; to walk as far as the quarry and back. Once, he challenged himself to go into Uncle Romesh's yard with the Alsatians. Looking back, it seems like a stupid thing to do, but the dogs weren't fully grown then and they weren't as bad then as they are now. He chose a time when Uncle Romesh and Auntie Rachel weren't at home and the dogs were loose, sleeping somewhere around the yard. He knew, as the dogs ran towards him, that the whole thing would be decided in the first few seconds; that either they would attack, or let him pass. And he knew, somehow, that he had to push his panic away and be calm; to truly control his mind and body and be fully calm. Even now, he is not quite sure how he did it, just that he did, and it felt like having a new power. The dogs sniffed him all over (their noses came up to his shoulders) and he stayed calm, truly calm. When he felt the moment was right, he casually set off walking towards the house, and the dogs stopped their sniffing and let him pass.

He won't be able to fight with these men, that much is clear; he will have to summon his powers, use some other tactic. He thinks of what he will say to them as soon as he gets this tape off his face. He'll say, look, fellas, what's going on? He'll say, no need for the rough stuff! I'm co-operating! I'm the co-operative type, easy-going! He'll say, you picked up small-fry here, you know! You must be mistaking me with another Deyalsingh, maybe the one who has the hardware shop? I hear them people have plenty money. My father don't have any money. But hear nuh. How about this. I was ready to skip town anyway. ('Skip town' sounds good, like something they say in the movies.) How about you let me go, and I'll leave Trinidad quick-quick, and just, *voom*, disappear? (*Disappear*.) You can tell everybody you killed me. No one has to know. I'll never tell, I'll never come back to tell. What you think? Sound like a plan? Maybe then they will let him go. He imagines how he will walk down the road in the bright midday heat, brushing the dirt off his elbows and knees. He will go to the coast and get someone to take him on a boat and he will go away. He realises that he cannot fully open one eye; in the ear on that side, all he can hear is a high-pitched whine. His whole body is hurting, as if he was thrown around while he was unconscious. Maybe he was; he cannot remember. He swallows carefully, concentrating on not being sick. They are driving fast. Outside, the road is quiet, there are no street-lamps any more. The sky is dark; night has come. He shuts his eyes. He will use this time to rest so that when the opening comes, he will be ready.

15

The road has been bumpy, potholed, slow; for the last half-hour or so, Paul has thought that they must be driving along a dirt-track. Now, the car comes to a halt; the driver switches off the engine, yawns, loudly and slowly.

'It's dark, man!' Treats says. 'See how dark it is?'

The men get out, open the trunk, rummage around. Paul has been lying, half-awake, for he doesn't know how long, but he doesn't feel rested, only exhausted.

'I thought we would reach here earlier,' Treats says. 'How we're going to get over to the place? Robert! Where are you? Put on the headlights, man. I can't see anything.'

'You fraid the dark?' the driver asks, mocking.

'Boy! I not shame,' Treats says. 'Of course I'm fraid. All kinds of things live out here, man.'

The serious man, the one whose name must be Robert, leans in through the window, turns the key in the ignition; the dark disappears. In front of the car is a fallen tree, the base of the huge trunk rotted away, the roots sticking up in the air.

'What we doing? We not going by the boss's house?' Treats asks.

'No, he said to stay away from there,' the man named Robert says. 'We're hiding out here until the father pays the money.'

Paul hears rustling of paper, of nylon sacking, feels the light thuds of objects being shifted in the trunk just behind where he's sitting. Then a clink of glass, a tearing of cloth, a sloshing, a smell of gasoline. Paul's heart beats faster; he looks from one side of the car to the other. There's a flicking sound as someone's thumb works at a lighter, and then a flash of light that steadies and grows, becomes a new presence, as if there were four beings now amongst them instead of three. Through the back window, Paul sees the serious man, Robert, holding up a glass Carib bottle, the piece of rag stuck into it, now doused in gasoline, making a bright flame. The other man, Treats, is standing facing a tree, his legs apart, his trousers sagging. They might be in a forest – although the trees are a bit sparse, and if they have managed to bring the car in as far as this, they must have come on some kind of road. Ahead of them, past the fallen tree, is something that could be a path, zig-zagging up a slope.

Treats opens the door for him. 'Come. Time to walk,' he says. He gets Paul's feet up on the seat, sticking out the open door; with a Stanley knife, he carefully cuts through the duct-tape, a line straight down between Paul's ankles at the front. He pulls at the ankles until Paul's feet are on the ground, and then helps him stand up, turns him around, and cuts the duct-tape carefully at the back. 'Don't run away,' he says. And then he adds, in a low voice like the voice that announces American movies, 'Out in the woods, no one can hear you scream.'

'Treats, behave yourself and come and take something to carry,' the driver says. He's set the flambeau down on a blue and white ice-cooler at his feet: next to the ice-cooler there's a gun, a radio, and a cardboard box with the red Crix logo on it. The man named Robert picks up the gun, checks it, then stuffs it down his trousers. He doesn't look like a bandit at all: he looks tidy, serious, like an office worker. He picks up the flambeau carefully with one hand, and then picks up the handle of the ice-cooler with the other. 'Take the box,' Robert says. He puts the cooler down, slams the trunk closed. He goes to the driver's side, turns the key, takes it out, puts it in his pocket. Paul watches as they both go back behind the car. For a half-second or so, they are both bent down – Treats picking up the box, Robert getting the ice-cooler – and Paul quickly looks around. But, before he can even make his legs move, Treats has him by the arm again, and they are walking to the front of the car, towards the fallen tree: another chance gone.

The man named Robert rests the flambeau on the trunk, wedges it into a little dip somewhere amongst the rotted-away flesh of the tree. Something – a bit of bark, or dried leaves – catches in the flame and flares up. 'Careful you don't burn the place down,' Treats says. Robert climbs up onto the trunk, carefully picks up the glass bottle, and stamps out the twigs that have caught fire. He sits, slides down the trunk on the other side, and then turns to face them, holding the light up so they can see. 'Send the boy next,' he says.

Paul gets one foot up onto the trunk and tries to put his weight on that leg, but it's hard without his arms to help him. Treats puts the box down. 'I'll push you,' he says. Paul tries again to get up on the trunk: this time, Treats holds him by the arms and pushes him up, until he is standing atop the log, a man on either side. He hesitates – is this another chance? – but Treats moves as if to push him forward, and Paul quickly jumps off, and lands on the ground next to the man Robert. Then Treats does what Paul was trying to do a moment ago: he puts one foot on top of the log, gives a push-off with the other foot that brings him on top, and then he jumps down to the ground. A roll of black garbage bags falls out of the box, and he picks it up and throws it back in. Robert turns and leads the way up the path, the flambeau held high; Paul follows, his eyes still scanning left and right for any sign – any sign of anything that could be helpful; and Treats walks behind him with the cardboard box.

There's a rustling from somewhere up ahead. Robert straightens up, puts his hand on his gun. Paul's heart beats fast: he halts, not sure whether to go forward or back. The men halt too. A creature runs across the path into the bush on the other side: Paul catches a brief glimpse of a glossy pelt, a furred foot.

'Ooooh!' Treats says. 'Oh Lord! That frightened me!' He laughs loudly. 'Oh Lord!'

'Lappe,' Robert says. He sets off walking again; Paul follows, and then Treats.

'I thought it might be one of them things,' Treats says.

'What, bogeyman?'

'No, man. Like, Mama Dlo and them. Or soucouyant. I fraid soucouyant!' He taps Paul on the shoulder. 'You ever seen soucouyant?'

Paul shakes his head.

'I seen soucouyant. Not too far from here, I saw one, as God is my witness. I was lying down minding my own business, and it was pitch dark, like now, and all I saw was this thing, looking like a ball of fire, coming towards me.'

'And what you did?' Robert asks.

'I closed the window, quick!' Treats says. 'I ran around the place, stuffing anything I could find into all the cracks, all t-shirts, socks, books, newspaper, everything I could find!'

'I don't fraid soucouyant,' Robert says. 'She want to come and suck my blood? She could suck it if she wants!'

'But you feel drained in the morning, man,' Treats says. 'You can't get out of bed, you's feel so *drained*, after soucouyant has sucked the blood out of you. You would never be the same again. You might still be alive, but only just.'

'I don't fraid her,' Robert says. He looks around, to check they are still behind him. He doesn't look like a bad man, he looks like a normal man, like somebody's uncle. 'It's douen that frighten me, man!'

'Yes, douen. Me too.'

'You know douen?' Robert says, looking at him.

Paul nods, but Robert keeps talking anyway, in the low voice that people use to talk about these things. 'The douen are the children who died before they were born,' he says, 'and they live out here, in the forest.' He comes to a halt, and they stand huddled together, by the light of the flambeau. 'And if you ever meet one, it will be easy to recognise, because you will notice straight away how the child has no face, and that the feet are pointing backwards. And if somebody calls your name when you're outside, and it's dark? The douen will steal your name and they'll steal your soul and you'll become one of them.'

There's an eerie silence, and then Treats bursts out laughing.

'Oh God, look the boy trembling now, man! You scared the boy!' Treats holds him by the shoulders, gives him a friendly shake.

The men keep talking as they walk up to the top of the slope; the path gets narrower and then disappears altogether, and all around them is thick bush. Paul keeps close to the man in front, to see by his light. He tries not to cry; there is no place for crying, here: he must keep his eyes open for his opportunity. He keeps remembering all the pictures he has seen in the papers, of men – two men, one at each end – carrying dead bodies out of bush just like this. But these men are not bad men; not very bad, at least. Not crazy. If they were crazy, he would have no chance, but with these men, he might have a chance, as long as he does not just fall apart and cry. He is big now; he must look after himself. As he walks, he peers at the ground, careful of where his bare feet are stepping: there could easily be snakes here, scorpions, centipedes, shinnies, in bush like this. Already, he's been bitten, just by little things, ants or mosquitoes, and every few steps he tries to lift one foot to scratch at a bite on the other leg. They go up a steep bit, all red dirt and roots and fallen branches, which Treats has to help him over; then down a steep bit, which he stumbles down; and then they are at a river. Robert stands at the edge, raises the flambeau again to look at the water: it is wide and slow in one part, fast and narrow in another. 'Here,' he says, and he goes towards the narrow part, which is white and frothing with the fast-flowing water. 'Wait. Hold on,' he says. He splashes through the water, picks his way over the rocks on the other side, and rests the cooler down. Then he comes back, holds Paul by one arm and leads him over the water. Treats splashes through the wider part; in the middle, he sinks to his shoulders, laughs, holds the Crix box above his head.

As they walk down the last stretch, Paul feels sand sting his face, hears the rhythmic rise and fall of breaking waves. The air is the big wide air of the sea. They arrive at the place, a sort of house, a half-built, abandoned house, just four brick walls and a floor, with holes left in the walls for the windows, and some galvanise sheets resting on top where the roof is supposed to go. The men put their things down by one wall – Paul gets a glimpse, as the flambeau comes in with them, of the other things scattered around the place: rubber boots, plastic drinks crates stacked up, bush-cutters, newspapers, flattened cardboard. The man Robert takes him outside and pulls down his pants for him to pee, and then pulls up his pants and walks him back into the house. Robert picks up something from the pile and goes outside. Treats drags the cardboard over to one side, humming as he goes. 'You thirsty?' he says. Paul nods cautiously. 'I'll give you some water just now.' Paul tries to stand still while he waits. He feels he might fall over. The man points to the cardboard and says it is for him. Treats goes to the pile of things by the other wall and roots around, straightens up with a roll of wire. 'Go over there,' he says, pointing at the cardboard. When Paul does not move, he says, 'You want to sleep standing up?' Paul is by the door; no one is behind him. Treats, sometimes, has his back turned. The next time Treats turns his back, he could run out the door, run back the way he came, or run in any direction as long as it is away. He stands watching Treats, his mind rehearsing the movements. But how far will he possibly get on his own? The men will catch him before he has gone ten yards, and who knows what they will do then. The best thing is to play along, and try to stay alive. Slowly, Paul walks over to the cardboard laid on the floor; it is damp, with dark stains in patches, smells bad. The man comes over with the wire: he works it around Paul's wrists, over the duct-tape, and then feeds it through the holes of the breeze-block bricks in the wall. 'Hold on,' he says. He carries the flambeau out. The light appears on the other side of the wall, through the holes in the bricks: the man takes the ends of the wire and ties it around something outside. Paul hears him talking to the other man, Robert; later, further away, he hears them open bottles of beer. For a while, he sits up, thinking that the man is about to come back with the water for him. His throat is so dry he can hardly swallow.

Every now and again, he waits for saliva to fill his mouth and he swallows it carefully and slowly, trying to let it wet his mouth and the back of his throat. He hears the quiet shuffle of cards, the quick slippery sound of cards being dealt. They must be a little distance away from the door of the house, but Paul can make out a flickering of light from the flambeau. He gets to his feet, quietly pulls at the wire tying his hands to the brick. It might be tied to a pipe on the other side, from the way he senses it sliding. It's fencing wire, he knows the one. Daddy has bought it often enough at the hardware shop and used it to fill in gaps in the fence and in the front gate. You need a heavy-duty wire-cutter for this wire: Daddy borrows one from Uncle Romesh when he needs it. Paul tries twisting his hands this way, that way, but he cannot get his hands loose. If only he could use his teeth, he would be able to bite away the duct-tape around his wrists, even that would be something.

He leans his head back against the wall. How long has he been away? It feels like a long time ago that he was sitting peacefully in the bush on his own; a very long time ago since he woke up this morning to get ready for school and walked down the road with Peter, in his clean school uniform, his schoolbag on his back, to get the maxi taxi. He wonders what they're all doing now at home, whether Mummy and Daddy and Peter are getting worried. One of the men, Robert, maybe, said that they were going to hide out here and wait for the father to pay the money. It is better not to hope for anything, better not to sit here hoping that Daddy will pay this money, however much it is. They can't keep looking after him. He will look after himself.

Sometime later, when he opens his eyes, the flickering light has disappeared; instead, there is the clear, steady light of the moon, shining through a gap in the roof. Perhaps the men have gone away. He gets to his feet and tries again to get his hands free. He pulls and tugs; something metallic clangs on the other side of the wall. He pulls harder, yanks, twists, tugs, not caring about the clanging. Nobody comes, nobody tells him to be quiet. He rests, tries again. Eventually, he sits back down, leans his head against the wall. Slowly, the shadows creep along the floor.

16

Clyde knows, as soon as he hears the man's voice on the other
end, what it is all about. He hears his own voice replying to the
man, replying in a calm voice, saying that yes, this is Deyalsingh,
Deyalsingh from La Sagesse; yes, he is the brother-in-law of
Romesh 'Hotsauce' Ramcharan. He keeps his eyes away from
Joy's. The light beyond the window is the bright, untroubled
light of mid-morning, the sky as blue as any other day. A lawn
mower hums somewhere along the Trace. The man introduces
himself politely, says who he is working for, and that they have
the boy, and that the boy is OK. He tells Clyde to get a pencil,
to write the number down. 'Just tell me,' Clyde says. 'I won't
forget.' But the man says to get a pencil anyway; people always
think they will remember, he says, and then instead they forget.
'Write it down, and then we're straight,' the man says. Clyde
reaches forward to the coffee table, takes yesterday's newspaper,
the ballpoint pen. Joy's hands are on her cheeks. He lays the
paper on his thigh, positions the pen over the margin. The man
speaks the number; Clyde writes. Over the phone, there's the
fizzing sound of a plastic bottle being opened, the quiet *glug-
glug* of liquid going down the man's throat.

'You wrote it down?' the man asks.

'Yea.'

'Good. When you think you could get it ready?'

'I'll have to see,' he says. 'It's a lot of money. I don't have that kind of money.'

The man licks his lips, screws the top back onto the bottle. 'Hear nuh,' the man says. 'I know about you, and you know about me. Not so? There's no secrets here.'

'I don't know about you,' Clyde says. 'I thought I was keeping far away from you people.'

'You see, this is what I mean,' the man says. 'Don't bother with this pretending-thing. You're wasting everybody's time.' He repeats the name of his boss, a name that everyone in Trinidad knows, and he calls out the man's full address, in Caroni, not far away from the industrial estate where Clyde goes to work every day. Clyde already knows the place, from pictures in the newspaper, or stories from others who have seen it: a compound with high brick walls topped with razor wire, and nothing around it for miles except the flat swampy land where once there was rice and now there are just weeds. 'So don't waste your time thinking you could fight anything,' the man says. 'Just focus on getting the money together. Cash, eh?'

'And what if I don't have the money?'

'You have it, we know you have it.'

'And how you so sure about that?'

'Your brother-in-law, man!' The man raises his voice, impatient. 'Hotsauce! He told us all about the doctor, and the doctor left you all his money and you haven't spent any of it yet. We know all about that. That's what I'm saying, don't waste your time . . .'

The man keeps talking but Clyde doesn't hear any of it. He nods into the phone, says, 'Right, right,' and, 'Well, we'll see.' By the time he hangs up, the lawn mower has gone quiet outside.

'What?' says Joy. 'What is it? Is he OK?'

'I think so,' he says. Together, they stare at the number written in the margin of the newspaper. He takes her hands. 'Romesh set it up,' he says.

Clyde holds her hands – hard, dry hands, the fingers cold – until she takes them away. She stares at the wall, her face blank. A fly lands on her shoulder; Clyde watches it walk across her t-shirt to her collarbone, rub its hairy hands together. The lawn mower starts up again. The clock on the wall ticks forward.

It is better to live without illusions, he thinks. Joy might not understand. Maybe women prefer illusions. There was a time, long ago, when he first saw things with this same clarity as he does now, when he and his own father were having some argument, right here in this room. His father had hit him with something – a plate, maybe, or a cup, something he had picked up from the dining table – and Clyde had felt the warmth gathering in his forehead as the bruise came up. Clyde's sisters watched from the kitchen. And Clyde looked back at his father and realised that his father was not so big and strong as he had once seemed; and he saw that as long as he was prepared to fend for himself, that there was no reason to stay here and continue like this; that he was, in fact, quite free to walk out the door and not come back. And so he collected his few things in a Tru-Valu plastic bag, and slipped on his flip-flops and walked out. And as he walked along the Trace, he realised that he was alone, and although it frightened him at the time, he also knew that it was the only way to be. This is what he feels again now, sitting next to Joy with the clock ticking on the wall and the lawn mower droning outside: that it was a mistake to expect anything from anyone; to behave as if anyone owed him anything; the truth of the matter is that anyone – friend, family, anyone – can betray you at any time, and you must be permanently on your guard.

Joy is shivering. 'Darling, you go and lie down,' Clyde says. He has to shake her shoulder continuously to get her moving. 'You didn't sleep much last night,' he says. 'Come on.' He gets her up, steers her past the dining table. In the kitchen, she turns to him, puts her arms around him. It feels awkward: she wants a kind of comfort that he's not in the mood to give. 'Clyde,' she says. She's crying. 'Where is he? What are they doing to him? Tell Romesh to tell them not to be cruel with him,' she says.

'They won't be cruel,' Clyde says. 'Why would they be cruel?' He tries to sound reassuring, but they both know his words are empty. The men will be cruel if they feel like it. 'Darling, go and lie down,' he says again, trying to propel her forward. 'Just lie and rest. I need to call Seepersad.'

She opens her mouth as if she wants to say something else. 'You rest,' he says, firmly. He says he will bring her a cup of sweet-tea. He gets her to the bed, pulls back the sheet, helps her lie down. 'You want the fan?' he asks. The room is hot but Joy is still shivering. He puts the fan on the lowest setting and sets it to face away from her, just to move air around the room. 'OK? Comfortable?' he asks her. She looks at him blankly. Her hair is messed up, sticking out in the wrong places. 'I'll bring the tea just now,' he says. He pulls the door shut as he leaves.

He's standing by the sink, stirring the teabag in the mug, when the phone rings again.

'Hi, Clyde, hi.' It's only Mr Bartholomew. 'I was just calling to see if Paul is back yet. I saw you didn't go out this morning at your usual time. You had any news?'

'News,' Clyde repeats. 'You could say that.'

'Oh Lord,' Mr Bartholomew says. 'What happened? Is he dead?'

'We don't think so,' says Clyde. He says it lightly, but he doesn't like Mr Bartholomew's tone. Who knows who else is involved in this thing? Maybe everyone is in on it, playing along, waiting for a percentage to fall into their laps. Clyde thinks of how, just two weeks ago, after coming home to the dark, silent house, he walked to Mr Bartholomew's gate and called out and asked for his neighbour's help. And all that night, the night of the break-in, Mr Bartholomew was here, all the neighbours were here, all of them had free rein to wander around his house.

'Wait, let me understand,' Mr Bartholomew says. 'It's a kidnapping? They kidnapped him?'

'Seems so.'

'Oh Lord, man,' Mr Bartholomew says, sadly. 'Oh my God. Man, what is this place coming to? But you-all don't even have any money! What purpose do they have in kidnapping your child?' He asks after Joy, after Peter; he asks if they have spoken to Paul, heard his voice; he asks if the kidnappers have sent any body parts or bloodied clothes; sometimes they do that, he says.

'I'd better go,' Clyde says. 'I have things to do.'

'Clyde, wait. You have people in mind to go and speak to? You want me to get my sister-in-law to call you? She's a lawyer. She might be able to help you. She knows a lot of people.'

'No,' Clyde says. He forces himself to speak normal-sounding words. 'I appreciate it. But no thanks.'

'OK. I'll let her know anyway, in case you change your mind. Think about it.'

The tea has gone cold by the time he gets back to the kitchen. He pours it out, refills the kettle, stands by the stove waiting for it to boil. But the phone rings again: Mrs Bartholomew this time, saying that she has just heard the news from her husband. She

[206]

wants to know what they have eaten today, whether they would like her to bring food; she asks where Peter is, where Romesh is, where Rachel is; she asks how much ransom has been demanded. Clyde thinks of Joy's blank expression, of her lying dumbly on the bed waiting for him to bring the tea. 'I better keep the line free,' he says to Mrs Bartholomew.

'Of course,' she says. 'Of course.'

But no sooner has he hung up when the phone rings again: Mrs des Vignes, the last house on the Trace, next to the Bartholomews. She asks if they know where the boy is; what time the kidnappers phoned; which gang is behind it; how much money was demanded; what contacts does Clyde have in the police force, the army; how are they going to negotiate? Clyde answers her questions dully. For the questions he doesn't have answers to, he says, 'I don't know,' to which she echoes, 'You don't know yet?' and he replies, 'Yes, I don't know.' 'You want me to call my nephew for you?' she asks. 'He knows someone in the police.' 'No, no. I don't want that,' he says. When he hangs up, he glares at the phone. He forgot to call Seepersad: Clyde was supposed to be at the industrial estate at seven, and it's now a quarter to eleven. Joy is still waiting for the tea. He presses his fingers to his eyes. The phone rings.

He grabs the receiver. 'What?' he shouts. 'Who is it now?'

There's a brief pause before the person says, calmly, 'This is Father Kavanagh.'

'Hi,' Clyde says. He rests his head against the wall. 'Hi, Father.'

'Peter told me that Paul didn't come home last night. I wondered if he was back home now?'

'No. He isn't. And I may as well tell you, since all of Trinidad will hear about it before the day is out. He's been kidnapped. You would think I look poor, and nobody would bother to kidnap anybody in my family, but they did. Somebody rang me with the ransom. So that's where he is. OK?' He waits, but Father Kavanagh doesn't say anything. 'You heard me? Kidnapped. Right now, he's with kidnappers. I have people calling me every five minutes wanting to know what's going on. Everybody offering me contacts.' Still, there's no answer. 'You hearing me?'

'Yes. I'm hearing you.'

The priest's silence gives him space to think. His breathing slows. He wonders if these priests are any different to anyone else; whether, after helping you, they turn around and demand some kind of payment.

'Father? You're there?'

'I'm here.'

'Could you do something for me?'

'What can I do?'

He explains the help he needs: just somewhere safe for Peter and Joy to stay for the next few days, that's all, somewhere in Port of Spain. They don't need to be together, he says, they can be apart, as long as they are both somewhere safe, and Peter can get to school, and has a quiet place to study in the evenings. 'That's all the help I'm asking for,' he says. 'I don't need any more help than that.'

'I'm sure we can find somewhere,' Father Kavanagh says. He speaks quietly, with no hurry.

'That's the only thing I need,' Clyde says. 'And if you can help, I'll be very grateful to you.'

'We can help, Clyde. We're happy to help.'

'Good,' Clyde says. 'Good. I'll get Joy to pack a bag for Peter and I'll organise to transport her to Port of Spain.'

'I could come, if you like. I'll speak to Father Malachy, get someone to cover my lessons.'

'OK,' Clyde says, uncertainly. 'But – you'll come by yourself, Father? Not with anyone else?' He pictures four or five priests crowding into his house, and trying to make him sing hymns or say prayers, or whatever it is that they do.

'Whatever you prefer.'

'I prefer you come alone, Father. That would be best.'

'Fine.'

'And tell Peter to stay at school. I don't want him coming with you. It's better he stays up there.'

Clyde feels better when he hangs up, but just a few moments later, the phone rings again. There is no way to turn the sound down on this thing: it is either silent or shrieking, no in between. He picks up, hears another neighbour's voice, puts it down again. And he still hasn't rung Seepersad, and he still hasn't made the tea. He takes the phone off the hook, meaning to pull himself together before he phones Seepersad but, after a while, he realises he is pacing up and down the room. He still smells bad, from yesterday. He should bathe. He should make the tea. He should get a gang of men together and drive to Caroni and storm the man's house – but he knows it won't do any good, that it will only end in a bodycount and things will spiral out of control, even more out of control than they already are. The only way is to do things alone. On the wall, the second hand of the Jesus clock ticks forward: an hour has already passed since he last looked at it. *Move!* he tells himself. *Do something!* He dials the number for Seepersad's office at the industrial estate.

'Deyalsingh!' Seepersad says, when he answers. 'Where are you? What happened?'

'I meant to phone you earlier to let you know I couldn't come in today,' Clyde says. 'But the time ran away with me. I'm sorry.'

'What happened? Something wrong?'

There is no point hiding it: Seepersad will hear it from somebody or other before the day is out. 'They kidnapped my child,' he says. 'Last night he didn't come home, and I thought he was at the nightclub, and then they phoned me this morning.'

'Oh Lord,' Seepersad says. 'I'm sorry to hear that, man. I'm real sorry.' He asks whether Clyde knows who is behind it, how much they have asked for. Clyde relates the details of the phone call: of the man in Caroni, the amount they have demanded. 'Clyde, man!' Seepersad says, with feeling. 'Clyde! What you going to do? You have a plan yet?'

'Boy, the phone hasn't stopped ringing all morning. I can't even hear myself think. I have to make a plan.'

'Yes, make a plan. Decide how you're going to handle it. You're looking for a negotiator? You want me to put you in touch with someone?'

'No, no,' Clyde says. He rubs his forehead. 'No.'

'Listen, I know you need some time to think things through, make your plans,' Seepersad says. 'I'll tell you what I can do. I can give you some money up front, OK?'

'No, no, man. I don't want any money. I never borrowed from anyone, I'm not going to start now.'

'No, it's not a loan. I'm saying I can give you some salary in advance, that's all. If you want it. You don't have to decide now. Your head still spinning. I can give you three months' salary in advance, if you want it. I'll give you cash. What currency they want? US or TT?'

'TT.'

'I could have gotten you US if you wanted, but TT is easier. So when you're ready, just let me know. I'll give you three months' pay in advance. And I could get someone to drop it up by you so you don't have to waste your time driving all the way down here. OK? I probably wouldn't come myself, I don't want anyone to think I'm involved, you understand. But I'll send someone.'

'OK. I'll think about it. Thanks.'

'No problem. Go and think.'

He puts the phone off the hook when he's finished talking to Seepersad. He doesn't want to talk to anyone else. He wants to stay in one place, gather his thoughts, make his head stop spinning. He thinks of Joy, still in the bedroom waiting for the tea. He puts the kettle on again, goes to the bedroom to speak to her, but she's fallen asleep. She looks strange: flat on her back, her mouth open, her face pale-coloured. He goes closer, checks to make sure she is breathing. He shuts the door quietly behind him.

Ahead of him is the boys' bedroom, the door ajar. The sun is shining outside, a normal, bright, midday sun; in the room, the light is normal, bright, midday light. Paul's bag is still at the foot of his bed where Peter left it, his trousers still folded at the edge. One white sock, balled up, sticks out from under the bed.

Clyde steps into the room. The stuffing is coming out of Paul's pillow; one end of his bed is sagging. On the windowsill there is the tell-tale brown dust of termites; he sprayed the window frames only last year – maybe it was the year before – and already the termites are back. And Romesh – Romesh! – gave him the number for a company who will do it all properly, who will cover the whole house with tarpaulin, and will fumigate the whole house, so that every living thing inside the house will die – all the termites, ants, cockroaches, jackspaniards, everything. If you have any plants or flowers, any fish or birds or anything like that,

Romesh said, you have to move them, because every living thing will die. That is the only way to get rid of the termites properly.

Under Peter's bed are all his piles of books: school textbooks, Webster's English Dictionary, World Atlas. Books that Uncle Vishnu, long ago, brought for Peter to read. Secret Seven books, *The Magic Faraway Tree*. *The Handbook of Common Tropical Diseases*. *Pears' Cyclopaedia 1962*. 'He needs books,' Uncle Vishnu said. 'Keep giving him books, anything you could find.' Peter has stacked up the books on a big piece of cardboard so that he can pull the whole thing out like a drawer. Clyde stoops to the floor and pulls out a book: *Electricity and Electromagnetism*. He flips through the pages, filled with strange triangles, squiggles and arrows, all with some hidden meaning.

He puts the book back where it was. He goes to Paul's bed, slowly sits down. The sheet is still tucked in, smooth. He looks around: aside from the Baby Blue walls, this room looks the same as it did when Clyde used to sleep in here as a child. The big window there, the small window there; the breeze through the breeze blocks near the ceiling. A lizard is on the wall above the window – one of those little rust-coloured ones with the white stripe along its spine. He watches the lizard's flanks rise and fall as it breathes.

Paul was in this bed the night before last, a little more than twenty-four hours ago; now, he is not. Clyde lies down, feels the sharp edges of the springs prick his back, his hip.

He has so much to do. So many phone calls to make, people to speak to, things to organise. But his head is throbbing and he cannot think. Maybe he will sleep for just a few minutes; then, after he has rested a little, he will get to work. He closes his eyes, but he does not fall asleep. He puts the pillow over his face to block out the light.

17

The sounds are unfamiliar. There are birds, but not the ones he is used to: instead, there are the small, jabbering sounds of some bird that he doesn't recognise, and a wheeling, squawking faraway call from birds somewhere high up. And instead of the gentle, cool breeze that flutters the curtains at home, now there is a constant shushing, the high-pitched sound of coconut fronds moving ceaselessly in the wind. He wonders if it was all a dream. It might all be a very bad, very realistic dream. Maybe he dreamt the men dragging him away in the bush, dreamt the long drive in the car, dreamt the walking through the bush with the flambeau. Please let it be a dream, he thinks. He opens his eyes.

It was not a dream. He is lying on a floor in a house, a sort of house, a half-built house. The floor is rough concrete, with ridges of brush marks where somebody must have tried to sweep it smooth as it was drying. The walls are grey brick. The red-brown cement that glues the bricks together is smudged in places, like when you put jam in between two layers of cake and press them together and the jam squelches out the sides. There are big square holes in the walls in place of windows, showing nothing but sky, a normal blue sky, just like any other normal day, the clouds white and fluffy. The air is the cool air of morning. Peter will be at school already. The bell might be ringing to signal the end of recess; soon, the boys will settle back at their desks, the school will fall quiet. Father Kavanagh is at the front of the classroom; Paul's desk by the corridor is empty. He closes his eye again, and then realises that the other eye isn't moving. In fact, it doesn't really feel like his eye is there at all; it feels like something puffy is there in its place, something dull and aching.

When Paul opens his eye again, a man is in the doorway. Not one of the ones from last night: this one is wearing old blue short-pants and carrying a sack over one shoulder. His eyes are big with shock. 'What is thissss? What going on here?' His eyes move from Paul, to the pile of stuff in the corner, to over his shoulder. 'Oh Lord have mercy. What is thissss?'

Paul quickly sits up. He is saved, at last. This man will untie him, surely. He shows the man his wrists, the wire wrapped around, fed through the bricks. He jerks his head towards the wall behind him. Somewhere outside, he tries to say – the wire is tied to something on the other side of the wall. The man has a hand over his mouth, he is backing away, looking over his shoulder, at Treats, who has come up behind him, dripping wet from the sea.

'You put this boy here?' the man asks.

'It's better you just go away, breads,' Treats says. 'Go away. You didn't see anything.'

'What mischief you making here?' the man asks. 'You're kid-nappers? You've kidnapped this boy?'

'Old man,' Treats says. 'Go. I'm telling you. Go quick.' He mentions a name that Paul has heard before, mentioned by grown-ups gathered in carports and patios, or waiting by the old bus shelter for the maxi taxi to go to school. A well-known man, a drug-lord in Caroni, who built himself a compound for his whole extended family to live in, twenty, thirty people.

The man backs away. 'This is evilness,' he says. His voice is quieter, further away. 'You-all are evil. Evil.'

Treats motions after the man, as if to wave him away. 'I'm doing him a favour!' he says. 'And he's calling me evil!' A pool of water is forming at his feet. He shakes his head vigorously; water from his hair splatters onto the brick walls.

Paul feels a tightness take hold of his throat. He must not cry in front of this man. Instead, he coughs. He looks hard at Treats, coughs again.

'Oh gosh, I forgot to give you something to drink!' Treats says. He goes outside, comes back with a Styrofoam cup filled with something. He kneels in front of Paul, sets the cup on the ground. 'Hold on,' he says again. He goes to the pile, finds the Stanley knife, comes back. Paul tries to stay still, tries to keep his eyes closed; his heart doesn't feel normal at all, it's beating and bubbling like a waterfall.

'Hold still,' Treats warns again. He jabs with the point of the knife. 'You ready?' There's a sharp yank. Paul's skin feels like it's burning where the duct-tape has come off. Another yank, and another, and another. Out of nowhere, tears appear in his eyes, stream down his cheeks. 'Be brave, be brave!' Treats says. He carefully picks up the Styrofoam cup and lifts it to Paul's lips. Paul drinks slowly, but the man is impatient, he tips it up faster than Paul can drink; it begins to dribble out the sides. 'Come on, I thought you were thirsty!' the man says. He laughs, pours the rest of the water over Paul's head.

'You want food?' Treats asks. 'You want a sandwich or something?'

Paul stares back at him, unsure what to say. All this time, he has been planning the words he will say. 'Hey, fellas!' He was going to say it in a relaxed and light-hearted way. But he cannot say 'Hey, fellas!' now. He's still thinking of the man in the blue shortpants: just a few minutes ago, the man was in the doorway, and he would have helped if he could. Another opportunity gone! How many more will there be? Treats taps him gently on the cheek, first on one cheek, then he lifts the other hand and taps the other cheek, quickly: tap-tap-tap-tap-tap-tap.

'Yes or no?' Treats says. 'Which one?'

Paul shakes his head.

'OK, then,' Treats says.

———

The gold-tooth one, Robert, is squatting in front of Paul. 'Hello.' The man pats him roughly on the cheek. 'Hello. Wake up. Who are you?'

Paul opens his eyes. It is daytime again. He is not sure how much time has passed. He looks straight into the man's eyes, trying to summon the energy to answer the right thing back. To smirk, maybe, and say, 'What, all this way you brought me, and you don't even know who I am?' Or: 'Why do you ask?' Something casual, something to throw the man off balance and create an opening. But his mind isn't working properly at all: it feels murky, swampy, like the lights have been switched off. The man's eyes are not crazy or evil, only focused on his job, whatever it is. A good man for the job. He would be a good government minister, somebody who could negotiate with the oil companies, a man who won't back down. His hair is very short, the hairline making a straight edge, neatly clipped. His body made of muscle. This man doesn't care about him one way or the other. 'Hey, fellas!' will not work.

'Which one are you? Are you Peter?'

Behind him, Treats says, 'They have two, one bright and one dense. The bright one was the short-haired one, definitely.' He says it like defin-ite-ly.

Robert grips Paul's chin and gives a little shake. 'Hello! Speak!'

Paul closes his eyes, confused. *You could talk? He could talk? He can't talk?* What should he say? Should he say he is Peter, or that he is not Peter? Robert slaps his cheek again.

Robert winces as he straightens up, holding his knees. He must be old, older than Daddy, even though his body is so muscly. He looks like he might be one of those men who run for exercise: you see them sometimes running along roads in shortpants and sneakers, sweat running off them like rivers. The two men stand right there next to him, talking; Paul hears Uncle Romesh's name. The men talk and talk: ten per cent, five per cent, long hair, short hair, bright one, dense one, right one, wrong one. The sun is coming in the window and shining right on him. The inside of his mouth doesn't feel like his mouth at all; it feels like a sponge that's been left out in the sun and has dried into something hard as stone. The duct-tape is off now: he could swallow, try to speak, ask for water. But he doesn't want to speak any more. The two men talking seem blurry, far away. He doesn't want to say, 'Hey, fellas!' He doesn't want to say anything, or speak to anybody. He shifts along the cardboard, trying to get out of the sun. He feels the cardboard growing soggy, warm, underneath him and he doesn't care.

'Oh gyad,' the men say. They screw up their faces, fan their noses, go outside.

———

Treats is walking towards him, a paper plate in his hand. He's still wet from the sea, sand clinging to his feet like grains of sugar.

'You want macaroni pie? I hearing your belly growling.'

Paul nods.

'Why you don't talk?' Treats asks. 'You frightened? Sometimes people is get frightened. I understand. It's frightening.' He nods, understanding but unworried too, getting a forkful of food from the plate. 'Robert forgot to bring ketchup. He brought the food from the boss's house today, but he only brought this, and he forgot the ketchup! I like my macaroni pie with ketchup.' He smiles widely. 'It's better with ketchup, eh? That's how you like it too?'

Paul nearly nods – the words are so normal, and actually, yes, macaroni pie is best with ketchup. Everyone can agree on that. But he stops himself and watches the man warily.

'You so frightened!' the man says. He laughs; he's having a good time. He holds the fork laden with macaroni pie in front of Paul's mouth. 'Here comes the aeroplane,' he says. Paul hesitates. The man might do anything with that fork: he could jab it in Paul's eyes, up his nose, scratch it across his face. The man is still smiling at him. His eyes are red-tinted behind the brown; his teeth are amazingly white: perfect teeth like the Americans on *The Young and the Restless*. The man wiggles the fork around. 'Here comes the aeroplane! You not hungry? If you not hungry, I wouldn't bother giving you food, you know.'

Paul opens his mouth and keeps a close watch on the man as he bites the food off.

———

There's a faint, sweet smell of weed from somewhere outside. The sun is coming through the gap in the roof and blazing on him. Paul gets to his feet, steps off the cardboard, stoops to the ground and manages to get hold of an edge. He props it up a foot or so from the wall, sits down behind it, and tries to angle it to give him some shelter from the sun. As soon as he lets go, it slips down, skates a few inches away. He picks it up again, tries to rest it against the wall like a tent, but it's too soft: it just collapses to the ground. He lies on the ground, pulls the cardboard over him like a sheet. The cardboard rests on his right eye, the bad one. He turns his head the other way, to take the pressure off. He breathes.

He hears footsteps outside. He closes his eyes, pretends to be asleep. Someone lifts the cardboard off: Treats. The other man, Robert, is the one who comes and goes; Treats stays here, swimming, smoking, lazing around.

'You were hot?' Treats asks, now, holding the cardboard.

The sun has moved a few inches to the side, but it's still right there, above Treats's head. Paul closes his eyes.

'Hello, I'm talking to you.' Treats nudges him with his foot. 'The sun was coming in?'

Paul nods. He sits up, leans against the wall.

'That's OK. So long as you don't try any tricks.' Treats is in a quiet, relaxed mood after the weed. He smiles widely at Paul. 'Easy peasy! Just do what we tell you to do, and everything will be *aw-aw-right*.' He sings the last bit, like the Bob Marley song.

Paul coughs. This is how he's been asking for water: he doesn't know exactly why he doesn't just say, 'Can I have some water, please.' He doesn't feel like talking. He doesn't feel like saying 'Hey, fellas!' or saying what his name is, who he is and who he isn't, or discussing how much money Daddy really has in the bank account, or whether Romesh 'Hotsauce' Ramcharan might be lying or not; he doesn't want any of that. He just wants water.

'Oh, you thirsty? You should have said. Hold on.' Treats goes outside and comes back with a Styrofoam cup of water. He kneels down next to Paul and holds it to his lips. 'Here,' he says.

Paul drinks, trying not to mind how close the man is, the black hair sticking out of his cheeks and chin, raggedy; the smell of him, the smooth, dark skin stretched taut over his muscles.

'There,' says Treats, grinning. 'Feel better?'

Paul nods again, cautiously. Treats's face is close. He comes closer, so his nose is almost touching, and opens his eyes wide, like a child might do if pressing his face to a mirror, or to a glass pane at the zoo. 'BOO!' he says, and he laughs. Inside his mouth, Paul sees the silvery strings of saliva stretching between his jaws.

Treats looks at him again. Paul wants to close his eyes, but he feels as if Treats is studying him with some idea in mind.

'You don't talk much,' Treats says.

Treats stands up, and Paul's heart begins to pound, because he seems to have some purpose. He looks through the hole in the wall, and then, satisfied, unbuttons and unzips his pants and withdraws his penis, greyish-black, flaky with dry skin. A mild whiff of urine. The man fixes his eyes on him intently, and manipulates his penis gently, with practised care. It is horrible, horrible; he is so full of revulsion that no words come to mind, only short, sharp breaths and a pounding in his chest. He closes his eyes but he can still hear the gentle stroking rhythmic movements of the man's hand. Then the man steps one foot over his legs, so that he is straddling him, and bends his knees to a half-stoop, and pushes his penis towards Paul's face. Paul turns his head away; the penis, hard, nudges his cheek.

'You ever taste some of this?' the man says. His voice is secretive. 'Open your mouth,' he says. Paul, eyes shut tightly, head turned away, shakes his head. 'Come, open, open.' The penis thrusts itself about Paul's face.

Treats steupses at him in irritation, works his hand up and down the shaft. Then he holds Paul's head with both hands, his thumbs digging between his jaws, like how you get a dog to open its mouth for medicine. 'Come, give me a little suck-down and I'll let you go. Robert not here. I'll tell him the man came back and helped you run away. Promise.'

The penis presses against his closed lips. Will he really let him go? He imagines himself walking down the road in the bright midday sun. His lips part. Treats gives instructions. Do like so and like so. Treats moves his hands from Paul's head to the wall behind, to keep himself balanced.

When they let him go, when he walks down the road in the midday sunshine, he will find somewhere, first, to rest. He will not go home. Mummy and Daddy will not want to see him; he doesn't want to see them. He doesn't want to see Peter, doesn't want to see Marc Aboud, doesn't want to see Candace. Father Kavanagh, perhaps. Paul knows, deep down, that it will never happen, but he allows himself to imagine it: how he will go to Father Kavanagh, knock on his door, and say, please may I rest here for a while. And his voice will be weak but he will not have to explain anything, where he has been or what he has done, and Father Kavanagh will just look at him and know everything and understand. He pictures Father Kavanagh standing by the door to the chapel and gesturing to it as if it were his own home. *Come*, he will say. *Rest here. You are welcome here.* Paul imagines himself lying on the smooth, cool tiles of the chapel floor, the sad faces of the saints in the stained glass windows above him, and allowing his eyes to fall closed for a little while.

18

Peter, sitting in the passenger seat, directs him – just with a terse, 'Left, here,' or 'Straight, straight' – but Father Kavanagh remembers the boys' cheerful chatter from the last time he drove to Tiparo in the rain. There is the tree where they wait for the maxi taxi in the morning; there is the blue-painted shop where they used to buy ice-lollies until the shop opened in the gas station; there is the old bus shelter where the vagrant sleeps, the rusting galvanise sheets scratched with children's names, and papered with signs announcing fetes, political meetings. And here is the turn-off to their little lane, the tarmac road cracked and potholed, weeds sprouting up in the cracks, the wooden telegraph pole leaning precariously, the wires pulled taut. The bush is so overgrown that from here it looks almost like a path into a forest than a road. He drives in cautiously and parks on the road just past their gate. If it weren't for the way the dogs bark, looking over their shoulders towards the house, he would think that there was no one at home.

There is a twitch of the curtain; then, after a minute or two, he hears a key turning in the lock of a door, and Clyde appears on the patio. He comes down the steps and picks his way, barefoot, along the drive, unshaven, unwashed, squinting up at the bright sky. He scowls at Peter.

'I said to stay in Port of Spain.'

Peter walks briskly past his father, ignoring the dogs trotting beside him. Father Kavanagh follows slowly. On the patio, bristling trails of ants surround the half-empty glasses left on the coffee table; ashes and cigarette stubs are scattered around the floor.

In the living room, Joy gets up, straightens her clothes. 'Hi, Father Kavanagh,' she says. 'You want a drink? A coffee?'

He shakes his head. He fights the urge to take her hand and say that he is sorry for her troubles; to ask where Paul is, whether he is OK, and what has been done to bring him home; instead, he presses his lips together, looks around for somewhere to sit.

'I apologise for all this,' Clyde is saying, looking around the room. 'We had a break-in not long ago and we haven't had time to get new furniture yet.'

Joy sits on the sofa, the end nearest to Clyde; Father Kavanagh sits at the other end, by the window.

'How much do they want?' Peter asks.

'Two hundred and fifty thousand,' Joy says.

Peter pulls out a dining chair roughly and swings it around to draw it up next to Clyde's armchair. He sits, folds his arms. 'Are you going to pay it?'

Clyde takes his time sitting down. 'How was the traffic coming down here?' he asks Father Kavanagh.

Peter stares at Clyde. 'How much is in the bank account?'

'I am dealing with this,' Clyde says. 'You worry about packing your bags. Make sure you take all the books you need for the next few days.'

'Tell me how much. I know where the bank statements are. If you don't tell me, I'll just go and look at them myself.'

Clyde rests his cigarette in his ashtray. He sits back, looks steadily towards the window.

Peter turns to Joy. 'Somebody, speak! How much is in it?'

'Uncle Romesh had something to do with it,' Joy says.

'He didn't just have something to do with it,' Clyde says. 'He set it up. I guarantee you.'

They all speak at once; Father Kavanagh, silent, sits up straight, his hands curled into fists resting on his knees. It is too complicated for him to follow it all, all the names and incidents they mention. The last time he was here, during the rainstorm, the small light of the candle seemed to draw them all together; now he feels as if he is watching the family being flung apart, all catapulting off in their different directions. Joy is still trying to defend this Uncle Romesh, saying that he will not let anything bad happen, repeating again and again that he is her brother, her family; Peter is on his feet, shouting, the veins bulging on his neck; Clyde says little, only drums his fingertips against his arm-rest, sitting on his throne behind a haze of smoke.

'You haven't answered me about the money,' Peter says. 'How much is in the bank account in England?'

'There's enough money,' says Joy. 'All morning I've been trying to tell Clyde to phone up the bank in England and get them to issue a bank draft for us. But he won't do it.'

'Why not?' Peter asks. He turns to Clyde. 'Why not?'

'You know why.'

'No, I don't. Why?'

Clyde grinds his cigarette into his ashtray, his composure vanished. 'Why do you think?' he says. 'Why do you think? Because the money is for you!'

'I don't want it.'

'And you think that's for you to decide?' Clyde's hands are trembling. 'You're such a big-man now that it's up to you to decide these things?' His hands go up, gesturing angrily in the air. 'This is not for you to decide!'

'I don't want it. I won't use it.'

'You say that now, but trust me, when the time comes, you will want that money.'

'I won't.'

'And how are you going to go away? How will you get out of here, when you're eighteen?'

'I'll find a way.'

'Is that so? Tell me what way you're going to find. I'm curious to hear it.' He pauses, glaring at Peter, and then goes on. 'Because, I can tell you now, if you have no plan, you'll never get anywhere. Fail to plan, plan to fail! You ever heard that? If you have no plan, you could forget it. Years now I've been planning this. Years. You think you could just ups and decide, oh, I want to emigrate, and the doors will open for you just because your name is Peter Dey-alsingh? The world doesn't work like that, I'm sorry to tell you.'

'I'll win the Gold Medal,' Peter says.

Clyde makes a little laugh. 'Is that so? And you don't know how many boys around Trinidad want the same thing?'

'I'll win it,' Peter says. He's standing in front of the window, looking straight at Clyde, unflinching, like a man. 'So I won't need the money. That's the reason I came with Father Kavanagh. I came to tell you that.'

They all wait. 'You standing here with all your big-talk,' Clyde says, when he speaks. 'You-all think you understand, but in reality, you don't understand. Even if you win – which, I grant you, you may well do – I still have to pay your first year's fees, you realise that? I have to pay it up front. You won't get the visa to go to the US unless you can show them a bank statement with money in it. If you win, the money will get paid back. But for you to leave this country? For you to get the visa, and get on the plane, and for US immigration to let you in? That money needs to be in the bank account. If there's no money, then Gold Medal or no Gold Medal, you're not going anywhere.'

'Clyde won't touch the money in England,' Joy says, hopelessly. 'I already tried saying the same thing. You could talk until you're blue in the face, but he won't use it.' Her nose reddens, she starts to cry. 'Excuse me,' she says. Father Kavanagh looks down at his knees. Joy pushes herself up from the sofa and walks past Clyde's chair, past the dining table and through the archway to the kitchen.

Clyde sits back, crosses one leg over the other, looks out the window. Father Kavanagh moves his eyes to the ashtray on the coffee table, where a cigarette has burned down to the end, leaving a soft cylinder of ash. Peter stares at Clyde; Clyde stares past him, out the window. In another few moments, Father Kavanagh thinks, they will both be on their feet, their hands at each other's throats. But as the seconds tick by, Peter's expression loses its certainty. Father Kavanagh straightens up; he has only one thing to say, when his turn comes, should there be an opportunity for him to speak. *Paul*, he wants to say. *What about Paul?* But Clyde holds up a hand to Father Kavanagh, as if to tell him to be quiet. 'I am telling you, leave this to me,' he says, to Peter. 'I will do everything I can.' Peter leaves the room quietly, and shortly after, they hear him go into his room and close the door behind him.

Clyde scowls at the window. He picks up his box of cigarettes, shakes it, rests it on the seat next to him. He crosses one leg over the other, taps his fingers on the arm-rest of the chair. His eyes flick to Father Kavanagh. 'I'm not just going to sit here all day, if that's what you're thinking,' Clyde says. 'You're looking at me like you think I'm just going to sit here all day and do nothing. I'm not going to do nothing. I'm going to do something.'

'What are you going to do?' Father Kavanagh asks.

'Once Joy and Peter leave, I'll get to work. I have a lot of people I have to see.'

'If there's anyone you'd like us to put you in touch with,' he says. 'Father Malachy asked me to mention to you. In case it might be of any help. There are many people who would be willing to help you.'

'You see,' Clyde says, the scowl coming over his face again like a cloud, 'this is why I didn't want people to come here. Because everybody wants to give me advice. Everybody so busy giving me advice!'

'Not advice,' Father Kavanagh says, quickly. He thinks of 'help', but 'help' is even worse than 'advice'.

'I didn't ask for your advice!' Clyde says. 'Look, I know why you're really here. You're here to tell me what you think I should do. Aren't you? Isn't that why you're here?'

'I'm here because you asked me to come. And because Paul is somewhere out there, all alone, and I want to help. I'm sorry if that offends you,' Father Kavanagh says simply.

'You want to tell me who I should speak to,' Clyde itemises on his fingers, 'who I should speak to, who I should borrow money from, who I should ask to negotiate for me. Not so?'

'No.'

'Let me explain to you,' Clyde says. 'Because I know you're sitting there judging me. Let me explain how things work in this country. What people will tell me to do in this situation is to identify who it is, which gang-leader or drug-lord or whoever it is.

They have different divisions to these things. And then you have to find who inside the police force is close to them, who could negotiate on your behalf. I say "negotiate", but what I mean is, the gang will take some, and the policeman will take some, and they share it out between them, and if you're lucky, you get your child back in one piece. Maybe. Nothing is guaranteed.

'The problem is,' Clyde continues, 'everybody will want a cut. Say you're lucky, and you get the child back. You might think, hurrah, problem solved! But let me tell you something. Problem not solved. After a little while – and it might be a week, a month, a year, who knows – after a while, all kind of collateral people will come out of the woodwork. Somebody who saw him, or saw the kidnappers, or who has information about the kidnappers – they will then go to someone else in the police force with that information, and they will want some money to stay hushed up, you see. So before you know it, you'll be in another situation – another kidnapping, or another break-in, or worse, and round and round it goes.'

Clyde glances over his shoulder, where Joy and Peter are standing in the kitchen doorway. He sits back, lights another cigarette, sucks hard on it, lets out a long, slow breath, all smoke.

'You see me?' Clyde says. 'All my years in Trinidad, I tried to stay out of this kind of trouble – to stay away from troublemakers, to not get tangled up in anything. I never wanted fancy cars, a big house, trips to Miami, London, Niagara Falls. I was just trying to live my life. Just to live a decent life. That's all. But you see this country? It's impossible to live a decent life in this country.'

'You're a decent man,' Father Kavanagh says. 'Don't—'

Clyde cuts him off, a hand raised. 'Stop. Just stop. You're trying all kinds of tactics, don't think I don't see it.'

'What tactics?'

'Tactics! Look, I've already made up my mind. With the money in England, I made up my mind about that long-time ago. I said, that money is for Peter. I said to myself, I said, nobody, no matter who they are and what they want it for, nobody on this earth is getting that money except Peter. And don't think that you, just because of who you are, that you're going to convince me of anything.'

'But Clyde, money comes and goes. Other things, once they're gone, will never be brought back. That's what you might have to live with. That's a heavy burden to live with.'

'You're talking to me about heavy burden?' Clyde says. 'You don't even know what a heavy burden feels like, Father. I could tell you what a heavy burden feels like. I already know.' He is pointing at his chest. 'So you leave it to me to decide whether I can carry it or not. Eh? Don't tell me what to do.' He stabs at his chest. 'I know. I know what I have to do.'

19

It is nearly five o'clock by the time Father Kavanagh sets off for Port of Spain with Joy and Peter. After they have gone, Clyde locks up the house, gets into his car and reverses out onto the Trace. A few boys are liming in the road by the gas station, sitting on the pavement edge, or on the broken-down brick wall; one or two stand up to get a better look at him as he drives by. A mile or so down the road, with a field of buffalo on one side and an overgrown, untended stretch of land on the other, he notices a section of iron pipe laying by the side of the road. He gets out to look: the pipe is not even rusted, three feet long, an inch and a half diameter; the size of a stick-fighter's stick, the kind of stick a man should always have to hand. He brushes the dirt off, puts it in the footwell of the passenger seat.

He drives to San Juan, an hour's drive in the rush hour traffic, to the place where a man named Desmond Maharaj works. At the desk, the secretary is sorting through a pile of receipts and writing tiny, neat numbers into the little blue-edged squares of the ledger.

'Is the boss upstairs?' Clyde asks.

'Who are you?'

'Tell him it's Deyalsingh from La Sagesse,' he says. 'He's upstairs?'

She organises the receipts into a pile and clips them with a paperclip, closes the ledger book on them. 'Hold on,' she says. 'I'll go and check.' She gets up and opens a door in the wall behind the desk, and Clyde hears her footsteps clumping up the staircase.

Heavy footsteps come down the stairs, and Mr Maharaj appears in the doorway. His skin is pale for an Indian man, the colouring of someone who spends most of his time inside an office, and pockmarked all over his face with acne. He has thick hair, the type that sticks straight up from his scalp. 'You're busy?' Clyde asks, as they shake hands.

'Always busy!' Mr Maharaj says. 'Come,' he says, leading the way up the stairs. 'We'll go in my office and talk.'

Upstairs, there's a grey office carpet, with yellowed blinds over the window, and a rickety kitchenette in the corner with a sink and kettle and a little fridge. Mr Maharaj gets him a glass of water from the sink and puts it on the desk in front of Clyde.

'So,' Mr Maharaj says, sitting down. He has a CEO-type chair, one of the ones that spins round. 'I heard about your problems. You know who's behind it? You have somebody negotiating for you?'

Clyde drinks all the water, sets the glass down. Mr Maharaj watches him across the desk; in between puffs of his cigarette, he works a fingernail at a pimple on his chin, or at the side of his mouth.

'Come, tell me,' Mr Maharaj says. 'What can I do for you? You're looking to borrow some money?'

'No. I don't borrow what I can't pay back. I want to sell the house.'

'You mean your father's house, there on La Sagesse?'

'That is the only house I have.'

'I remember the location. It has an empty space next to it, not so?'

'That's right.'

'And that's the one that has only bush on the other side, and the mountains going up behind, right?'

[231]

'Yea.'

'People not very fond of that location,' Mr Maharaj says. 'Because of bandits passing through there.'

'Well, look, you tell me. You interested or not?' He mentions the names of other men who have expressed interest in the past: three, four names, all wealthy men.

'I'm not saying I'm not interested,' Mr Maharaj says. 'I'm only stating a fact, that people don't find that a desirable location.'

Clyde taps his fingertips on the desk.

'How long you have to get the money?' Mr Maharaj asks.

'They haven't said,' Clyde says. He reaches for his box of cigarettes in his pocket: empty. 'Who knows with these people?'

Mr Maharaj slides his box of Marlboros across the desk to him. 'Take, take,' he says. 'Take all.'

'How much could you get me by tomorrow?' Clyde asks.

'Tomorrow?'

'Tomorrow. How much?'

'In cash?'

'Yea.'

'In cash, the most I could get you tomorrow would be forty thousand. I can get you some more, another forty thousand, but I have to get it from Miami, it will be at least a week, maybe ten days.'

Only forty thousand? The kidnappers have asked for two hundred and fifty thousand. He didn't think he could get as much as that together – but he was hoping to get at least half of it, somehow. Forty is not much at all. 'You can't make it a bit more? The house is worth at least eighty.'

'It might be worth eighty, boy, but you want cash, and you want it today, and I don't even know if you have any kind of paperwork to prove the house is yours in the first place.'

[232]

'Boy, I have the Deed, don't worry about that.'

'OK.' Mr Maharaj sits up straight, rests his forearms on the desk. 'It's up to you. I can give you forty tomorrow if you want it.'

Clyde screws up his face. 'Forty? You can't make it forty-five, or fifty?'

'Look,' Mr Maharaj says. 'Normally this is not how I buy houses, you know! Normally I have lawyers and all kind of thing. I'm trying to help you, because of the situation you're in. I doing this as a favour.' Clyde opens his mouth to say something, and Mr Maharaj says, hastily, 'I know, I know, you don't want any favours. It's not a favour.'

Clyde puts his elbows on his knees, rubs his face with his hands. Mr Maharaj goes to the kitchen in the corner and comes back with something wrapped up in tinfoil. 'Look a chicken sandwich,' he says. 'Take it to eat in the car.' When Clyde still doesn't speak, he says, 'Go and think about it. But if you want the forty tomorrow, you need to ring me this evening, so I could go to the bank first thing tomorrow. I wouldn't send anybody: I'll go myself. OK? Give me a call when you decide.'

'It's all right,' Clyde says. He stands up and reaches a hand over the desk. 'I decided.'

'OK,' Mr Maharaj says. 'OK.' He's smiling like he's happy to make the deal, but Clyde doesn't smile back, and then Mr Maharaj stops smiling too. They discuss the remaining details standing up, turned towards the door.

'Deyalsingh,' Mr Maharaj says, at the top of the stairs, as they're about to part ways. 'You don't have to rush to leave the house, eh? Take your time. Take all the time you need.'

———

'I know who you're working for,' Clyde tells the man from Caroni, when he phones that evening. 'But who are you?'

'You could call me Six,' the man says.

'Six? Six what?'

'Six. Just Six, man.'

'What kind of name is that? You don't have a proper name?'

'Hello,' the man named Six says. 'Don't make me vex here. You're not in charge. I'm in charge.'

'I can't raise all that money,' Clyde says. He keeps his tone businesslike. 'I just can't raise it. I'll bring you what I can. OK? I sold my house, I'm going to sell my car. I'll empty my account in Republic Bank. That will bring it to about fifty or sixty thousand. I'll have it for you hopefully tomorrow, or the next few days. These things take time.'

'Fifty? Like you think this is joke or something?' the man says. 'You need to bring us the full amount. *Two*-fifty, man, not fifty.'

'I don't have it, that's what I keep telling you,' Clyde says.

'That's not what your brother-in-law is saying. So which one is lying, you or him?'

'Well, it must be him,' Clyde says, 'because it's not me.'

The man steupses. 'You think this is a joke?'

The next few days are a blur. One morning, when he gets up, he eats a slice of bread from the loaf; in the evening, when he comes back, there are only crumbs left, the plastic bag full of holes, puddles of bird-mess on the counter. One day he showers; another day he only wets his hands and rubs them across his face. One day he remembers to give the dogs water; another day he forgets. Some evenings, he sits on his back-step for a while, smoking a cigarette; other evenings, he lies on his bed and wills himself to go to sleep.

But they are not all the same days. Three days go by, maybe four. Every day, he drives by Romesh's house, looks at the locked doors, the empty carport, the dogs patrolling the fence. He drives by Rachel's father's house, the one that, at Christmas-time, is covered with lights. He rattles the gate, calls out to ask if Romesh is there, but whoever comes to the gate – they always send the women, one of Rachel's sisters, or Rachel's mother – says that no, Romesh is not there, and neither is Rachel. On the third or fourth day that Clyde visits, the woman tells him that Rachel and Romesh have gone on a little holiday. 'Is that so?' he asks. 'Where to?' And the woman – a good-looking woman, her hair styled, and wearing eyeshadow and lipstick – thinks for a moment before she replies that they have gone to the States. 'Why you don't just tell me that they're too frightened to speak to me?' Clyde says. 'You think I look like I'm going to break down your gate and come in and kill somebody?' The woman doesn't bother to try to keep going with her lie. 'If I wanted to break down the gate and kill some-body,' Clyde says, 'I would have done it already. I just want to speak to him. So many years we've known each other, I thought he would at least speak to me.' The woman looks embarrassed. 'Well,' Clyde says, walking away. 'He knows where I am.'

During the daytime hours, he is busy driving up and down Trinidad. He goes to Republic Bank in Port of Spain to empty his account – he has to take the money in four separate visits, for security, although each time they pack the money into a suitcase, which, Clyde thinks, is a dead giveaway to anyone who might want to steal from him. He goes to an autodealer to agree a price for his car; to the furniture store in Arima to sell the fridge, the freezer, the stove, the dining table and chairs. He goes to Des-mond Maharaj's house and reverses into his driveway, and puts two sacks full of cash into the trunk of his car. Mr Maharaj invites him to come in and eat something, or at least have a cold drink; when Clyde declines, Mr Maharaj tells his wife to get some food for Clyde to carry with him, and she goes into her house and comes back out with an ice-cream container crammed with rice, curry and coleslaw, and a clear sandwich bag filled with Indian sweets, and another one filled with plums. She opens the car door and puts the food on the passenger seat. Maybe she notices the iron pole, because she closes the car door and quickly goes back to the house and doesn't come out again.

In the evenings, back in his own house, Clyde waits for the man Six to call and, every time, he says that he is raising as much money as he can, and that there is no other money, that there must have been some misunderstanding, but there is definitely no other money.

'OK, here's the plan,' the man named Six says. 'Take what you have to your brother-in-law, and he will bring it to us.'

'He hasn't been home,' Clyde says. 'He's hiding from me.'

The man phones him back to confirm. 'Take it by him in the morning. To the house on Hibiscus Drive, or whatever it's called.'

'Bougainvillea Avenue.'

'Right. Bougainvillea Avenue. Take it there. Everything's arranged.'

'I hope he's not going to pull out a gun on me or something,' Clyde says. 'You-all setting me up here, or something?'

'No, no,' the man says. 'At least, I don't think so. Don't worry about that,' he says. 'We will deal with him. You just bring the money.'

The next morning, Clyde hauls the sacks into the car and drives the half-mile to Romesh's house. The Alsatians are locked up in the dog-house in the back. He opens the trunk, gets the sacks out onto the ground; he had no idea money would be so heavy. Romesh appears in the doorway, just in his shorts, no shirt. He stands in the doorway, holding the sides of the doorframe. His eyes go to the rice-sacks, and then to the neighbour's patio, where the pilot's mother-in-law is watching them, her nipples visible through her thin nightie. She quickly goes back into her house, and they hear her door being quietly closed, and then locked. Clyde drags the sacks in.

At the bottom of the steps, he takes a sack in each hand, and comes up, his muscles straining. At the top, he rests the sacks on the floor. The recreation ground is empty: it's mid-morning, the men at work, the children at school. Clyde leaves the sacks where they are and walks into the living room. The place looks just the same as before, nothing has moved since Clyde was here a few nights ago.

'Where are you?' Clyde calls. Cautiously, he walks over the glossy tiled floor, past the huge dining table to the kitchen. Romesh is by the back door, as if readying himself to run away.

'Anybody else here?' Clyde asks. 'Rachel home?'

'No.'

'Sayeed's at school?'

'Yea.'

'I told the man Six how much there is,' Clyde says. 'So don't thief any. They know how much is supposed to arrive.' They stare at each other. Romesh takes a step back. 'What per cent they giving you, boy?' Clyde asks. He moves towards Romesh. 'Eh? Five per cent? Ten per cent? You don't feel ashamed of yourself?'

'Clyde, you need to give them the full amount.' Romesh's voice is scared.

'You frighten now?' Clyde asks. 'It's only now you're realising things serious?' Romesh's eyes are big, like a child's. 'You thought you would get your bit of money, and then everything would come back like normal? That's what you thought? Eh?'

'Things got kind of muddled up,' Romesh says, finally.

Clyde needs to get out of here before he loses his temper. There are implements all around that might find themselves in his hand: knives, scissors, screwdrivers. Clyde turns, begins to walk away.

'Clyde,' Romesh calls from the back door. 'I'm not joking. You need to get the full amount for them.'

'Tell them that's all they're getting. Tell them to let him go. You think you could do that?'

'But Clyde, what about all Uncle Vishnu's money? Give them that.'

'It's not Uncle Vishnu's money,' Clyde says. 'It's not my money, or your money, or anyone else's money. It's Peter's money.'

He parks his car at the gas station and gives the keys to the shopkeeper for the autodealer to collect later. Then he walks home along the Trace, the melting tarmac sticking to the soles of his shoes. Now that the cash has been handed over, all the transactions completed, he feels exhausted. The dogs crawl out from under the house, wagging their tails, shaking the dust off their coats. Slowly, he climbs the steps to the patio. Inside, he has to fight an urge to lie down. Better to keep moving: keep moving, don't stop, don't think, don't weaken, don't think about what might happen if the money is not enough. He goes to each room in turn, shutting windows, switching off lights. He slides the shoebox from the high shelf of his cupboard, takes out the documents he needs to keep: all the birth certificates, his marriage licence, the bank statements from Barclays Bank in London, Peter's award certificates from St Saviour's; all the death certificates he has accumulated, for his father, Uncle Vishnu, Mousey. He holds the thick, creamy paper in his hands, runs his thumb over the raised edges of the registrar's seal. One day, he thinks, someone will hold a similar piece of paper in their hands, and his name will be written on it. The room is spinning; he should lie down. But if he lies down, he will think; and if he thinks, he might change his mind; and he must, above all things, not change his mind. He slides the documents into a plastic bag. He takes a few clothes, his toothbrush, his razor. He forgets to close the cupboard doors behind him; they hang open, clothes lie crumpled on the floor.

Outside, he calls the dogs, unbuckles their collars. He moves the old cupboard door away from the gap in the fence behind the coconut tree. He leaves a full bowl of water for them under the steps in the shade.

There is nothing else to do now but sit in his armchair waiting for the phone to ring. Maybe the money will be enough; sometimes these kidnappers just take whatever they're given and let the person go. But every time he thinks it, he also thinks: but maybe they won't. Maybe, maybe not, maybe, maybe not. His mind goes round and round in circles, confused. He cannot understand how he got to this point. He is quite sure that back at the beginning, when the boys were born, he was determined, above all else, to be a good father. Now, somehow, he has ended up here, and there seems to be no way back.

'Deyalsingh,' the man named Six says, when he rings. 'You only sent us this little amount of money.'

'That's all I have, man. I have nothing left. Let the boy go. It's plenty money.'

The man steupses. It sounds like he's scratching his head.

'It's plenty,' Clyde says. 'Seventy-five thousand dollars? That's a fortune! Let him go. You haven't harmed him, right? Let him go. You don't have to bring him anywhere, just let him go, he will find his own way back.' He waits but there is no answer. 'Eh? What you say?'

'I have to see what the boss says.'

'I had to sell my house,' Clyde says. 'I have no house. I'm going up to Port of Spain. You could reach me through the priests.' He waits. 'OK? So when you let him go, you'll call me there and tell me?'

'I don't know, man,' the man says. 'I have to talk to the boss.' The man sighs and hangs up.

Clyde slides his feet back into his slippers, picks up his plastic bags. He locks the patio door, puts the key up on the top breeze-block brick for Paul, in case he comes back.

In the front yard, he looks around for the dogs, calls their names, but they do not come. He closes the gate behind him, and sets off along the Trace towards the gas station. At the tree where the maxi taxi comes, the vagrant is sitting on a tree-root scooping out the insides of a breadfruit. He fixes his eyes on Clyde as he walks past. A car drives by, slows down; the driver studies him in the rearview mirror before he drives on. It must be coming up to four o'clock: the shadow cast on the tarmac is the same size as his body, the same shape. As he walks along, one mile, two miles, the sun lowers, his shadow lengthens. He is glad when he reaches the bend in the road, and the shadow disappears.

20

In the half-built house by the sea, different things have come and gone each day. First there was the ice-cooler, the Crix cardboard box, jaliter bottles of soft drinks, newspapers, a pack of cards; other days, there were sheets, towels, rolls of toilet paper. One day there was a grey bucket; another day it was gone. Most days, there has been food: things bought from food vendors, wrapped in tinfoil or greaseproof paper; sandwiches in cling film; cooked food in Styrofoam boxes: barbecued chicken drumsticks, pork ribs. But today is different. All morning, the men have been clearing out, taking up armloads of stuff and trudging back to the car. They haven't spoken to him; they haven't offered him water; they haven't looked at him very much at all.

Now, laid on the floor against the wall of the house, there are garbage bags, horse-feed sacks, duct-tape, a dull-black handgun and a stack of dusty reddish bricks. With tools like these, there will only be the happy picture, the 'before', if Mummy and Daddy can find one. He wants it to happen soon; it is terrible to lie here and wait for it to happen. He knows it will be quick: the man Robert promised him. Earlier, Treats picked up the gun and pointed it at him and said, like it was a game, 'Pow! Pow! Pow!' Paul screamed – he screamed a lot, and they covered his mouth with duct-tape again – and the man Robert told Treats to stop playing the fool. And then Robert touched him on the shoulder and said that it would be just one shot, and that it would be quick.

When they drag him outside, he tries not to listen and not to look, but he still hears them talk, about where to put him to make the least mess. They take him down to the beach, down close to the water where the blood will seep away and disappear. He closes his eyes and listens to the waves and the sound of the wind in the trees. He tries not to think about where they all are, and what they're all doing – Daddy, Mummy, Peter, Father Kavanagh; he tries not to think about how mad Daddy will be when he hears that Paul couldn't look after himself, that he failed in this, his first task as a grown-up – as a sort of grown-up. Robert said he would make it quick, but this is very slow. Very, very slow. Very, very, very slow. This is going on forever. He tries to stay calm, and to trust that the man Robert will make it quick like he promised. He listens to the sound of the waves, to the water that is waiting for him. And he can't say why, but he thinks that maybe this water really does care about him, that this water wants to take him in its arms; and, either way, it is beautiful water and if he has to end up somewhere then it may as well be there.

21

They are at the airport: the old airport, the one with the waving gallery upstairs and the big breeze-block hall downstairs. It is the sort of place that should be bright and airy, but it is not. The walls are painted a lifeless green, their lower flanks soiled by years of greasy hands, sweaty backs, sticky patches of spilt sweet-drink, the fluorescent yellow of curry stains. The lights, fixed to the iron bars of the roof thirty or so feet above them, have just flickered on a few minutes ago, but it was better before, in the dim twilight. Peter, standing quietly next to his mother, thinks that he has never seen her look so tired, so old. Under the electric light, the dark smudges under her eyes look like bruises. She glances up as a man in a string vest brushes past her, and pulls her handbag to her front, hugging it to her belly.

The hall is filling up. A few feet from where Peter and his mother are standing, there is a glass door over which is a white, backlit sign with the words: 'Departures – Salidas'. In front of the door are two metal barriers, the kind that appear at Carnival or Independence Day parades, arranged to create a makeshift corridor up to the glass door. Two air hostesses push through the crowds and stalk past the barriers in their stockings and high-heels and jaunty little neckties to take up their posts on either side of the glass door. They speak into walkie-talkies, and then busy themselves with chatting and smoothing their hair, ignoring the onlookers.

The passengers are gathering, saying their last goodbyes to their families. A lot of the people here have no connection to the departing flight, but are just here for the spectacle: they jostle against the metal barriers, trying to get into a good position to overhear the farewells, study who is on the flight to New York today, and what their business is there. Nearest to Peter is a short woman in a too-tight t-shirt, eating pholourie from a grease-stained paper bag, staring at him unashamedly. Her eyes have been over him top to toe several times already, taking in the new jeans, the new sneakers, the new t-shirt, the knapsack over his shoulder, just like the ones American students wear on TV.

Inside the knapsack are several important documents, which he checked and re-checked at home in Port of Spain before they set off for the airport. A bank draft, from Barclays in England, for thirty thousand US dollars; several hundred in cash to see him through until the draft clears; and a letter addressed to US Immigration at JFK, from Harvard International Student Services. The letter is his favourite, on that creamy, watermarked paper, with the crimson and black crest at the top. It is signed by someone called Dr Evan Waszowski, and lists his phone number and that of his assistant; below the signature are the words, written in swift cursive: 'Please call my cell phone in the event of any problems at immigration.' The s's finish with a little flick so that they look more like the number 8; the crosses on the t's extend with a flourish. Evan Waszowski is a busy man, an important man, but he will take a phone call in the middle of the night and vouch for Peter if needs be. That is something.

He and his mother stand in silence, looking towards the little booth where his father is waiting in line to pay his departure tax. A hundred TT dollars it costs, and everyone has to pay it, otherwise they won't let you through. His father has one hand on his hip, stepping out to the side of the line to observe what is happening at the counter, the blue hundred dollar bill folded in his hand. There is plenty of time: they have only announced the flight once so far, and it will probably be late anyway, knowing BWIA. Peter watches him, hoping to catch his eye and signal that there is no rush. He bites his lips together, runs his hand through his hair, folds his arms and unfolds them again, taps one hand against his thigh. When it is his turn, he slaps the blue note on the counter; the official stamps the receipt and slides it under the glass. Peter watches his father snatch the yellow chit from the counter, sees how he closes his fist around it as he walks back to meet them.

'You have everything?' his father asks.

Peter takes the scrap of paper from his father's hand. The three of them huddle together.

His father counts the items off on his fingers. 'Ticket?'

'Yes.'

'Boarding pass? Passport?'

'Yes. Yes.'

'Bank draft?'

'Yep.'

'The visa? And the letter?'

'Yep.'

'All your travel instructions?'

'Yep.'

'And the cash. Keep it safe.'

'I will.'

And just like that, after all these years of waiting, they are here. Later, whenever Peter thinks back to this moment, he imagines himself with his head bowed and his arms raised at his sides: one hand trying to hold back the past, the other, the future, as Moses might have held back the sea. In that quiet space between those high, dark walls, if only he had enough power in his arms, he would have held the world back from them, created somewhere to keep them all safe, keep them together. But he cannot. Already, the moment is passing; already, his father seems to be shrinking before his eyes; already, he is no longer his father, but an old man at the end of a long journey, laying down his burden.

Peter has a lump in his throat, but he swallows it back: crying has no place here. Paul has played his part. Daddy has played his part. The rest is up to him: he, now, must play his part. He turns to his mother first. Her fingers grip his shoulders; against his chest, he feels her swallowing and swallowing again.

Then, his father. The onlookers lean closer.

'All the best,' his father says, as they shake hands.

He turns to go. The country bookies hiss as he walks up the makeshift aisle towards the security guard: *Bye bye, travel safe. Make us proud.* The guard takes a good look through his passport, not for any official reason, but just out of sheer macociousness, and glances over his shoulder at his parents, sizing them up. Peter takes his documents back, steps through the doorway, pauses a moment to reorder them. He can feel the eyes on his back, of his parents, the onlookers, everyone waiting for him to turn and wave goodbye once more. But all that is over now; he must think only of the task ahead.

22

That October, as soon as the exam results are in, Father Kavanagh drives to the little house the Deyalsinghs rent in St James, in western Port of Spain, a brown envelope on the seat next to him. He pushes open their gate, waits on the tiny patio for them to open their front door. Joy looks through the burglar-proofing bars of the window and waves. Clyde unlocks the door and steps out to the patio: he looks at the envelope, puts his hand to his chest.

'Come in, come in, Father,' Clyde says. Father Kavanagh knows he doesn't like talking on the patio, with the passers-by so close on the busy pavement just in front. Clyde sits on his armchair – he brought his armchair from La Sagesse, and eventually had it reupholstered – and Father Kavanagh pulls a rickety plastic chair from the table. Clyde holds the envelope, glancing frequently towards the bedroom, where Joy is getting dressed.

When she comes out, she sits on the arm-rest next to Clyde, and he puts on his glasses to read. Father Kavanagh waits. He knows there isn't much to see: a single sheet of headed paper from the Trinidad & Tobago Ministry of Education; a few type-written lines, slightly askew. 'OFFICIAL confirmation from the Ministry. Gold Medal awarded to: Peter Deyalsingh. School: St Saviour's College, Port of Spain.' Beneath, there's an illegible signature in blue ballpoint.

Earlier, there was cheering and clapping in the school office, and Father Malachy held the envelope above his head like a trophy. Now, Father Kavanagh sits quietly on the little plastic chair while Clyde and Joy stare at the letter. 'He got it!' Joy says. After a long while, Clyde says, 'He got it.'

Father Kavanagh makes them a coffee, and soon the phone starts ringing. Father Malachy calls to make sure the news has reached them, offers his congratulations. The Minister of Education calls. The Maths teacher from St Saviour's calls, Peter's primary school teacher calls, Sister Frances from the primary school calls, their neighbours call, their relatives call, the *Trinidad Guardian* calls, the Principals of the other schools call. Congratulations, they all say. Congratulations, congratulations, congratulations.

'Father, you could do me a favour?' Clyde asks. He's looking a little dazed.

'Of course.'

'I want to go and lie down a little while,' he says. 'Could you answer the calls for me?'

Father Kavanagh takes over on the phone. 'I'll pass on your good wishes,' he says to each caller, writing down their name on a piece of paper. He speaks to a Mrs Bartholomew, who used to be their neighbour; a daughter of a certain Mrs des Vignes, lately passed away. Joy brings him a plate of food, stands next to him as he eats.

Joy came to Rose House a few weeks ago and asked for his help. She needed to speak to someone, she explained, some men, but she could not go alone. 'If you come with me,' she said, 'they will see I just coming to talk, not to make trouble.'

'And why not go with Clyde?'

'I can't take Clyde, Father,' she said.

They went to where one of the men was living. The man was wearing only jockey shorts, sitting on his bed. He looked like a normal sort of man; Father Kavanagh thought he might have passed him in the street. He was eating pepper mango from a little plastic bag: his forefinger and thumb were red with the stuff.

'I not here to make trouble,' she said. 'I not here with police, or any big gang of men. It's just me and the priest. But he wouldn't tell. He's not allowed to say anything, that's his religion.'

The man sat with his elbows on his knees, his knees wide apart, sucking on the mango pieces.

'What you did with the body?' Joy asked the man.

At first he denied it, but she said again that she only wanted to know. 'I need to know,' she said. 'That was my child, you know! And we are Hindu. We have rituals and thing.'

Eventually, the man said that they threw the body into the sea. 'Deep deep,' he said. 'You wouldn't find him.'

Joy asked, in a loud voice, like she was trying to make herself feel brave, 'He suffered a lot?'

'No, no,' the man said. 'I am not cruel like that. He didn't suffer.'

Father Kavanagh walks through the house to the bedroom. 'Clyde?' he calls. The door is ajar, he can see Clyde's bare feet at the end of the bed. 'Clyde?' He pushes the door a little. Clyde is lying on his back, one arm limp on the mattress, the other hand pressed over his eyes.

Father Kavanagh moves the clothes from the chair, sits. He sits the way he does for Confession, squarely in the chair, his hands clasped loosely in his lap. The fan is off and it is hot in the bedroom, the curtains still drawn, the bedsheets rumpled from last night's sleep. He closes his eyes to block all this out, prays to God to show him how to help this man in his hour of distress.

'If you ask for God's forgiveness,' he says, gently, 'He will grant it to you.'

The man may be crying, it is difficult to tell with his hand pressed over his eyes like that. Father Kavanagh reaches out and takes Clyde's hand. Clyde grips hard; Father Kavanagh grips back, surprised at the strength in his own arms, so little-used these last few years. Without the hand covering his eyes, Father Kavanagh can see now, plain as day, the tears escaping, running down his temple.

———

They hadn't expected to see Peter back until next summer at the earliest, but the government scholarship money has been paid in early, and now there is money for everything: the Harvard tuition fees, Peter's meals at the university cafeteria, his books, clothes, medical insurance and spending money, and two plane tickets back to Trinidad every year. He's only been away since the end of August, and he's back already for the Christmas vacation, wearing his new American clothes, the Harvard t-shirt and Nike sneakers, and smelling of mouthwash and aftershave. He got his driving licence over the summer, before he went away; now, Father Kavanagh, in the passenger seat of the Deyalsinghs' car, watches him drive. So many young men of this age want to show off, he thinks: they drive with one hand hanging out the window, or they swerve last-minute to avoid potholes, or drive too fast round corners. Peter does none of that. He has both hands on the steering wheel, he frequently checks his mirrors, even though at this hour there is hardly anyone else on the road. It is early morning, the sun not yet up.

At Maracas, there is just one car in the car park, with the headlights on; they are going further along the north coast, to Blanchisseuse. The road narrows and presently the asphalt paving gives way to a dirt and sand track. The vegetation on either side is sparse, scrubby, dotted with tall coconut trees, their silhouettes eerie in the dawn light. They park in a clearing and walk down to the sand. Peter brought a torch, but they don't need it: the first rays of the sun are reaching over the hills behind them, the sky waking like something catching fire.

They have already discussed what he is here to do. Clyde and Joy didn't want to come. 'That is not Clyde's kind of thing,' Joy explained, 'but is something I need for myself. I need to know somebody said a prayer, so his soul could rest in peace.'

Peter sits on the sand and takes off his sneakers. No one else is here, except for a little brown and white dog nosing around by a rubbish bin. It sniffs in their direction, then sits on the sand, watching them. Peter tucks his socks inside the shoes, rolls his trousers up to just below the knee. 'I should have brought bathing trunks,' he says. He puts the car key into his shoe, straightens up again. Father Kavanagh removes his shoes, hitches his trousers up just past his ankles, stands. Peter watches him quietly, and then he walks down the beach to the water's edge. Already the light is brighter, he has to shield his eyes.

Father Kavanagh follows him slowly, feeling as though he is walking towards the edge of a cliff. The sea might be shallow at first, where he can stand with the water up to his ankles, but after that, the bottom drops away to a great nothingness, and there will be only the strong pull of the current and the crashing force of the waves. He stops at the edge, where the foam rushes up to his toes (how fast it moves!) and then sinks into the sand and recedes.

'Here,' he says. 'Let's stop here.'

Peter is already in up to his knees. He looks back, the breeze rippling his hair. Father Kavanagh wants to reply in a calm voice that he cannot swim, that he does not like water. But in his mind he sees the dark, murky depths, the treacherously rising swells. The cool foam, not white but pinkish-gold in this light, touches his toes; he draws his feet back.

'Come,' Peter says. He comes back, his rolled-up trousers already darkened by sea water. 'Take my hand.' Behind him, the sky is glowing. Father Kavanagh reaches slowly towards him. And he sees now what Clyde has always seen – that, indeed, Peter is not one of us, that he is made of gold, pure gold.

Father Kavanagh takes his hand, and he follows Peter as he steps through the water into the sea.

Acknowledgements

I'm deeply indebted to my sister, Jennifer Adam, for reading every draft of this novel, and for many hours of discussion over Skype. For reading and giving critical feedback, thanks also to Jeremy Taylor in Trinidad; Jo O'Donoghue in Dublin; Ardu Vakil at Goldsmiths; Jacob Ross, who mentored me in 2016 as part of a scheme run by Cathy Galvin's Word Factory in London; Willy Kelly; Alice Kelly; Mary Adam.

Thank you to my agent, Zoë Waldie, at Rogers, Coleridge & White, for helping this book make its way into the world.

Thank you to Mitzi Angel for the right words at the right times, the space, the title. I feel honoured to be a part of the Faber & Faber family: thank you, Stephen Page, Alex Bowler, Louisa Joyner, Rachel Alexander and Maria Garbutt-Lucero.

In New York, Alexis Washam provided detailed and insightful comments on the manuscript; I'm grateful to her and the whole team at SJP for Hogarth for their passion and belief in this book, especially Sarah Jessica Parker, Molly Stern and Rachel Rokicki.

To my family: thank you, Mom, Dad, Ian, Jenny (again), and Judy, for your support and encouragement over the years; thank you, Sophie and Benji, for sharing the kitchen table with my stacks of papers, and for sharing a part of your childhood with this book; and thank you, Nick, for making it all possible.

Suggested reading group questions
for *Golden Child*

1 How does the wider family in the novel, with their various social hierarchies, play into the plot?

2 Uncle Vishnu's death, and Romesh's response to how he had been helping Clyde's family, is a key turning point in the novel. How important is Uncle Vishnu's influence on the family, and how does his death affect their fortunes?

3 What do you think about the way Paul is treated? When Father Kavanagh assures Paul that he is normal, what effect does this have on Paul, and also on Father Kavanagh's and Clyde's relationship?

4 Masculinity is a key theme in the novel. How much does it affect the choices made by the characters?

5 What do you think about the sacrifice that is made for Peter's sake? Can it be justified? What does it say about a parent's obligation to their children?

6 What do you think about Joy's choices and actions? Do you think she was right to keep Peter and Paul together at school? Do you see her as strong, or weak, or inexplicable? Why do

you think she doesn't argue more with Clyde towards the end?

7   Clyde and Joy appear to be Hindu, yet they don't practise their religion, and they send their boys to Catholic schools instead. To what extent does religion represent a social hierarchy in the novel? Which religion is at the top of the hierarchy? Which is at the bottom? Why?

8   What did you think about Father Kavanagh's role in the story? To what extent is he a 'white saviour'?

9   Trinidad is described as having a thriving petrochemicals industry, and several characters are very wealthy, yet the Deyalsinghs live in quite humble circumstances. Why is this? And to what extent does corruption in the society play a part in the lives of all the characters?

10   To what extent do you think the characters are influenced by the time and place in which they live? Do you think they would have made the same choices if they were living, for example, in contemporary Britain?

11   *Golden Child* asks many complex moral questions – how did you feel about Clyde's choice? What does the final scene of the book say about his decision? How did you respond to the end of the novel?